Briarwood Publications, Incorporated

SOMETIMES

YOU GET

KILLED

Sharon Carton

BY

SHARON CARTON

Copyright © 2000 Briarwood Publications Inc.

First Published 2000
Briarwood Publications & Sassy Cat Books, Inc.
150 West College Street
Rocky Mount, Virginia 24151

All rights reserved. The use of any part of this publication, reproduced, transmitted in any form, or by any means, electronic, mechanical, photocopying, recording or otherwise, or stored in a retrieval system, without prior consent of the publisher is an infringement of the copyright law.

SHARON CARTON

SOMETIMES YOU GET KILLED
ISBN 1-892614-30-8

Manufactured in the United States of America.

Printed by Briarwood Publications, Inc.

To my parental units, who made me.

Acknowledgments

Okay, my units forced me to dedicate the book to them because of THE RULE, but there are other people I want to thank: Before I get to the ones who are going to fight over the order, let me extend my love and gratitude to my Sentinel friends, who for years made me feel like a writer and a member of a family. Tonya, you kept me in print even when I rebelled, and it's a debt I can never repay. Okay, the Others: the three women who made my life what it was the past three years, my coven (no, I am not a devil worshipper, not that there's anything wrong with it); Kelly, who made me feel like the Second (or first) Coming, Natasha, no better vetter or friend could I have hoped for, and Claudette, who treated me as if this was predestined. My witch, Sapphire, who gave me hope and spells; my shrink and friend, Betty, who kept me out of lockdown; my niece who doesn't understand that once published, a writer is no longer crazy but amusingly eccentric; my awful job which made me desperate to get the hell away (and I'm sorry, but it's so built on the hellmouth); Leslie, who was the Jack to my Ernie, Carol who explained the other side and got me autopsy pictures; my sister, who lets me be the subversive one; Elvis Costello and Thich Nhat Hahn and the Dalai Lama and the Circus Boy Carmen; Howard, Randolph and Joel, on the short list of whom I would call the morning before I went postal; Susan, the kewlest person still practicing law, and if it wouldn't humiliate me to say it, the wind beneath my wings (yeah, but you gotta give me snaps for not having seen the movie), and to Sharon, who showed me there's an exit door in Hell. Finally to Barbara, who stopped me from going under that third time. Oh, and thanks to the Academy, too. It was an honor just being nominated.

Sharon Carton

Chapter One

I didn't kill Luis Mendoza's nephew. I wasn't even glad he was dead. But that doesn't mean I didn't see it as the answer to all my problems.

Not that I had all that many problems, not lately, anyway. Even my leg, injured in a fall through a plate glass door on a case a few months back, had not required any further surgery, to the surprise of the doctors and the infinite relief of yours truly. So all things considered, I was a happy man.

That's not the kind of thing I normally like to call attention to. The gods don't like people to be too happy; it makes the powers that be feel they haven't been doing their job. Acknowledging my happiness was recklessness of the highest order, tempting fate, daring the gods to do something about it. A Jewish friend called it "putting a *k'nehura* on yourself." My Italian father, who didn't like seeing his wife or kid — or anyone else — looking too happy, called it making an ass of yourself. My mother, Irish and brazen with it, couldn't have cared less what anyone, including the so-called gods, thought of her.

Still, it should've told me something, something along the lines of this won't last, can't last, isn't real. And it wasn't, I guess you'd have to say, though I *felt* happy enough. I'm not sure that counts, since things went to hell so easily, so quickly, that my feeling that life was on the right track must've been wrong. I mean, things must've already gone pretty far along the road to disaster without my noticing.

There's no denying I was ignoring some of my life's more unpleasant realities. Like the fact that I was

Sharon Carton

only a few years short of forty and my career as an investigator still consisted of jobs where the risks or boredom factors far outweighed the compensation I was able to collect. And like the fact that Ernie Darwin, my associate and friend, was steadily self-destructing on drugs. Throw in the fact that the Mets were finding new ways of self-destructing, too, and I guess it becomes clear why both Ernie and my lady friend Annie have an annoying habit of referring to me as "the happy little moron."

Annie, that's Annie Royce, is a teacher and administrator at The New School for Social Research downtown. Annie is scholarly and thoughtfully placid, with a maddeningly even temperament despite her flaming red hair. On her good days, she can provide me with reason to live; on her bad days, her penchant for pedantry can make me feel like one of the fourteen-year-old kids in the junior high school classes she used to teach. Ernie, a former lawyer who now works for me, is several years younger than I am, deep and certifiably manic-depressive, with no manic episodes in recent memory. Me, I'm shallow, undereducated and, for the last several months, content as a cow.

I'd gone through a bad few weeks the previous Fall, but after that I went back to my old fuck-the-world-I-feel-fine self. Jack Migliore, The Sequel. Annie Royce, she of the penetrating intellect and phlegmatic personality, was back in New York after an interminable year teaching English Lit and Freshman Comp at the University of San Diego. If you think her return didn't contribute to my renewed sense of well-being, then you know me about as well as I knew myself when I let her go without a struggle. Now she was back, I was working, if not profiting, and enough was right with my world that I was willing to ignore what wasn't.

Like Ernie. My friend had had one helluva winter. Last Fall, he had renewed his love affair with Alice Morrissey, the grand passion of his law school days, as we

Sometimes You Get Killed

investigated a murder which we later learned she had committed. Something obscenely familiar had happened to him a year earlier. He had recovered that first time; now, his depression was just getting worse with each passing week. Emotional stability had never exactly been Ernie's long suit, but I just kept hoping he would come out of this.

About two years ago Ernie Darwin had called me from Washington, D.C., where he was working as an attorney for the Defense Department. A few years before that, Ernie had decided to give up the law, and for a brief stint he served as my operative. His restlessness wasn't satisfied by the career change, though, and soon he quit me to wander around Spain for a while before he finally lit in D.C. When his boss at Defense was murdered, Ernie, for various reasons, became a suspect, and I came down to D.C. to answer his SOS. As it turned out, he'd been relatively innocent, his guilt being limited to screwing the married woman who'd done the actual killing, and honing a nasty little drug habit picked up abroad.

After I managed to clear him, and the sympathetic police lieutenant on the case got Ernie into drug rehab, Ernie moved back to New York and came back to work for me. All in all, it was working out pretty well; Ernie had a way of alternating between being a useful associate and frustrating impediment in our cases, an enjoyable companion as often as he was an insufferable pain in the ass. I came to value his friendship, even as I despaired of ever turning him into a self-sufficient investigator. It seemed we would have to settle for our version of a symbiotic relationship, my sanity complementing his lunacy. It was a tidy little arrangement, one I expected would last until one of us killed the other.

The problem these days wasn't that he was inflicting his sorrowful and extremely disturbed person on my merry little universe. The problem was that, in some distant orbit, out of the corner of my eye, I could still see him trying to avoid me, and that was even worse. Ernie was in deep shit. Sometimes it seemed like my job was damage

Sharon Carton

control, keeping Ernie out of the trouble for which he showed such a great predilection. His job was easier, being limited to introducing me to all the metaphysical and unseen mysteries of the intangible, psychological and philosophical phenomena which heretofore had remained outside my sentience. Annie's job, in case you were wondering, consisted of teaching me words like sentience, how to spell them and how to use them in a complete sentence. We all led a full life.

In March, Ernie the errant lawyer got busted. It wasn't his first arrest: That had come about a year and a half earlier, in Arlington, Virginia, when the charge had been murder. As I told you, back then he'd been innocent — of that crime, anyway. He had, of course, been guilty then of the charge on which he was arrested this past March: felony Possession of Controlled Dangerous Substances. He was guilty now, too, of compounded bad judgment: He had offered the coke to an undercover cop with no sense of humor or proportion. Because Luis Mendoza, the cop in Arlington, had had both, Ernie had no priors and was able this time to plead down to misdemeanor Possession. He got a $250 fine and 150 hours of community service.

The fine he borrowed from me; I have no idea where he was getting the money for the drugs. I had no idea, either, where he was getting the emotional wherewithal to do the community service, since he was as tapped out psychologically as he was financially. My best efforts at keeping him solvent in both regards by keeping him working weren't an overwhelming success. For that, Ernie had no trouble just saying no.

It didn't help much that Alice, his erstwhile girlfriend, had recently been all over the newspapers and television, as she was being tried for murder. Ernie and I had worked on the case last year, and it was that unpleasantness that had sent him seeking solace from his old habit. He had had enough difficulty coping when it was just a private truth; when it hit the press again as she went

Sometimes You Get Killed

to trial, Ernie could barely come up for air.

Just when it looked as if his life couldn't get any worse, Ernie got served with notice of a disciplinary proceeding that the New York State Bar was bringing against him. Ernie was a mostly nonpracticing, mostly former lawyer, but these past few months he hadn't even taken on the occasional freelance legal research or appellate work that came his way. Now it looked like he would no longer be refraining by choice.

Given the hardline anti-drug stance of the Bar these days, he'd be lucky if all he got was a suspension instead of being disbarred. He had appeared unrepresented to face the criminal charges, and wasn't even bothering to mount a defense to the disciplinary action. He told me he didn't care because "number one, I'm guilty, Jack, so what kind of defense could I raise," which showed a glimpse of why he was now a detective rather than a lawyer, "and number two, I haven't practiced in over a year, and have no intention of going back to it, so what does my Bar membership matter?" Number three, as obvious as it was unarticulated, was Ernie's belief that he neither had nor was especially interested in any kind of a future, so what was there to salvage?

I never had to ask him why he'd been doing the coke, although it wasn't his drug of choice. Ernie preferred anything with a dulling effect, anything that might put an even greater distance between him and reality than he customarily enjoyed. He'd been popping so many barbiturates in the last few weeks that it now took a jolt of powder up his nose to jump start his heart every day. As far as I knew, after a year of complete abstinence, he was now indulging freely in pot, hashish, assorted downers, and the aforementioned cocaine, the last of which I had twice caught him free-basing. As far as I knew, he hadn't yet gone back to playing with needles. Maybe he didn't have the price of a hypo. Maybe the AIDS crisis was not without its up side.

And what was I, probably his best friend and certainly his only sane one, doing to deal with this sad situation of a once promising life gone wrong? I had begun my own private suicide watch when what seemed like the neatly packaged solution to all his problems came to me via a telephone call from that cop in Arlington, Lieutenant Luis Mendoza.

"New York," said a voice I hadn't heard in about a year, "you probably don't remember me...."

As a matter of fact, I did, blessed with fantastic recall and a special reason for not forgetting this particular cop. "Yeah, I remember you, Lieutenant, but you seem to have some trouble remembering my name. Am I the only New Yorker you know, or are we all 'New York' to you?"

"Gimme a break, Migliore," Mendoza replied, and he sounded like he needed one.

"Why not, I owe you."

"Oh no, what you owe me I got bigger plans for."

"Huh?" All right, fantastic recall but not exceptionally quick on the uptake.

"And you ain't the only New Yorker I know, you know. I heard about your partner in crime."

"Ernie? I didn't know it made the out of town papers. You read the *Times* just to keep tabs on your special projects?"

"With him it wasn't hard. You know what kinda strings I hadda pull to get him into that program?" I got the feeling he wasn't trying to be hard-nosed with that last bit; he was only justifying in his own mind having to ask someone for a favor. He wasn't the type of man who found that easy to do.

"Strike one," Mendoza went on, "now he's got a record. Strike two, he's about to lose his license. You guys just hanging around waiting for him to strike out, or you got some kind of plan?"

Well, sticking close to Ernie so I'd be there to call the ambulance when he overdoses isn't exactly what you'd call a plan, so I just said, "I'm open to suggestions."

"Good," he said firmly, "'cause I got one. I got a

Sometimes You Get Killed

job for the two of you. It's custom-made for you and that asshole you call a partner, which is good because you owe me, like you know and like you said, and 'cause, if I'm being honest with you," he said in a rush, as if embarrassed by this part, "I didn't really know who else to ask."

Mendoza was right. Just because Ernie hadn't killed his boss at Defense didn't mean that some other cop, given the same damning evidence, wouldn't have been satisfied with letting the state prosecute him. And when I heard Mendoza's story, I had to agree he was also right about the deal being custom-made.

"My nephew," he began gruffly, "died last month. He was...my sister says he had changed, he was having some problems. I don't know."

I was confused. "What kind of problems? How did he die?"

Mendoza hesitated. This was the part he'd been dreading. "Don't gimme any mouth, all right, on this, until you know the whole deal. He died...they're telling me he died of an overdose of barbiturates."

I was silent. What could I say? God, how that must've hurt the cop to admit.

"That ain't all of it, Migliore. All of it is where he died, and where is in a drug and alcohol rehab center in Florida. That's where my sister is, South Florida, and the kid-"

"He O.D.'d in rehab?"

"That's what they told me, yeah, but it's bullshit, bullshit it'd happen there and bullshit it could happen anywhere. I know that kid. He was clean."

When I would put the proposition to Ernie a few days later, his first question — though not his first or even his second or third comment, which I'll get to later — was, "So what does he want us to do, get evidence of negligence for a lawsuit against the clinic?" With Mendoza, I had had a slightly different bent. "You got any reason to suspect foul play?"

Sharon Carton

"Don't gimme 'foul play.' The kid was murdered. If it was drugs, it wasn't self-administered."

"Look, Lieutenant, take it step by step. The kid — whatever you may've known about your nephew, he must've had a problem with drugs, right? Maybe it was a small one he or your sister wanted to stop from getting bigger. Maybe."

"It had to be Inez's idea, because this place was like one of those places where somebody, like a family member, you know, has to have you committed, sign you in, you know."

"Tough Love?" I said, mentioning the only program of that type I'd heard of, which, as far as I knew, was for minors. I had gotten no indication of his nephew's age.

"No, well, like that, for adults. Berto was twenty-three. Anyway, I'm telling you he was straight, no pot, no pills-"

"How recently had you seen him?"

"I spoke to his mother-"

"No, that's not what I asked."

"All right, so it's been a while...."

I sighed. "Lieutenant, I know what you were thinking. Ernie and I go down there, I get him committed by posing as family, and together we prove your nephew was clean and someone murdered him. Am I close?"

He answered with what must have been a silent nod.

"Okay, so just listen to me. It'd be a great job. I'd get Ernie into rehab again on this pretext and after a few days or weeks of running up a tab, I'd come back and tell you just what you already know but don't want to believe. I have too much respect for you to take you up on this."

"New York, don't let me down. You're the only-"

"Why?" I interrupted. "You telling me there's no professional courtesy in South Florida? You can't go down there and get the inside dope?" I asked, flinching at the inadvertent pun.

"I'm telling you I been warned off. Up here, down

Sometimes You Get Killed

there. Nobody's giving me shit. All I'm getting is the cold shoulder."

"As in investigation-in-progress?"

"As in case closed. Bunch of fucking rednecks down there. Their way of thinking, one less spic junkie don't exactly give them sleepless nights. Officially I'm getting nowhere, so I figured it's time to go unofficial. You two clowns are as unofficial as I can get. Besides, there ain't too many drug addicts or private cops, much less pairs of 'em, I can trust-"

"Or call in a favor from," I said resignedly, "yeah, I know." I paused, weighing his objectivity, which was nonexistent, and my options, which were even fewer. Less. Whatever. I mean, who could benefit from an undercover assignment in a drug rehab program more than someone who failed it the first time? And who better to have him committed than his partner, who was only too aware that Ernie had been certifiable for some time now. "Okay, Lieutenant, I'll talk to Ernie about it-"

"No, you gotta talk him *into* it."

"Same thing," I joked. "No, really, I'll talk to him about it, and get back to you in a coupla days. That's the best I can do."

"No it ain't, Migliore," he said, his voice heavy with disappointment, "but I'll take it anyway."

"Fuck you, Jack."

All right, so Ernie wasn't exactly thrilled with the idea.

"I'll take that as a yes."

"You can take that as a no and shove it up your ass."

"Darwin," I said with mock surprise, "I don't understand. I happen to know for a fact that your social and professional calendars are somewhat underbooked, so it can't

Sharon Carton

be that you don't have the time. How can you resist such a golden opportunity to repay a deep obligation to a man through whose good graces you are not now serving time for homicide, and thanks to whom, also, you so successfully cured your tiny little drug problem last year in that rehab program he got you into?"

Ernie just shook his head, a small smile curling his lips. "If Annie heard that sentence, your love life would be somewhat underbooked."

"Yeah, it's true, according to her 'sex-for-syntax' regime. So, what do you say? We do owe him, you know."

"Yeah, and this has nothing to do with me, right? Like the two of you didn't get together and cook up this little scheme to get me into a drug program again?"

"Uh huh, right, Mendoza asked his nephew Adalberto to overdose in a Florida clinic so Ernie Darwin could get his act together. It's so obvious, I shouldn't wonder you saw through it."

See, one of the most reliable aspects of Ernie's character is that, when all else fails, go for the guilt. I don't know why it worked with him. He's not Catholic, he's not Jewish, and he never had a mother to prime him on its finer points. Ernie, whose mom died when he was a toddler, was raised by his stepfather, Charlie, or by various social agencies episodically filling in for the uninterested Charlie when Charlie's relatives were unavailable. So who initiated Ernie into guilt?

"That's not fair, Mig," he said, now shamed into compliance. "It sounds so paranoid when you put it that way. Besides, I never said I wouldn't do it."

"No, that's true. It's just that I don't know all the foreign languages you do, Ernie, so I didn't know fuck-you-Jack is translatable as I-accept-the-suggestion. What is that, Mandarin Chinese or Szechwan?"

"It's prison slang," he smiled, "picked up from that night you made me spend in Riker's before you bailed me out."

Sometimes You Get Killed

"And you didn't believe me when I told you it'd be a learning experience."

Chapter Two

It takes special genius for a New Yorker to wangle an all-expenses trip to South Florida in mid-July, when the Mets aren't in Spring Training and the sun is making its rare annual appearance up north. Ernie flew down to Fort Lauderdale ahead of me to get us a hotel room, get settled, and spend a few days visiting an old friend of his in Miami, while I took care of some important details here in New York. The most important detail was explaining to my skeptical friends that hating to fly is not the same as being afraid to fly. I had one of those skeptics, NYPD Detective Jeff Fenton, call the clinic to clinch Ernie's admittance on such short notice. While the Chief of Staff down there, a Dr. Samuels, had been a bit recalcitrant when I'd telephoned, the cop connection did the trick, as it had done similarly in Arlington a year ago.

It took a little over thirty-two hours for me to make the drive, stopping once for a meal and twice more for pit stops. The air-conditioning in my 1976 Nova is temperamental at best, and by the time I got off I-95 at Griffin Road, the last of six Lauderdale exits, and headed east for the beach, I was drenched in my own sweat, my hair dripping beads of perspiration onto the back of my neck in a South Florida variation on the Chinese water torture.

Ernie had booked us into a modest, somewhat dingy hotel on A1A, the beach road, following my strict instructions not to get carried away on Mendoza's budget. Ernie had grudgingly agreed to one double room since, as I had heartlessly reminded him, he wouldn't be there past the weekend. When I entered the room unannounced, he was sucking on a joint which he claimed was rolled with pot but

Sharon Carton

which I suspected, from the glassy look in his eyes, was hashish. The only surprise was my reaction.

"You're not, like, pissed?" Ernie got more articulate when stoned.

"Nah," I said truthfully. Well, half-truthfully. I was trying to be nice, and determined to enjoy what I fully expected to be no more demanding than a working vacation. Besides, I usually need to be surprised to be angry, and Ernie's response to anxiety was predictable. "What the hell," I told him, "it's your last weekend, knock yourself out."

"Hey, no, really," he said, after about five minutes of intense concentration. "This is homework."

"'Homework?'" I repeated.

"Yeah, for the job. You know, like maybe they'll ask me to describe the effects of, you know...."

"Pot, asshole, you said it was pot."

"Yeah, pot," he grinned.

"Uh huh, so you wanted to refresh your notoriously poor short, mid- and long term memory."

"Uh, yeah," he said, then giggled about ten minutes later.

I showered and changed into cut-offs and a tee shirt, not bothering to unpack anything else from my duffel bag. Then, leaving Ernie still giggling, I went for an exploratory walk on the Lauderdale beach. I headed north; it was nearly five o'clock but I only got about a quarter of a mile before the heat and humidity drove me into the ocean. It was gorgeous. No other word for it. This wasn't like the beaches in New York. You couldn't even have convinced me it was the same ocean.

I swam for about a half-hour, then walked along the shore, lighting a cigarette from the pack I'd buried in the sand with my wallet and keys, until I got to a street called Sunrise Boulevard, where that section of the beach seemed to end. I crossed the road and headed south back toward the hotel along The Strip, a string of fast food

Sometimes You Get Killed

restaurants and shops selling tee shirts, skimpy neon bathing suits and cheap souvenirs.

I encountered Ernie in the patio of The Strip's McDonald's. Clear-eyed, chatty and famished, he was scarfing down a cheeseburger, amid the remains of two Big Macs, double fries and a chocolate shake. While I have to struggle to keep off the pounds, Ernie, who has a couple of inches on me, maintains his stick-thin build with the help of an out-of-control metabolism and controlled dangerous substances.

In between bites, he told me about his visit to Catherine, his friend in Key Biscayne, and informed me that we had plans to dine with them the following evening.

"You back on this planet?" I asked wryly.

He grinned, abashed.

I shook my head. "Ya feel better, don't you?"

"Yup," he said, nodding vigorously, his mouth full of food. "You wouldn't like to remind me why this is such a negative thing, my doing drugs and all, would you?"

I shrugged. "Funny, I'm always ready, willing and able to quit smoking while I'm exhaling the last drag of a cigarette, or to start a diet when my belly's full. Dope doesn't work that way, huh?"

He swallowed his last bite of cheeseburger, and tidily drew a paper napkin across his ketchup-stained mouth. "Must be something to do with its addictive properties. You know, I feel good now, I felt bad before: Why wouldn't I want to repeat the medication when the symptoms reoccur?"

"'Medication,'" I echoed, making a face.

"Speaking of which...." He reached over and grabbed a Merit from my crumpled pack, lighting it with my disposable. "So what's the plan?" he asked without enthusiasm.

"You go into rehab, get inside info on the clinic, which info I use to solve the case-"

"Case? Oh," he remarked, feigning surprise, "you still sticking to that story, Mig?"

15

Sharon Carton

"Drop dead, Darwin."

"Nice alliteration. So, you telling me you really think Mendoza's nephew was force-fed his vitamins?"

I sighed. This was the tricky bit, the part of this "case" I wasn't clear on myself. "Let's just say he seems to have died under mysterious circumstances, and we're gonna try to solve the mystery."

"Yeah. Right." Ernie made a snorting noise. "If that's your story, you just stick to it, Jack. Nobody can fault you for consistency."

"The hobgoblin of legal minds," I put in.

"That's *little* minds."

"That's what I said." I was trying to distract him from the "case," which, yeah, I couldn't help thinking about in quotation marks, but he wasn't cooperating. He resumed questioning me about our strategy — not because he cared, but to prove that I didn't have any — and even though he was still in a good mood symptomatic of the artificial aftermath, I didn't want to get drawn into it. "Tell me about tomorrow night."

Saturday night we drove into Miami to meet Ernie's old friend and her husband for drinks and dinner at Bayside Marketplace, South Florida's answer to the South Street Seaport. Ernie had known Catherine Olwine since one summer in the late 1970's, when they'd both worked for the Department of Justice, Cathy as a law clerk while taking night classes toward her J.D. at George Washington, Ernie as a summer intern between his second and third years at Brooklyn Law. Cathy had gone on to prosecute for the U.S. Attorney's Office in D.C., leaving only to join Flowers, Derby and Lindner, a profitable Brickell Avenue law firm, where she was now a junior partner.

Last year she had married Ricardo Alvarez, a Cuban-American five years her junior. They were an

Sometimes You Get Killed

attractive if incongruous couple: the blonde Cathy hyper with the litigator's restless intensity; the languid, curly-haired Ricardo, or Richard, as she called him, whose smooth Anglo features belied his heritage, all tepid insouciance. He was as casual and passive as she was kinetic. I asked him what he did for work.

"The family business," he answered easily. "Fruits and vegetables."

"And he teaches tennis on the side," Ernie supplemented, later adding privately that between his work as a tennis pro and in his father's company, Ricardo was pulling down a tidy annual income in the low six figures. If I'd known that Saturday night, I wouldn't have fought so vigorously, albeit unsuccessfully, for the check.

With typical Migliore delicacy, I asked Ricardo what he knew of the fabled South Florida drug traffic.

Cathy looked ill at ease, glancing at Ernie, who apparently had few secrets, but Ricardo reacted with aplomb. "I see a lot of coke among the tennis people, but that's about it."

"You ever do any?" I pursued, just making conversation.

Cathy laughed. "Are you kidding? Mr. My-Body-Is-A-Temple? No self-respecting YUCA would sully himself-"

"'YUCA'?" I echoed.

"Young Upwardly-mobile, or Urban, or Upscale, Cuban-American," Ernie explained, adding, "and don't even mention drugs to Cathy," Ernie offered. "She still lives by the prosecutor's purist mentality."

"I made some inquiries," Catherine said, making a smooth, if callous transition, "into this place you're going into."

"Oh yeah?" Ernie said, instantly uninterested.

"What did you hear?" I asked.

"Nothing," she said quickly, "good or bad, except that it's pretty exclusive, in both senses of the word.

17

Sharon Carton

Expensive, to a literally prohibitive extent. Who's footing the bill?"

See? I'm not the only one with no tact. "We got a partial waiver of the fee," I responded, "owing to the desperation of Ernie's case."

She accepted the lie for what it was, and let it drop. I had no idea how much Ernie had told her about this second effort at rehab. He had been lectured, at some length and with some frequency, on the meaning of the word "undercover," but Ernie had never given me any reason to believe he had absorbed this concept any better than he had the rest of my tutelage.

After dinner, we strolled by some of the shops, stopping finally by the bandstand on the water where a magician was performing.

"How long you been here?" I asked Ricardo.

He smiled, showing me the white teeth of a nonsmoker. "All my life," he answered in his unaccented English.

"First generation?"

"Mm-hmm. My father got out smart, in "56. He's not political. He just came for the economic opportunities."

"You like it here?"

"I don't know anything else."

"No, I mean Miami."

He considered. "Same answer, I guess, though I've traveled a bit with the tennis. What's not to like: the sun, the ocean — I just got my P.A.D. certification, diving, you know? My family's here, so why would I want to live anywhere else?

I started to mentally catalogue the reasons people chose to live in places without palm trees and palmetto bugs, but fortunately realized before the list got articulated that the question had been rhetorical.

"Ask Cathy what she thinks," Ricardo was saying, "she's lived a lot of other places, but she swears by South

Sometimes You Get Killed

Florida."

Catherine was engaged in a heated discussion with Ernie a few feet away. I couldn't catch any of their conversation.

"What's Key Biscayne like?"

"Beautiful, man," Ricardo assured me. "Why don't you guys come out tomorrow and spend the day? We could take a ride on the boat, do some fishing, pack some food, make a day of it."

It sounded great, and I told him so. "I don't know," I mused aloud, "sounds like a dangerous amount of clean living."

Ricardo laughed, throwing back his head. I guess when you spend your time in fresh air and sunshine, exercising regularly, not smoking, and eating fruit and vegetables, you have energy to burn on surplus bodily gestures like that.

Don't get me wrong; I found him likeable, Cathy too; it just felt like we were from different worlds. I wondered if it was more than just geographical. I wondered also what Ernie possibly had to talk to Cathy about. He was speaking with more animation that I usually saw on his face these days, and I was curious about the topic of conversation. I leaned into it, catching scattered words here and there. It was all legal stuff, and I was struck with sadness for Ernie. He really did like the law, and being a lawyer, even if he didn't care for practice. I remembered suddenly how much he had enjoyed his stint as a law professor while working undercover at the Manhattan Law Center on that Alice Morrissey case last Fall. How depressing it must be for him to face losing it all, after the amount of work it must've taken to get there. No wonder he's seeking chemical sanctuary.

No, I reminded myself, wrong chronology. The chemical sanctuary came before the arrest and the threat of losing his license. Face it, I thought, Ernie's depression wasn't the cause or effect of the drugs. Everything — well,

19

Sharon Carton

at least this current misery — had its origin in the disastrous investigation at the law school: Ernie falling in love again with Alice, his old law school girlfriend; Ernie being scammed by her; Ernie learning and then proving that she was the murderer; Ernie going off the deep end....

And even though it had been Ernie who had gotten us involved in the case, it was because of me that he'd been in New York working as an investigator in the first place, and because of my skepticism that Alice hadn't gotten away with murder. So it all came back to my feeling responsible for looking after Ernie, as I tended to feel with him, in part because of our deep bond of friendship, in part because, after all, he needed someone to do for him what he couldn't — or wouldn't — do for himself. So I would get him through rehab, as Mendoza had done before, and maybe then I could stop feeling so damned guilty for having such a good time.

"Were you ever lovers?"

Ernie was in a bad mood on the drive back to Fort Lauderdale from Key Biscayne Sunday evening. I wasn't so much trying to figure out if it was due to jealousy over Catherine's new husband as I was trying to provoke an argument. Once I got Ernie agitated over something, it was an easy transition from anger to amusement. Anything was better than this sullen, morose silence.

He shook his head.

"Oh," I said casually, "I was just wondering if she might've killed Mendoza's nephew."

All I got for my trouble was a sour expression. Ernie had a history of falling in love with women involved in our investigations, women with unsettling homicidal tendencies. Our mutual friend Jonah Barnes had once suggested to me that I might do well to pinpoint the object of Ernie's affections on subsequent cases in order to solve them.

Okay, so the joke had never exactly been calculated

Sometimes You Get Killed

to amuse Ernie, and it was getting pretty old, anyway. I still wondered whether there might've been something else bothering him. I knew the closer he came to Monday the tenser he would become. But he'd been surprisingly ebullient with Catherine and Ricardo. It was only on the drive home that he clammed up.

Maybe he had started to reflect on the disparity between the lifestyle his old friend was enjoying and his own. The Key Biscayne condo was spacious even by South Florida standards, with an airy living room whose wrap-around window opened up on a magnificent panoramic ocean view. Ernie and I had spent a lot of time exiled onto the terrace to smoke, forbidden from polluting the apartment's pristine atmosphere. The decor was predominately antiques, though I didn't know enough about interior decorating to tell that the furniture was anything but old and expensive. The apartment seemed warm and inviting, but I had the impression that was a carefully engineered illusion.

It wasn't like the house in which I'd grown up, where kids and animals grew up by breaking things that were bought based on their replaceability. This place wasn't garishly opulent or gadget-heavy; I just got the feeling that every item had been chosen carefully, with less regard for need than for aesthetics: Did they like it? Did it match? Those weren't the same questions I used when shopping: Did I already have something that did the same thing? Could I afford it?

Ernie's approach was a variation on my own: Do I have room on my bookshelf? Do I have enough cash in my pocket? Ernie had always seemed content with his austere living arrangements; if he had enough cash for books, cigarettes and drugs, his life was complete. He didn't live any better when he was earning than he did when down on his luck. I think money confused him, required choices he wasn't prepared to make.

I had no such ambivalence. I knew exactly what I

would do if I ever made money. I was primed, if not qualified, for success. Yet my jealousy of people like Catherine wasn't strictly financial. I envied their potential; I envied the way they had translated that potential into reward. Their lives were linear, directed, realized. In my own life I saw a lack of preparation, the failure to learn, to acquire the skills and knowledge to make me the person I wanted to be. With each passing year I mourned the failure to complete the man, to make up for the intellectual inadequacies.

Ernie of course had had all the education. Did he look at Catherine and see someone who had fulfilled her early promise, while he had wasted every opportunity? He hadn't wanted material acquisitions, but he must've been ambitious at some point in his life. Had he lost the desire when he lost the drive? Maybe he didn't know. Maybe seeing Catherine, the fulfillment of a dream he must have shared at some time, served to stir the doubts, the self-examination and self-flagellation that in Ernie were always close to the surface.

I don't think he begrudged his friend her accomplishments, but he was too self-critical by nature not to compare and regret. He may not have wanted what Catherine had; more likely, knowing him, he was blaming himself as much for *not* wanting it as for not achieving it.

If that was true, the best thing for him was to get involved in this new case. If there was a case, solving it would make him feel like a success. If there wasn't, he might get from rehab the promise of a new start.

Or at least, that was what I was still telling myself.

Chapter Three

Monday morning I drove Ernie to the rehabilitation clinic for his nine o'clock check-in. I followed the directions I'd been given on the telephone by the receptionist, a Debbie Galesseo, nice Italian girl. We took the beach road south until it turned into the 17th Street Causeway, then south on U.S.1 to State Road 84 west for about fifteen minutes. We drove in silence — at least, I made inane small talk and Ernie sat in mute terror beside me.

"You okay?" I asked finally, knowing he wasn't. He had been sick in the hotel bathroom most of the night.

"No," he said, mustering a weak smile, "I'm scared shitless."

"Why?"

"Ah."

"What's that supposed to mean?" I said, instantly on the alert.

"Just as I thought," he charged, almost smug in the certitude of his despair. "You think I'm scared about the job, which if you had one ounce of insight you'd know I wasn't, but you think I am and you can't understand why, which proves that there's nothing to be afraid of about the job, which proves you don't think it was murder, which in turn proves you're not putting me in here to solve the murder, but rather to get me clean. *That's* what the 'ah' meant," he finished, suddenly exhausted by his burst of communication.

He was right. "That's bullshit, Darwin. You're babbling, which makes sense given the dearth of viable brain cells you have remaining."

Sharon Carton

"You mean extant, not viable, and dispute my logic, asshole, if you can."

Well, at least he was talking. "I couldn't figure out why you'd be scared, because you're one tough sonofabitch, Darwin, invulnerable to harm and impervious to pain. No, really, I couldn't understand it because you've got such great back-up in yours truly."

"Uh huh."

"Or," I said, ever flexible, "if you want the truth, what really surprised me was that the thought of someone coercing you into death by overdose didn't appeal to you."

"Jack...."

"Oh, fuck, Ernie, I don't know why I said 'why.' A verbal reflex. Small talk. I belched and it sounded like 'why.' I was really just clearing my throat. I had been reciting the alphabet silently and when I opened my mouth to say I could well understand your being terrified, I had just reached the letter y and it popped out before I could shift mental gears."

I turned to glance at how he was taking all this. There was a sour grin on his face, and he was shaking his head. I decided this was a good sign, and quit while I was ahead.

We were greeted in the parking lot by the Director of the clinic, Dr. Roger Samuels. The sign on the building said only, "The Center." I shot a look at Ernie, who said nervously, "Very Zen, don't you think?"

I didn't. It reminded me of this eerie punk sci-fi movie I'd seen a year or two ago, where all the food the characters ate came in packages generically labeled "food," and so on. My impression didn't improve when Dr. Samuels walked us through the lobby, past walls plastered with ominously bland Big-Brother platitudes like "The Center - where you don't have to want help to get it." Roger noticed my grimace, and smiled equably. "Do they strike you as trite? You might be surprised at how clichés often give our patients an anchor to hold on to."

Sometimes You Get Killed

He apparently meant it, and to this day I admire Ernie for not turning tail and bolting. Roger was a man of medium height and build, in his early forties I guessed — or maybe the salt and pepper modified crew-cut prematurely aged him — with a clean-shaven earnest face and manner to match his gap-toothed welcoming smile and bright blue eyes behind wire-rimmed glasses. I knew the type: one big happy family mentality, as long as everyone in the family practices 100% homogeneity. He had distinctive hand gestures that made him look as if he were engaged in excited prayer, and, when speaking, he rocked back and forth on his feet, almost as if dovening, leaning improbably forward, uncomfortably close into his listener's face. I thought it comically fitting when later that morning I heard staff and patients alike referring to Samuels as "The Reverend."

"Yes, we pattern ourself after the 'tough love' program, except, of course, our patients are adults. It's not one's parents who enroll one here, but someone who has acquired power of attorney over that adult."

"Voluntarily?"

"In almost all cases, yes. It's just a legal fiction perpetrated for purposes that suit that patient and the community. Your brother-in-law hasn't objected to the arrangement, has he?"

Ernie, my "brother-in-law," was sitting in the reception area filling out forms, his favorite pastime. Nobody likes it, usually because we can't decipher them. With my lawyer friend, the problem was rather that each question poses some kind of existential mystery to him, as if the answer to any one individual inquiry could make the difference between self-realization and self-deceit.

"No," I replied, "he knew he needed help, and as I told you on the phone, he needs the enforced discipline of a place like the Center."

"Well, we're a very small clinic, so we have to be extremely selective in filling vacancies," Dr. Samuels said in his carefully enunciated style. I was finding myself

25

Sharon Carton

hypnotized by his mannerisms. As deliberately as he chose his words, the Reverend nonetheless had a tendency to stammer, as if with the weight of sincerity, his hands clasped in front of him, as he nodded vigorously in the pauses to convince the listener that emotion ran deep even when words were not forthcoming.

"Yeah, well, you've got a great enterprise going here. Very reasonable rates," I lied, "for a privately funded operation. It's no wonder you're in demand."

"I appreciate that, Mr. Migliore. I think your brother-in-law will do well here. I think everyone involved will be satisfied by his stay here."

Ernie had just walked up to join us, and favored me with a forced and sickly grin. "When do I get locked up?"

The Reverend's smile never reached his lips. "The doors aren't locked until well after dinner, Ernie. Until then, you have free run of the grounds."

"He's really locked in his room?" I said, disconcerted.

"It's a timed pneumatic system," Roger explained. "State of the art. The staff can enter the rooms without keys, but the patients cannot leave except during what we call 'changing of the guard.'"

"Which is when?" I was asking all the questions. Ernie was brooding, and tuning everything out.

"Five minutes before every hour, for a five-minute period."

"So everyone scrambles to get from one place to the other in those five minutes?"

"Only to leave. They can enter any room they like, at any time."

"What's the point? I mean, it doesn't keep the patients locked up."

"No, but it restricts their movements. It makes life easier for the control booth."

"Excuse me?"

Sometimes You Get Killed

Dr. Samuels pointed to a small room in the main corridor. "That's where a designated monitor sits during the lock-up hours. He has video hook-ups to every room in the Center, and can pull up a view on his screen in three seconds."

"So he — this monitor person — only has to watch for escaped ... prisoners for those five minutes."

"Basically. There are some bugs in the system. We're working on it."

I wondered if he was thinking about Adalberto Santiago, Lieutenant Mendoza's nephew. "And the staff's movements are so restricted, too?"

"Oh, they have keys," the Reverend said airily, taking an electronic key-card from his breast pocket in demonstration. Then he stopped walking, and turned to face us with a look of sincerity that raised the hairs on the back of my neck. "Now, you both understand the rules, I trust. First time you're caught holding, in possession of drugs or alcohol, that is, you're out. Any other rules violations will result in forfeiture or suspension of privileges, including rights regarding Sponsor Days, telephone communications- "

"Wait, Sponsor Days?" I interrupted, looking at Ernie. He had a sad, distant look on his face, as if he was unhappy but trying to pretend he were someone else, someone who wasn't.

"We allow," Roger clarified, "our patients' sponsors to visit for a sort of open house one day a week, on Thursdays."

"Are you telling me I'm only allowed to come here once a week? And he's not allowed out?" This I didn't like.

We finally had Ernie's attention, and he was now listening closely to Roger's reply.

"That's correct. And, I might add, sponsors are the only permitted visitors."

"No way-" Ernie began.

"You have to understand our position, gentlemen,"

Sharon Carton

Roger interrupted. "We allow only sponsors because of their demonstrated loyalty and responsibility toward the program. Allowing multiple visitation would undercut the clinical therapeutic environment, not to mention severely undermine security. Ours is a rigidly regulated environment, and we have found it to be a salubrious one for our patients."

I hesitated. For all the reasonableness of his words, I didn't like or trust him, not yet, anyway, and the idea of abandoning Ernie to the care of this humorless and inflexible man for a week at a time troubled me. Even if the "murder investigation" was largely a pretext, as he legitimately suspected, that didn't mean I felt comfortable not being able to check up on him — and this place — more often than once a week.

"I don't suppose he can come and just not see me?" Ernie offered weakly.

"Other than on Sponsor Day? No," Roger said, without an inch of compromise in his voice.

"Jack," Ernie began, looking at me beseechingly.

I was confused, but Roger jumped in with, "There is, of course, telephone access at any time other than lock-up. There are no phones in the bedrooms."

"He can call or be called any other time?"

"That's right."

"Ernie?"

"Why don't you discuss this privately in the coffee room?"

"No fucking way in hell I'm going to fucking do this, Mig. There's just no fucking way-"

"Ernie, Ernie, you're splitting infinitives, you must be upset."

"Come on, Mig, I don't need a place like this to get straight. I'll quit on my own."

"Ernie," I said patiently, "You're confused. You're here undercover, remember? This is a job, not a punishment."

Sometimes You Get Killed

"Oh, get real, Jack. We both know the real reason I'm here. You don't think Santiago was murdered any more than I do. We can repay Mendoza and look into this thing without my checking into this hell-hole."

"How?" I had him, and felt mildly guilty. Did I really want to do this? I didn't know.

Ernie was silent for a few minutes, then, "Don't ask me questions like that. That's your kinda stuff. I'm only supposed to ask you that, and you tell me. You know, like asking people questions, looking stuff up, going to scenes of the..." his voice trailed off.

"That's right, Ernie," I said, going in for the kill. "I'm the professional here, and I know how to conduct an investigation. In this case that means you go into this place, look around, talk to people, get to know the cast of characters."

"And you?" he challenged.

"I talk to Santiago's family down here, the police, anyone on the outside who might know anything. You've got the important job of-"

"Why can't we ask these people questions without my going inside?"

"Because that's obviously what the cops did, and we're looking for a little more information than they got. Come on, Darwin, get tough. I'll be here day after tomorrow. If you decide by then that you can't stand it, we'll pull out and no harm done. Or, or course, if you don't survive until then, I promise to avenge your death."

"Yeah, and to take good care of my videos of the '86 Series, huh," he said dryly.

And so it was decided, only because he was too dispirited to put up a good fight, and because I was too pushy not to take advantage of that.

Roger introduced us briefly to Dr. Paul Rios, who took Ernie off for his in-take physical, while Roger continued my tour of the facility. Rios was a pudgy man,

29

Sharon Carton

balding with cherubic features, the kind of person usually described as "tubby" rather than "portly." His coarse laugh seemed friendly enough, though it had a disconcerting way of inappropriately punctuating somber discussion. I decided not to take offense, if only in appreciation of the way it invariably prompted Roger to wince with each uproariously braying affront to his sensibilities.

We left Ernie in Rios' hands, and I tried to affect more interest in the operation of the Center than I genuinely felt.

"How many patients do you have?"

Roger didn't hesitate with the Center's statistics. "Currently eight, including one woman, Sofia Cisneros. She had become close to another young lady who was just discharged. Our therapist, Louise Fischman, is working with her to ease her over the transition."

"Louise Fischman — is she the only shrink on staff?" I asked.

"No, she's an M.S.W., a social worker, not a psychiatrist. We have one Board-certified psychiatrist, that's Dr. Gregory Tessler, I don't think he's in his office right now, and one psychologist, Dr. Kenneth Khoragian, a Ph.D. Christine, his wife, Kenneth's that is, is a counselor here. Paul Rios you just met, he's an M.D."

"And I've met Debbie, the receptionist. Is that it?"

"Yes, including myself, for the staff. I'm trained as a psychologist, but I function mainly as an administrator."

"Seven staff members, eight patients: nice ratio."

"It promotes a family dynamic we find useful for recovery. Something akin to a parent-child disciplinary deterrence factor."

"Ever lose any?" I threw in casually.

Roger stopped short. "Excuse me?"

"Anybody ever flunk or drop out?"

"Ah. Our success rate is tremendous, 73.4%, well above the national average, but hardly ten out of ten. Ah," he said again, stopping in front of a door with "Dr. K.

Sometimes You Get Killed

Khoragian" inscribed on it. He knocked, then, without waiting for a response, opened the door and stuck in his head. "Kenneth?"

A shrunken, wispy figure of a man was sitting on the front of his desk, gesturing intently to an attractive, brown-haired woman with the longest legs I'd ever seen. I assumed this was his wife, Christine. They both looked up at us.

"Kenneth," Roger said, "this is Jack Migliore, who just brought in our newest guest, Ernie Darwin, cocaine, cannabis and barbiturates. Jack, this is Dr. Khoragian and Louise Fischman."

Ah, indeed. Not Khoragian's missus. Maybe, if there was a God, nobody's missus. She walked a few steps toward me to shake hands, and gave new meaning to the word willowy. Her light brown hair fell in soft waves to her shoulders, and her mouth was wide yet full, and turned up now in a warm, welcoming smile that lit up her brown eyes. She'd only taken a few steps, but she walked well, slowly, gracefully, with an undulating rhythm that made me wish she'd had further to travel.

Khoragian, on the other hand, was less pleasing, aesthetically, at least. His elongated head, topped with closely cropped curly dark hair, seemed out of proportion to his stunted body. His face bore an objectionable goatee and laugh lines circling dark, scowling eyes. From the grim expression tightening his features, I believed the scowl and not the wrinkles. It was instantly plain that he was not pleased to see us, but I couldn't tell whether it was me or Roger who offended.

"What have I interrupted?" Roger said with bland good humor which almost obscured the touch of malice obliquely conveyed.

Khoragian grimaced. "A complaint about Paul."

"That's Dr. Paul Rios," Louise Fischman offered me helpfully.

Roger evidently didn't like the public airing of dirty

31

Sharon Carton

laundry, and explained tersely, "That would be Miss Cisneros."

"You know about this already?" I asked.

"It could only be Sofia," Louise Fischman told me, smiling easily, without ill-will. "Paul has a rather...physical approach to some of our women patients and staff. Not everyone appreciates his touchy-feely style. Sofia has complained about it in the past, and she's communicated to me that she doesn't feel the problem has been remedied."

"Never mind," Roger said, anxious to abort this conversation. "He's with Mr. Migliore's brother-in-law now. I'll speak to him about this later. Sofia tends to overreact."

Roger hustled me out of Khoragian's office, and I could swear the psychologist flashed me a nasty look as I closed his door behind us.

"Dr. Rios means no harm," Roger tried to assure me. "He's never unprofessional; he's simply a Latin, well, you know, used to more physical body language. Some perceive it as too intimate, but there's nothing sexual in it."

"Uh huh."

"Paul was born and raised in Cuba, but trained here. He's Jewish, too. Top of his profession. Very good ties to the Jewish and Cuban communities. We've put together an admirable staff here. Very unique."

I flinched at the solecism, Annie's training having had its impact. Or possibly what I objected to was Roger's demographical approach to people. One woman patient, one woman shrink, one woman counselor, and of course a one-woman support staff. One Cuban doctor satisfying two minority quotas. A real bonus.

Roger went on. "Notwithstanding the usual assortment of personalities and idiosyncratic quirks, everyone seems to really enjoy everyone else. We all get along here so well."

Okay, so I wasn't convinced. Maybe I was thinking

Sometimes You Get Killed

that Roger was selling too hard. Maybe I was being the skeptic I was being paid to be, seeing suspects where I was being told to see friends and lovers. Maybe I was confused, too, about whether I was a detective looking for clues, a detective pretending to look for clues while I was really there just to get Ernie some help, pretending to look for clues as much as I was expected to pretend not to. Maybe Ernie needed help, but so did I. I figured we were both fairly fucked up.

"What would I do with a gun?"

"Ernie, don't ask me questions like that." I was by that point feeling so guilty for leaving my forlorn friend at this madhouse of pleasantries that I had offered to bring him my gun when I showed up on the next Sponsor Day.

"And don't you think that'd be kinda suspicious?" Ernie added.

"From what I've heard about South Florida, you'd stick out more if you didn't have one." Truthfully, I was almost relieved. Again, I didn't really imagine Ernie to be in any physical danger, except maybe from the affections of Dr. Rios. I saw it as posing a greater danger to place a loaded handgun in the possession of a severely depressed man being deprived of his daily dose of illegal substances. "Look," I suddenly said, "if there *are* any drugs around, I mean, if someone does offer you something, just hold out, okay? I mean, if you decide you don't want to quit, or can't quit, don't take anything here. Remember why you're here."

"Jesus, Mig," he said, annoyed, "you'd say anything to keep me clean."

"I'm just saying Mendoza's nephew died in here of an overdose. Or apparent overdose. Maybe he got hold of some bad drugs."

"All right, all right. So let's pretend I'm here to work. What exactly am I supposed to do while you're out gallivanting in the free world?"

Sharon Carton

"Talk to the other patients, to the staff, to anybody you can. Get a mental picture of this place, and see if you can unobtrusively find anything out about Santiago. Just be subtle."

"You're telling me to be subtle? What, have you actually found the word in a dictionary in the past few hours?"

"Excuse me?"

"I already heard about you ogling the therapist, Louise Fischman, but I haven't seen her-"

"How did you...?"

"Never mind."

"Yeah, well, since you brought it up, I might as well tell you that I'm just waiting to see which of the women here you fall in love with. Then I'll have Santiago's killer."

Tactless revival of the old joke, especially since his most recent passion was the woman now on trial in New York, and he was still hurting over it. Ernie was right: I was about as subtle as I was sensitive, and I could no more resist a jab than Ernie could a sexy murderer.

Besides, I wasn't feeling any too tolerant of my friend's sensibilities. I'd had a brief talk with Dr. Rios about Ernie's physical. I'd had no idea — I guess I hadn't wanted one — of how deep he'd gotten into drugs again. Maybe fear of AIDS had been keeping him off the needle, but these days you didn't need to inject to get in trouble. Crack and pot and hash were cheap enough, and Ernie had enough contacts in New York to keep him in pills and powders of every color and persuasion. I'd guessed at the variety, but never imagined the frequency and scope. There was no question he'd gotten himself addicted again. It had been easy for me to hope he could keep it recreational, but it wasn't in Ernie's nature. He didn't want entertainment, he needed to survive. You look for thrills to highlight, when everything else is safely, if dully, taken care of. For Ernie, he needed help taking care of every day. You don't do that with an occasional joint or snort at a party; if you're like Ernie, you never even get to that party.

34

Chapter Four

After leaving Ernie at the Center, I drove south to Miami for a late afternoon meeting with Alberto Santiago's mother, Inez, Lieutenant Mendoza's sister. Her English was good, but heavily accented, which is better than some people have said about mine.

Inez Santiago was a woman in her early forties, slightly heavy set, with short black hair tinged with shocks of grey. She was dignified in her grief, stolid and unyielding.

"I only agree to see you," she told me firmly, but not with any palpable hostility, "for Luis."

"Your brother explained what I'm here for?" My telephone conversation with Mrs. Santiago the day before had been brief, polite but not friendly.

"He say Berto does not die with drugs. He say he pay you money to prove this."

"Well, sorta. I'm mostly here to find out the truth, whatever that turns out to be. You're a widow, Mrs. Santiago?"

"Yes. From twelve years."

"Do you have any other children?"

"No. I have no children."

I hesitated. "You mean since Berto's death?"

"Since before this."

"Excuse me, I'm sorry?"

"He leaves home when he has eighteen years. Moves away from home. From then I have no children."

"I'm...I'm sorry, I don't understand. There was some trouble between you, so he left home?"

"No, no trouble," she said emphatically, "but he leaves home. So I have no children."

35

Sharon Carton

"Well, it's not unusual for kids to move out on their own-"

"Yes, here it's not, you right. Here there's no family, no closeness. Not like Cuba. So he leaves home and goes away to Fort Lauderdale, with the beaches and drinking-"

"And drugs," I suggested gently. "Did you ever see Berto using drugs?"

"At home he doesn't use *basura*, trash."

"What about after he left?" This was like pulling teeth.

"I don't see him when he leaves. One, maybe two times a month, some months no. We don't speak a lot when he does."

"So he could've gotten involved in drugs after he left home? He was gone, what, five years?"

"Five and a half. I don't know what he does when he's at the beach. All I know is he was brought up to be a good boy. He was too...free, *demasiado independente*, but a good boy. He knows right from wrong, always he knows this, so why would he use trash?"

"What about friends? Do you know any of his friends?"

"What friends? When he's a boy, he has nice friends. Then he grows up, all of a sudden his old friends are no good no more. If it's *cubano*, it's no good, Miami no good. Now he's Al, no more Berto. So who knows what friends he has at the beach?"

It wasn't much to go on, and it wasn't too promising. Alberto could have fit the profile of a drug user, if there was such a thing. Independent, bright, alienated from family and old friends, rejecting one way of life, looking for another. His mother didn't provide any leads regarding his new life in Fort Lauderdale, but I didn't get the impression she was hiding anything; she just didn't know. She had loved her son, but as he'd grown up, they'd grown apart, and it had hurt her.

Sometimes You Get Killed

"Do you think he died of a drug overdose, Mrs. Santiago?"

She took some time answering, as if impressed by my wanting her opinion. "He gets drugs in a hospital, they tell me, then dies from taking too much. This doesn't sound like my Berto, but I don't know why this hospital would lie to me. Do you, Mr. Migliore?"

I didn't, but I liked the way she said my name, so I said, "No, Mrs. Santiago, but I'll try to find out if they were."

I couldn't think of anyone to have dinner with, so I drove a few blocks into Little Havana and had a *chuleta de puerco* at a cafeteria on Calle Ocho, Eighth Street, in the Cuban neighborhood filled with the only people on the East Coast conservative enough to name an avenue after Ronald Reagan.

Later, I drove back to Fort Lauderdale, listening to the tail end of the Mets game on the radio, then sat out on a deck chair in front of the hotel, and watched the ocean until I was sleepy enough to go to bed.

On Tuesday, I got up early and went for a walk along the beach and a quick, indescribably enjoyable swim. Yeah, I could get used to life down here, I thought, which I later learned was not quite so easy to say *after* ten a.m. in a South Florida July.

After a large breakfast in the hotel coffee shop, I changed into some clean slacks and a short sleeve shirt and headed north and west to the address on Broward Boulevard of a police station Mendoza had given me. Waste of time. I didn't get to see the police report, or the medical examiner's report. All they told me was what I'd already gotten from Mendoza: death from accidental overdose, barbiturates by intravenous injection.

How did they know it was accidental, I asked them.

No evidence of suicide or homicide, a history of substance abuse: What else would it be?

37

Sharon Carton

It wasn't so much that they had convinced me as I saw nothing to be gained from arguing. Maybe Ernie's depression was catching. I'd caught it once before — well, no, that's not fair. I'd gone through a slump, which isn't the same as saying I'd come down with Ernie's case of terminal existential *anger.*

Tuesday afternoon, sitting by the hotel pool, I was not unhappy so much as confused. Did I suspect foul play, or was I just humoring Mendoza, not to mention taking his hard-come-by money, to serve my own purposes? No, scratch that, I wasn't confused. I knew exactly why I was in Fort Lauderdale, and it had nothing to do with Alberto Santiago. It had a little to do with Mendoza's paycheck; I'm not going to underestimate that. But taking a job for the money was only the excuse, the reason I was able to do what I was doing. It wasn't what I was doing.

I wasn't used to such ambivalence, and it was making the case feel foolish to me, awkward and amateurish. I was going through the motions — for Mendoza, for Ernie — and that's not the way I usually work. I can't function with divided purposes. The only trick I do is to obsess, to get into a case to such an extent that I'm there when the event in question happened, or in the mind of the person I'm looking for, or whatever. I don't have brains, or, truth be told, a fantastic memory, or great physical prowess. My sole distinguishing talent is focus, or concentration. It comes from liking my work, or from being just the happy little moron that Ernie and Annie accuse me of being. If I were brighter, or more sophisticated, maybe I'd have more on my mind than whatever case I'm working on. But I don't. So when I had to approach a case I didn't believe was a case, I couldn't get started. No ideas came to mind, no avenues to pursue, no leads to follow. There's nothing more to competence than confidence, and when I didn't believe in what I was doing, I couldn't believe in myself. I had always known the reverse was true, but this one was a new experience for me.

Sometimes You Get Killed

Embarrassment — I prefer that to guilt — kept me from telephoning Ernie that night. Something told me that whatever he'd have to say wouldn't make me feel any better about the reasons I'd taken the case. Maybe I have a short memory, but I didn't think I'd ever felt this conscience-stricken before Darwin deigned to reappear in my life. I used to be really comfortable with my insensitivity; it was one of my chief pleasures in life. Now I had to worry about doing the right thing — if I didn't, my work didn't get done, my life felt crooked, and my cigarettes didn't taste right. I used to be a happy man. Now I had to ask someone else for permission.

"So?"

"Yeah, and I weave great basket, too." Ernie giggled maniacally at his own joke.

"Funny, Darwin. Is that like giving great phone? Okay, so I take it you're telling me you're bored here."

"Bored? Bored, Jack? How could I be bored at a place so solicitous of its patients' feelings, a place whose credo is 'The Center, Where You Don't Have to Need Help to Get it,' a place so creepy that -"

"I think you got that slogan slightly -"

"-that I'm almost glad I get locked in my room at bedtime. Fuck, I'm thinking of requisitioning a fucking night-light."

I smiled. "Creepy how?"

"Defense Department creepy."

"'Paranoia will destroy ya,'" I sang.

"I'm serious, Jack."

"Well, what do you expect? It *is* a hospital, more or less. Sick people live there. One of 'em even died there. Maybe it's haunted."

"Yeah," he said earnestly, ignoring my sarcasm, "but it's not like haunted house or morgue creepy. I'm

Sharon Carton

telling you, I feel like I'm back in Arlington, wandering the halls of the Pentagon. It's like everyone else is in uniform and I'm buck-naked."

"Ernie, Ernie, get a hold of yourself. You know what this is. You feel guilty about being undercover. You know you've got a secret, just as you did back at Defense, and it makes you feel out of place. Your warped little mind twists things around until you start to think everyone else sees through you, or that they have something on you. Classic."

"And of course I must be paranoid, because nobody here has any secret, right?" he said dryly.

"Oh." Too late, I realized my slip. "So, you were saying something about being bored?"

"Was I? I can't imagine why. No, it's very exciting here. I caught the murderer early Monday evening, so I've been free to enjoy the myriad of other invigorating and stimulating entertainment available to one here."

"Such as? Wait," I stopped myself. "Back up. Pretend you're a real life investigator and start with the good stuff."

"Oh, you mean like solving the murder? Sure. Let's see, it must've been close to seven thirty. We'd just had our typical South Florida 'early-bird' dinner, the epicurean delights of which I won't digress and tell you about, when it hit me."

"What hit you?" I asked, ready to volunteer my fist for the job.

"The truth," Ernie said. "About Santiago's death. It wasn't murder."

"Accidental overdose?"

"Intentional — and reasonable, I might add — suicide."

"Okay," I sighed, "you're being subtle, at least I think you are, but I can't be sure because, as you pointed out, it's a concept far beyond the level to which I've evolved. But let me see if I've gotten this straight. You're absolutely

Sometimes You Get Killed

miserable here, you hate it, which probably made you even more depressed than normal in this protracted — dare I say interminable? — depressive stage in your manic depressive life. As a result, you more than likely have been rendered completely dysfunctional-"

" 'Rendered completely dysfunctional'? Did you really say that, or has my mind been so totally blown by this place that even your limited caveman vocabulary is coming out sounding like psychobabble?"

"-and," I went on, ignoring him, "that probably means you haven't done a lick of work in two whole days here. Am I right, or was this not a complete and utter waste of what I will only euphemistically refer to as manpower?"

For that I got a short laugh. "Okay, okay. But I did work, honestly. You just wouldn't believe this place."

"In what way do you mean?" I was surprised about him working, but I don't know if it was because I didn't think he'd be up to it, feeling the way he obviously did, or because I didn't think he thought I thought he'd been put there to do anything except stay clean. Or maybe I didn't think there was any work to be done.

"I mean," he explained, "I thought there was politicking and backbiting at the law school, you know, MLC," referring to the case in which he'd gone undercover as a law professor. "It can't compare to this place. Bickering, rivalries, intrigue, sex, violence: This place has everything."

"Uh, excuse me, Ernie, but did any of these things have anything to do with Alberto Santiago?"

"Oh. You mean like the case?"

I sighed. Nothing changes in my life. "Yeah, like the case. You remember the case?"

"Yeah, sure."

"So?"

"Huh?" He gave me a blank look, having apparently lost the train of conversation.

"So? So?" I, in turn, had lost my patience.

Sharon Carton

He giggled. "Yeah, with neat, even little stitches, and I weave good basket, too."

"Ernie...." I said, warningly.

"Okay, okay. Yeah, in one sense, but no, in another. See," he went on rapidly, having caught the look on my face, "I didn't get any new information about Berto's death. But I have learned a bit about the survivors, you know, the people here now."

"The other patients?"

"Yeah, and the staff, too. I'll start with the good guys first-"

"Oh good, as long as you've been approaching this with professional detachment."

He stopped. "Yes or no?"

"Okay, all right, go ahead."

"Louise Fischman, I like her. She's my therapist, and-"

"Wait, you like her? How do you mean that?"

"What do you mean? I just like her, she's a nice lady."

"Okay, scratch one suspect. Go on."

"Fuck you, Jack," he said heartily. "Anyway, she's warm and perceptive and reassuring without being patronizing. Very calm, deliberate, I guess you'd say, and she has this way of saying simple, or I dunno, even simplistic phrases as if they'd just come to her, as if they meant something special, just for you."

"And you like this? It sounds like Roger's platitudes."

"No," Ernie said, "not with her. You feel like she's working with you, like trying to find some great truth, but with him it's a con. The patients call him 'the Reverend' because he's so false and preachy about this place. He acts as though he's your friend while he's shoving the knife in your back."

"What about the other patients? What're they like?"

Sometimes You Get Killed

He shrugged. "Not as bad as I'd thought. I made one friend, Davy Rittenby. Very old New England family, but he's pretty down to Earth, except that he's Republican. Told me the only difference between a Democrat and a Communist is that a Communist knows what he's doing. You think he was joking? Anyway, he's pretty sensible for a kid, I mean, he's only like 25 or 26, something like that," said the ancient 30-year-old. "Most of the dirt I got on this place came from him."

"Ah, speaking of dirt, what about Santiago's death? Did you find out anything about him?" I tried desperately.

"Not much. It was his first time here, and he'd only been here about two weeks when it happened. He'd been admitted for dependence on crack and downers-"

"Wait, by whom?"

"Huh?"

"That's the way the Center operates, right? That's why I had to indulge in this myth about you being the kid brother of the woman I wedded and bedded. So who signed him in, who was *his* brother-in-law?"

"Oh, some friend of his named Nicky Something, Nicky-" he paused, "....DeBiasio. He's the one they called when he died, too, that's how I heard the name. Davy, that's Rittenby, said you never saw, sorry about this Mig, never saw such an unemotional Italian. The others remarked on it, too, that the people here took it harder than he did, or seemed to. Though I have to tell you, that's not saying much. They're a phlegmatic lot, at least as far as the death is concerned. I mean, if you were a patient where another patient died, wouldn't you leave?"

"What did they say about the way he died?"

"Berto? O.D.'d in his room. No one knew how he got the barbiturates, you know, like from whom or when, and no one thought he'd been suicidal. So everyone, I mean patients and staff I've heard from, and I haven't gone around asking questions or anything, not directly, but everyone seems satisfied it was a tragic accident."

43

Sharon Carton

"What kind of person was he?" I asked, hoping to getting a picture to offset what I'd gotten from Berto's mother.

"Berto? I dunno, nice. Problems like anyone else, I guess."

Really helpful. "Do you think they're lying to you?"

"Lying? About Berto? Fuck, no, why would they? I mean, I don't believe a thing the Reverend says, just on principle, but like Davy or Louise Fischman, why shouldn't I trust them?"

I sighed deeply. There was a resiliency to Ernie's ignorance, or innocence, which amazed, angered and scared me. You couldn't say he rebounded, exactly, from crises; it was more like he sort of forgot. Oh, he was still depressed as hell; he just couldn't quite place why. Unlike me. Hell, I got burned by somebody once back when I was eleven, and I'm still pissed at the world.

It made me mad because I saw it as a disease, Ernie's forgetfulness. It was like those drugs they give women about to go into labor; the women don't hurt less, but they can't remember the pain when it's all over. I think that's a cheat. If you hurt, there's a reason, and remembering that reason, using that reason, may be the only good thing to come out of the pain.

And finally, Ernie's amnesia scared the shit out of me because he was trusting again, and would continue to do so. Dumb for anybody, anytime, according to my philosophy, ridiculous given Ernie's history of being betrayed, but life-threatening if the case turned out to be anywhere near as serious as Mendoza seemed to expect. Oh, what the hell, I thought, I'd be there. I'd gotten him through worse, right?

Ernie took me for a walk around the Center's grounds. The place was clean, without a hospital's sanitary odors, and the lawn well-cared for, if weedy. South Florida in July didn't boast of lush green carpets. There was no garden, and inside or outside the complex, there didn't seem

Sometimes You Get Killed

much to do.

"How do you keep your dirty little hands and minds occupied, Darwin?"

"I dunno," he mused. "This is only my third day, and I'm supposedly doing something here above and beyond what everyone else is doing, and I'm bored out of my fucking gourd."

"I'll bring you a new gourd next week. What about the other patients? I mean, what do you guys do all day, besides peeing into little glass bottles to prove your righteousness?"

"Well, there's therapy twice a day, individual in the morning and group in the afternoon. That's only two hours a day, plus meals, of course."

"Yeah, so? That leaves a whole chunk of time to yourselves."

"We talk, y'know, mingle. I dunno. That's why it's so boring. One good thing, though, well, I dunno," he temporized. "I think it's good, but I don't know if objectively it could be universally perceived as a positive-"

"Ernie...."

"Okay, okay, it's just that I started writing again," he said, embarrassed, not looking at me.

"No kidding." Ernie used to write what I would refer to disparagingly as "weird little short stories," but a couple of years ago his first effort at a detective novel had had a part in implicating him in the murder of his boss at Defense. He retired his pen after that, and I was pleased to see him back at it. I considered him safer when some of his lunacy spilled over onto a printed page. "That's great," I said sincerely, then eased into, "Does that mean you're willing to stay, see this through?"

"For twenty-eight days?"

"Or until you solve the case, whichever comes first."

"I don't know," he said slowly. "I guess so, for a while longer, anyway. A month feels like too long, but so

Sharon Carton

far, okay. It's not as fascist as I thought around here. Controlled, but not structured, you know?"

I nodded.

"And," he went on, "unless you count the Reverend's preachy wholesomeness, there's no religion to speak of, either. Can't say the same about that place in Virginia Mendoza got me into. All the same, this place makes me crawly sometimes-"

"So you said."

"Well, between the paranoia of being watched while we sleep and the claustrophobia of not being able to come and go as we please.... Well, that's half true; I mean, we can enter, we just can't exit. What was I saying?"

"God only knows. Go back to the part about being watched. Who watches you?" I asked, having forgotten about the monitor in the control booth.

"They take turns, rotating for two weeks. It's, wait, I made a point of asking about this, oh yeah, ten p.m. to six a.m. The monitor of the week sits in that control booth on the first floor for eight hours."

"Just watching you on those little screens?"

"Yeah, or sleeping, or jacking off, I don't know. How many times can a guy look at people sleeping?"

"Okay," I said firmly, "your assignment for next week is to find out who was on monitor duty the week Santiago died. Or do you already know?"

"Huh? No, God, that's a good question. Nobody said."

"Surprise, surprise. See if the little Snoop-of-the-Week is still on staff, for starters, and if so, how come? That would seem a major gaffe, wouldn't you think?"

"No shit."

"And what *time* he died."

"Didn't you get that from the coroner's report?"

"Medical Examiner's, and no, they wouldn't show it to me, or the police report either, for that matter."

"Do they know who you are?"

Sometimes You Get Killed

"An investigator, you mean? Yeah, but not anything about you. As far as they know, I'm down here on my own."

"Let's hope they don't share with the folks here."

"No shit. Nah, they won't check up on me. They couldn't be less interested — in me, in Berto Santiago, or in the Center."

But Ernie had just pinpointed a serious problem with this investigation. As far as the Center was concerned, we were both in undercover roles. How could I ask the questions I wanted to, needed to ask, when I was just some addict's brother-in-law? And why had Mendoza told me I had to be a relative — Santiago had been checked-in by some friend. I was feeling as though I'd painted myself into a corner with my little scheme.

"What's in there?" We had just passed brown double-doors, hiding what seemed to be the largest room I'd yet seen at the Center. I backed up to peer through the window of one of the wooden doors.

Ernie looked bored. "Oh, that. It's, what do you call them, with weights and mats and-"

"A gym? They call them gyms, Ernie, although I understand it's a concept you're only familiar with in the abstract."

He made a face. "No, *you* know, it's called something else nowadays."

"Health spas?"

"No, it'll come to me."

"It'll have to, 'cause it's sure as hell you won't go to it."

"Universals," he said, remembering. "Isn't that it? Anyway, you've never seen such healthy degenerates, working out and going for runs out around the grounds. It's disgusting."

"It'd give you something to do," I said mildly.

"What is this, Darwin Self-Improvement Month? I don't see you entering any marathons."

"I don't have to," I said. "I keep in shape, doing

Sharon Carton

things like, now I'll go slowly so you can make a mental note of these terms for future reference, they're spelled just like they sound, now here they come, walking, playing softball, playing b-ball, playing-"

"Yeah, yeah, okay. Just stop nagging. Besides, I might be driven to doing some of this physical activity."

"By what? I thought everything was going so well," I said sarcastically.

"Sexual frustration."

"You've only been here two days."

"Yeah, but it's driving me crazy."

"Short trip," I said without sympathy.

"No," he smiled, "it's hearing about all the sexual healing that's going on around here. I think that's why everyone's always working out; they need to build their stamina."

"Okay, let's have it. Who's in the sack with whom?"

"Well, maybe I was exaggerating." He suddenly seemed embarrassed. I had an inkling why, but I let it go, smiling to myself.

"All I know" he was saying, "is Khoragian's wife hits everything that moves, and the rumor is she's gender neutral."

"Bi-sexual?"

"Yeah, or so I've heard. Understandable, from what I've seen of Khoragian, but I don't see what that's got to do with the case."

"Nothing, I guess." That was a switch, Ernie needing to bring me back to focus on the job. I really *was* confused. "Did she have anything to do with Santiago?"

Ernie shrugged without much interest. "Don't know. Haven't heard anything to that effect, but I can ask."

"That would be nice," I said dryly.

"Well, what about you? Have you made any pretense of working?"

Stung, I embellished on my minor league efforts of the past few days, making it sound as though I was making

Sometimes You Get Killed

progress, however slow.

It didn't take long, even with my exaggeration. I had done little, with even less success. This case was starting out, at least, differently than my normal case. It wasn't just working an alien environment, though that was bad enough. No friends, no contacts, no familiarity with the terrain: All robbed me of my customary work style. Not knowing my purpose — well, I've already described how that was handicapping me.

It wasn't that I lacked a *plan*, per se. I'm never that organized. I usually just dive into a case, annoy some people, and wait for the suspects to get sufficiently pissed for their tightly constructed lies to start unraveling.

What was so different about this case? Maybe there was no case. "Give me a list of the staff and patients," I told Ernie. "I'll start checking them out." I had no idea how, or, more to the point, why I would do something like that, but it sounded like a good thing to say.

It seemed to satisfy Ernie, who was always gullible but not usually such an easy audience. He knew me too well to accept my words as gospel. Maybe he was unused to the excess oxygen, unadulterated by illegal substances, getting to his long starved brain. My own brain was feeling pretty airy those days, but at least Ernie had an excuse.

Chapter Five

I had one week before my next visit to the Center, and two sets of ersatz leads to work on, Ernie's list of staff and patients, and the name Nicky DeBiasio, the man who had checked Alberto Santiago into the clinic. The list I gave over the telephone to two friends in New York, Jonah Barnes, a young former London cop who now headed a small, private security operation on the Upper West Side of Manhattan, and NYPD police sergeant Jeff Fenton, who normally served as my source of favors and information. Both were dubious about the amount of help their normally rich resources could prove in South Florida, but they said they'd make some calls.

Nicky DeBiasio was something I figured I could play with on my own.

And play was all I did. I called Information in Dade, Broward and Palm Beach counties. I went to the Post Office off Federal Highway, just south of State Road 84, and spent a few hours poring over the telephone directories. Nothing: No matter what spelling I tried, Nick DeBiasio wasn't to be found. Directory Assistance told me they could find no such name, not that there wasn't such a person with an unlisted number.

At that point, I started to feel productive, because of rather than notwithstanding the defeat. Missing Persons was good, Missing Persons was something I knew. I began to feel like I was doing something real, like there was a genuine mystery. In retrospect, my enthusiasm was exaggerated; I had no reason to think that Santiago's sponsor was a local resident. It was just a necessary assumption I

51

Sharon Carton

had to make, without which functioning would've seemed futile.

By Friday, I was intrigued enough to go back to Broward Boulevard and confront the police with my inquiries.

"What're you asking us to do, Mr. Migliore, put out an APB on this guy?"

I was speaking with a Lieutenant Wilbur McSherry, a short, burly man well into middle age. His affected display of ingenuous bemusement seemed designed to mask profound indifference.

"No, Lieutenant," I said with a straight face, "but I'll keep that option in mind. My concern right now is to establish that this guy exists." In truth, I was starting to wonder belatedly whether the dizzy Darwin had just gotten the name wrong.

"And in what way did you think the Department could aid you in that endeavor?" Past tense, as if by this time common sense would dictate that I knew better.

"Well, I think for starters we could check the file on Santiago-"

"What file is that?"

"Don't you keep records on suicides? I mean, I don't know how things are done down here, but in New York suicides are investigated as homicides."

"Oh, yeah? Well, we've heard about the advanced techniques used in the big cities up north, but they haven't all caught on down here yet."

"Gimme a break, Lieutenant-" I began.

"The Santiago case was investigated and closed, Mr. Migliore. Accidental overdose. Why're you trying to prove it was different?"

"I'm not trying to prove anything, Lieutenant. I'm just trying to learn the truth. If it was an accident-"

"It was."

"-then fine. I'm just doing a job here, same as you, so how about some cooperation?"

Sometimes You Get Killed

"I don't have any information to share with you, Mr. Migliore. If I did-"

"Would you just check the file to see if a Nick DeBiasio claimed Santiago's body, and if you have an address or phone on him?"

"If I do, will you leave me alone?"

I nodded. People were often willing to do me favors for just such payment.

It took about twenty minutes, but when Lieutenant McSherry returned, he was markedly more cooperative. He apologized for the delay, explaining that he'd had some trouble locating the file. He didn't bring the file with him, but instead produced a small slip of paper with a phone number on it. "It's a local number, and I'm a little reluctant about this. You gotta give me your word, Mr. Migliore, that you won't harass this guy."

"I just want to ask him a few questions, Lieutenant, not interrogate him."

"What can he possibly tell you?"

"I don't know," I said honestly. "Santiago's mother seemed out of touch with the realities of her son's situation. Maybe DeBiasio can give me a clearer picture of just how bad his drug problem was."

"We know how bad it was."

"Events seem to suggest," I said, picking my words with care, "that it was a lot worse than his family believes possible."

"That surprises you?"

I shrugged. "Families can be wrong. So can appearances. It's my job to figure out what's what."

"And you think talking to this DeBiasio will help?"

"Can't hurt. He must've been close to Santiago, to have gotten the kid into rehab when nobody else even knew he had a habit."

"Well," McSherry said, unconvinced, "just don't give this guy a hard time. I shouldn't even be giving you the number, but maybe this'll satisfy you that there is no case

Sharon Carton

here."

At the very least, McSherry was probably thinking, it would get me out of his office. I thanked him, took the piece of paper, and drove back to the beach. From my hotel room, I called the number McSherry had given me.

The phone was picked up on the second ring. "Yeah." It was a flat, no-nonsense voice.

"Is Nick DeBiasio there? My name is Jack Migliore."

"This is Nick. Do I know you, Mr. Migliore?"

"No, but I represent Luis Mendoza, the uncle of Adalberto Santiago. I'm looking into Mr. Santiago's death."

"What do you mean, 'looking into'? Doesn't the uncle know how Al died?"

"Well," I temporized, "he knows what he's been told. He's just not satisfied that's the full story."

"If you mean did Al O.D. at the rehab clinic, that's the truth. I oughta know; I had to go claim the body."

"Yeah, well, I'd really prefer not to go into it over the phone. Can we meet somewhere? Let me buy you a drink tonight." The phone was silent. "How 'bout dinner? I'll pick you up. Where are you? You'll have to give me directions, but-"

"All right," DeBiasio said heavily. "But I'll meet you."

"Pick a place. I'm in Fort Lauderdale, on the beach."

"All right," he said again. "There's a street that runs perpendicular to A1A, that's the beach road. It's called Las Olas Avenue. Take it west about two miles. Restaurant's called Paesano's. You on an expense account?"

"Yeah."

"You'll need it." The line went dead.

He was right about the restaurant being pricey, but it turned out I was paying at least as much for the food as for the atmosphere, so I considered it a fair deal. McSherry

Sometimes You Get Killed

kept me waiting about ten minutes, during which time I entertained myself with the first Scotch, and the second pack of cigarettes, of the day. It was boredom that made me chain-smoke; after the first twenty, a cigarette became more a matter of rote than pleasure.

When DeBiasio showed up, his looks provoked a stab of ethnic instinct that made me discredit the man as a fellow Italian. I was only half-Italian, the other half being my mother's Irish, but there was something about DeBiasio's appearance that didn't fit with his name. Then I stopped, chiding myself for stereotyping, knowing I was looking for inconsistencies to justify my working an elusive, or illusory, case.

Nick DeBiasio had limp, dark brown hair and matching eyes. His skin was pale — I had yet to encounter a bronzed sun-worshipper in South Florida, though Ricardo Alvarez had come close — and his wide pores mottled with blemishes. His large, thick nose looked like it had been broken at least once. He was six feet tall, give or take an inch either way, and when, still standing, he reached across the table to shake my hand in greeting, I saw that he was carrying about twenty pounds too much for his medium frame.

"Jack Migliore?" His voice was as unemotional as it had been on the telephone.

"That's right. Thanks for coming." I studied his face further. He seemed to be in his early to mid thirties, which would make him a decade older than Santiago.

"No problem. You wanted to talk about Al?"

All business. "Would you rather wait 'til after dinner?"

"No. Get it over with," he said tonelessly. "I like to enjoy my food."

It shows, I thought. "Okay." I signaled the waiter for another Scotch, and DeBiasio ordered a Michelob. "You were friends with Berto, uh, Al?"

"That's right."

55

Sharon Carton

"For how long?"

"I'd known him about two years. We met at a bar on the beach."

"You know," I admitted, "I don't even know what he did for a living."

"At that time," DeBiasio recited without inflection, "he was tending bar. Where we met," he added, in case I'd missed it. "He held a lot of jobs over the time I knew him."

"Like what?"

"Tending bar, doing yard work, delivering pizzas, that kind of thing."

"He had no skills, I take it."

"No education, no real ambition. He was smart enough, but at heart he was just a beach bum, not interested in much. Undisciplined."

"And you?"

"What about me?" he asked without suspicion.

"What are you interested in? What do you do for a living?"

"I'm a waiter in a restaurant on the Intracoastal right now, but I'm saving up to buy my own place. Another year or two..." his voice trailed off.

"What can you tell me about Al?"

"He was going to come work for me. I figured it would straighten him out."

"You talking about his drug problem?"

"He was using pretty heavily. Not when I first knew him, but over the last year or so."

"What about you?"

"What about me?" he said again.

Jesus. Talk about pulling teeth. "Did you do drugs together?"

"No." Still no emotion.

"Well," I joked, "did you do drugs separately?" for which I got a blank stare. "I mean, were you doing any drugs, too?"

Sometimes You Get Killed

"Oh. No, I've never been into that."

"No, I guess not."

"What makes you say that?"

"Well," I reasoned, "if you were on drugs, you probably wouldn't have sponsored Berto for drug rehab."

"Oh. No, I guess not."

I was getting nowhere fast, which made me peevish. "Where'd you get the money?"

"What?"

"The money. The Center's pretty exclusive. How could you afford it?"

"Look," he said, growing impatient at last, "I was just his sponsor. I didn't have to pay for it."

"Well, do you know how Berto managed it, then?" I pressed. "I mean, he couldn't have earned much at the kind of work he did."

DeBiasio hesitated. "He borrowed it from me."

I was starting to feel like I was trapped in the kind of conversation I normally had with Ernie. "So," I tried again, "where did you get the bread?"

He shrugged. "Savings."

"Your restaurant money."

"That's right. That provided the bulk of it."

"And the rest?"

"Family. Friends."

"Berto's?"

"Mine."

"Uh huh." I tried to think of something else to ask. He was numbing my brain with his stilted, Dragnet delivery. Besides, I was getting hungry, and tired of chain-smoking. "What about Al's friends? Can you give me a list of-?"

"He didn't really have any. None that I knew of, anyway. Just me."

Oh, fuck it. "One more question. Why is it you were called to claim the body, instead of Berto's mother? She's next of kin, after all."

Sharon Carton

"I guess the Center gave the police my name. How would they've known to get in touch with her?"

"Did you? Get in touch with her, I mean?"

"No," he shook his head. "I didn't have any way to reach her. Al never gave me her number."

"How did she get word then, I wonder."

"I told the police he had a mother somewhere in Miami. I guess they took it from there. Probably found her in his address book or something."

"Yeah, probably."

He hadn't said or done anything suspicious, but I didn't like him, didn't trust him. Which doesn't justify my poor performance: I hadn't even remembered to ask him why, according to the telephone company, he didn't exist.

Chapter Six

For the next couple of days I did nothing but hang out at the beach and field phone calls from Ernie. Mostly he fed me tidbits of useless gossip about personnel at the Center. He seemed to be growing inured to the sanctimonious Reverend and the Spartan discipline of rehab. If he was feeling the effects of deprivation, it didn't come across the telephone wire. Besides, I had reason to believe there was something other than short story writing that was keeping him entertained.

In one of those phone calls, the sole thrust of Ernie's conversation was a brief, weird dialogue he had had with a fellow patient, whose name he didn't mention. It had convinced Ernie that he was incarcerated in a funny farm, though he didn't use it as an excuse for permission to leave.

"This guy, I didn't recognize him but I know all the staff so he had to be a user, anyway, he came up to me and says, now these were the exact words, not that it was easy to remember them, because they made no sense, which made it something like memorizing a completely random series of numbers, as opposed to a set of letters which combine to constitute a meaningful pattern, commonly known, of course, as a word-"

"Ernie...."

"Well, anyway, he said, 'Friend of the bride or the groom?' As a question." He paused.

"Well?" I prodded.

"That's it, that's what he said. Or asked. What do you make of it?"

"I don't know. What did you make of it?"

"I didn't know. It felt like a test, you know, like in

Sharon Carton

those World War Two movies where the American posing as a Nazi is spoken to in English instead of German to see if he instinctively responds in his native English."

"I don't get the connection, Darwin."

"Oh, I forgot. I mean, when I said those were the exact words, I wasn't being quite accurate."

"He said something else?"

"No, that's exactly what he said, but he said it in Spanish."

"Oh." Ernie knew the language, having studied it in college and having spent time doing a lot of nothing but drugs in Spain in the early 1980s. "Are you sure you understood him?"

"Yeah, perfectly. My Spanish may be rusty, but I'm sure that's what he said." I heard Ernie muttering under his breath in Spanish, as if he were repeating to himself the odd question.

"So what did you say?"

"Loosely translated, I told him 'neither, I just get off on weddings.' "

I smiled. "Was that the right answer?"

"I don't know. It sorta killed all further conversation."

After he'd hung up, I thought about what this might've meant. Ernie's looks — fair hair, grey eyes, even features — are too white bread for someone who didn't know him to assume he could converse in Spanish. Besides, there was a spookiness about the tendency even I had noted for Spanish to be spoken as a kind of secret-code language at the Center. Just a coincidence, or a prerequisite for employment and treatment? Then I decided I was being paranoid just because, outside of English, all I could raise were a few curse words in Italian and the minor Yiddish every New Yorker has learned by heart. After all, this was South Florida; Fort Lauderdale was just a stone's throw from Miami, where you can see Cuba across the water on a good day. Why shouldn't even the Anglos have mastered a few

60

Sometimes You Get Killed

key phrases in Spanish?

But who the hell were the bride and the groom?

The calls stopped after the weekend, which gave me hope that Ernie was either completely acclimated, busy or dead. It didn't seem as if anything was getting accomplished, which made me feel a bit guilty about Mendoza. I considered calling him, but all I had to report was that his nephew reportedly had had a bad enough drug problem to lend credence to the Center's story of his death. I didn't see what good such a phone call would do, and I figured it could wait until I had something a little more promising, or at least more substantial, to share.

That's not really why I didn't call. Every day, every hour that went by without my actively working to solve Santiago's death made me feel more neglectful. It reminded me that there would've been a dozen things I would've been doing... if I'd felt differently about the job. Like I said, I might not have been the brightest investigator, the most industrious or talented, but I'd always been dogged enough to get the job done. Orneriousness more than insight or energy, I guess, but when I took a case I worked it until it made sense. Now my mind was blank. I don't think there was a dearth of leads — it was a case, like any other — but I couldn't get my mind working on it. I had to hope Ernie, at least, was doing more in the Center than staying clean and gathering gossip.

On Tuesday afternoon, I got a phone call from Roger the Reverend. He had bad news, telling me I wouldn't be able to see Ernie the next day.

"Why the hell not?" I demanded, wondering which clinic infraction my iconoclastic friend had committed.

"He suffered a transient negative episode-"

"And what the hell's that?" I snapped. Okay, so maybe I'd misjudged Ernie, but I wasn't sure.

"It's...he experienced an adverse reaction to the

Sharon Carton

medication-"

"Medication? Medication? I put him in there to get him off 'medication', not to substitute new drugs for old."

"Mr. Migliore, calm down. Your brother-in-law will be fine. He's fine now," Roger amended, "just a bit under the weather. He's resting quite comfortably. You must understand, medication follows a prescribed course of supervised treatment. What your brother-in-law had been doing was self-medicating, using narcotics to treat his own real or perceived maladies — sadness, anxiety, depression. Our goal at the Center is not merely to purge his system of the symptomatic effects of his emotional problems, to wit, the narcotics.

"Rather," he went on smoothly, "our program is as successful as it is because we treat the problem and effectuate a permanent cure. It almost always involves medication on at least a short-term basis, in Ernie's case, an anti-depressant and a low-dosage major tranquilizer."

"You're giving him downers? Christ, that's-"

"It's not that simplistic, Mr. Migliore. You're probably thinking of the so-called minor tranquilizers like Librium and Valium. The trank your brother-in-law was started on is really something usually used in larger doses as an anti-psychotic, called Stelazine. In extremely low amounts, as we're giving Ernie, it has a tranquilizing effect."

"So if it's such a safe dosage," I said, not mollified, "why did he have a bad reaction to it?"

"Well, I'm not a physician, but any medication is subject to divergent side-effects, of varying intensities in different patients. Sometimes it's of a physiological origin, while sometimes it's interactive rather than intrinsic."

"Are you saying Ernie may've taken something here that, when combined with his medication, gave him a bad reaction? What could cause that?" I couldn't help thinking that, for all the suspicions this was arousing about the Center, it lent credibility to the story that Berto had

Sometimes You Get Killed

overdosed; he wouldn't even have had to get the drugs from the outside.

"It could've been caused by ingesting unauthorized substances-"

"Drugs?"

"Unauthorized drugs, or alcohol, sometimes cause the effect we've noticed your brother-in-law experience, but it could just as probably have been caused by some inherent chemical condition unrelated to the ingestion of extrinsic substances."

I considered this. "You're still telling me it's possible Ernie got hold of some drugs — all right, or alcohol — on the grounds."

"It's extremely unlikely, Mr. Migliore. We search our patients' rooms, and persons, regularly, but visitors are not subject to such a regimen. Slips are possible in the most secure of arrangements."

Professionally, I wasn't unmindful of the implications for the Mendoza case, but personally I was as concerned about Ernie's still having access to drugs as I was about his being handed them on a daily, albeit prescribed, basis.

"What about the potential for abuse? Of his medication, I mean."

Dr. Samuels smile could be heard through the wire. "Hoarding is an ever-present danger, but we try to create circumstances which make hoarding both difficult and unnecessary. Don't forget that medication is only part of their treatment, coupled as it is with intensive psychotherapy. If they want more pills, all they have to do is tell their doctor why they feel they need it. If it's appropriate, the course of medication is altered, refined to fit their needs.

"Moreover," he droned on, "the medication is not on the order of methadone, as a substitute for their addiction. We treat them by resolving the problems that made them turn to drugs or alcohol. For some people,

Sharon Carton

short-term medication while they're here aids the therapeutic process. For others, we learn that there are genuine chemical imbalances causing or fostering the problems, thus requiring long-term treatment, usually a combination of outpatient counseling and supplemental, controlled medication."

I was torn. What Dr. Samuels was telling me made a certain amount of sense — he had a credible delivery of even the most self-serving crap — and so I could feel some measure of confidence in the treatment Ernie was receiving. On the other hand, distilling what Samuels was saying, there was, first, the possibility that Ernie had gotten hold of drugs here, meaning Berto could've done the same. Did this impugn the integrity of the program, or did it support the story of Berto's overdose? Were the two mutually exclusive?

Second, something had happened to Ernie. Did I believe Samuels enough to let it slide, or was I suspicious enough to force the issue, to jeopardize, even abandon, the case, and insist on seeing Ernie, or just pull him the hell out of there?

Maybe Dr. Samuels sensed my hesitation. "Why don't we do this, Jack? Today is Tuesday. Come back in three days. That's Friday," he added, obviously not sure I knew the days of the week, "and we'll fit in a visit. We'll make a special allowance to accommodate the special circumstances."

I hesitated, then relented. "All right. I'd appreciate that." It had been just the right suggestion on his part. Had he known that, if he'd offered me Monday, it would've seemed too far off to reassure me?

"Well, I can see, and appreciate, your concern for your brother-in-law. I admire and respect you for that concern. I want you to recognize that we respond to that."

Funny, I liked him even less after that — I'm not sure why — but I also felt slightly appeased. I thanked him, and waited for Friday.

It never came.

Chapter Seven

Ernie's voice was breathless and hoarse.

"I can't talk," he whispered.

"Then why'd you call?" I said.

"I mean on the phone."

"I know. So why'd you call?" I was being disagreeable, but he'd woken me out of a sound sleep. It was late Tuesday night, or early Wednesday morning, rather. I reached for a cigarette and my light.

"You've got to come out here. I have to talk to you," he said, an unusual urgency in his tone.

"What, now?"

"No-"

"It's only Tuesday." I looked at the clock-radio on the night table. "Make that Wednesday. It's not fucking Parents' Day 'til Thursday."

"Come anyway, okay? Okay?"

"Shit. Wait a second. All right. I'll sneak in tomorrow night. What's the set-up?"

"Huh?"

"Guards, night watchman, Dobermans: What do I have to get past?"

"Oh." There was a pause, and I started to drift off again. "Nobody patrols. There's just the booth. Paul Rios is on duty. He's why you have to come."

"He's the one who was on the watch when Santiago died?" I guessed.

"Look, I can't be seen out here now-"

"How'd you get out of your room?" I wondered suddenly, still not fully awake.

"That's not the problem," he said. "Just get here

Sharon Carton

tomorrow night."

When he hung up, he still hadn't told me enough for me to decide whether Ernie was blowing this development out of proportion. I wondered if he was stoned, legitimately or not, when he placed the call.

I walked into the Center, softly whistling the title track from the Eagles' "Hotel California," the place that was "programmed to receive/you can check out any time you like/but you can never leave." You had to like a place that left its doors open to the public, where you needed a key to exit, not to enter. Getting out I would worry about later. That would just be a matter of timing. Like high school: Bell goes off; everybody changes rooms. I could handle that.

According to Ernie, Dr. Paul Rios was sometimes referred to, sniggeringly, by the patients as "Dr. *Dios*," or "Dr. God." It was a play on his name and his lowly stature at the Center. Perceived as a small man, intellectually and emotionally though certainly not physically, Rios was amusingly self-important, but harmless and largely ineffectual. Also known as "Dr. Touchy-Feely," prone to coercive hugs he held uncomfortably long. As I found out later, his nickname led Ernie to the knowledge that Rios had been in the monitor booth the day Santiago died; one patient informed Ernie that, on that night, God had been ensconced in Heaven, surveying his realm and not seeing, or not caring about, one of his children injecting himself with a fatal dose of barbiturates.

Rios had agreed to meet with me at midnight. It meant blowing our cover, but in Ernie's judgment (odd how rarely those two words find themselves in the same sentence), Rios was one of the good guys, or at least nonthreatening: If we had to let someone at the Center in on our secret, Rios was probably a safe place to start. Worst come to worst, we'd just pull Ernie out of there, depending on what Rios had to tell me.

Sometimes You Get Killed

The Center was a residential facility, with dormitory apartments for the staff in back of the main building. Ernie told me that the staff retires to their quarters for the night well before eleven. Allowing an extra hour for stragglers, I figured I had a good chance of being undetected showing up at midnight. Ernie's weird phone call had me curious: Was he taking this phony case bit that seriously? He had seemed to be onto my ruse until now, so why all the melodrama? Or maybe Dr. Rios really had something he wanted to tell me.

I had no trouble reaching the surveillance booth on the second floor unobserved. I swung the door open, but no Dr. God. The pneumatic door swung shut behind me, and I turned instinctively, fighting a twinge of claustrophobia. That's okay, I told myself. Dr. God had the keys, and would let me out.

Except Dr. God wasn't there. The computer-operated monitors were turned off; Dr. Rios' half-consumed mug of coffee was there, but not the doctor. I sat down at his computer table to wait for him, and looked around me.

At the blank computer screens. At the locked door. At the wall clock telling me God was not infallible, because he was now ten minutes late.

At the feet of Dr. God, who wasn't even immortal, because when I stood up and followed the trail of those feet, I found that they led me to Dr. Rios' throat, which had been slit from ear to ear. God wasn't late; God wasn't sleeping or even bored. God was dead.

I jumped up, fighting the rising gorge, telling myself there was nowhere to be sick. Then, unthinking, I pulled at the door; no luck, of course. *You can check out any time you like/but you can never leave.* It sent me back to the body of Dr. Rios, looking for his keys. Someone else had already gotten them, someone who, obviously, had gotten to Dr. Rios before I had.

The phone, I suddenly thought, and lifted the receiver of the telephone built into the computer board. Nothing, unless you count dead silence. I desperately

Sharon Carton

scanned the board to figure out why, until I opened a panel door and found a series of switches, one of which was labeled "PH". The switch wouldn't budge; apparently, Dr. Rios' killer now had the key to that, too.

I forced myself to calm down, to realize that, until the next bell, until gym or milk and cookies or home ec, neither God nor I would be going anywhere. Then I realized that the same was not true of someone else. Someone who I guessed knew Dr. Rios planned to meet me tonight. Someone who knew enough about what Dr. Rios was going to tell me to make sure Rios didn't. Couldn't. Someone who maybe also knew, therefore, who I really was, why I was there. Why Ernie was there.

Oh, Jesus.

It took me nearly ten minutes to figure out how to get the computer up, and to get Ernie's room on the screen. Relief flooded through me as the screen showed Ernie sleeping deeply on his stomach, his face turned away from the camera. I slumped back into Rios' swivel chair, weak-kneed with the suddenness of fear leaving my body. I even smiled to myself, shaking my head at the thought of someone out to get Ernie. One dead body — all right, two if you count Mendoza's nephew — didn't mean Ernie was next. Besides, there being someone out to get him seemed so superfluous, or redundant; Ernie always managed to sabotage himself so much better than anyone else could.

My eyes studiously avoiding the inert form in the room, I took a sip from Rios' coffee cup. It was still warm, like Rios himself. More relaxed, I took a deeper gulp as I started using the computer to scan the Center. The hallways were empty, and room after room was occupied by a sleeping patient.

Before too long the coffee was gone and I was feeling sleepy. It had been so long since I had allowed myself to look that I had almost forgotten the corpse at my feet. On a small counter in the corner of the room sat a four-cup minidrip coffee maker. It had enough coffee left in

Sometimes You Get Killed

it for one more cup, which I poured into Rios' mug. I took a small sip of the bitter, scalding dregs. It needed sugar, but I didn't see any. I sat staring at the screen; there was nothing of interest, nothing moving. Where was Rios' killer? Had he fled the building? Did he kill Rios because of something Dr. God had seen, or because of what he was going to tell me? If the killer knew Ernie was a fake, would that pose a threat to the killer? Not necessarily, I reasoned, and felt my eyes closing.

After a few minutes I roused myself enough to get up and try the door again. It opened. My mind all fuzzy, I couldn't remember what Ernie had told me about the door schedule. My watch showed it was nearly one a.m.; had I fallen asleep? I hadn't heard the click of the door lock being released, but maybe that's what had awakened me.

I made straight for Ernie's room. He was still lying on his stomach. "Come on," I shook him, "wake up, we gotta get outa here." He didn't respond, so I roughly rolled him over onto his back. His eyes were open and staring blankly, his throat cut like Rios', ear to ear. I screamed, and woke up still in the chair in the monitor booth, being shaken by Dr. Khoragian.

"Get up," he was shouting angrily, "what the hell are you doing here?"

I bolted out of the chair and grabbed for the door closing slowly behind Khoragian. "Rios was murdered," I called behind me, "get the cops!"

The coffee had been drugged, I realized in disgust. Its effects coupled with the fresh memory of my nightmare filled me with a heavy dread as I raced down the hallway. I slammed open the door to Ernie's room and grabbed his arm. He rolled over limply, and I saw him breathing, his mouth slightly open.

"Wake up, you asshole," I said, grabbing his arm to pull him out of bed.

His eyes opened confusedly, and he murmured a word of protest.

Sharon Carton

"Rios is dead," I told him, as I tried to get him on his feet. The dazed look on his face and the loose-limbed lack of coordination told me he had been doped up, or else he was still in the throes of his nightly medication.

"Jack?"

I didn't answer, and he shook his head, muttering, "I'm zoned."

He was wearing a dingy white tee shirt and shorts, not exactly street wear, so I grabbed his old jeans, draped across a chair in the corner of the room, and struggled to force him into them. His black Converse high-tops were in plain view under the bed, but I didn't bother; middle of July in Fort Lauderdale, at least I wouldn't have to worry about him getting frostbite.

No sooner did I let go of him than he slumped like a rag doll across the bed. I pulled him back up off the bed and reached for the doorknob.

"*Fuck*," I cursed feelingly.

We were locked in.

Then it dawned on me. And I had called Ernie an asshole? I pulled my Colt Python from my jacket pocket and shot out the lock. The noise was ear-splitting in these close confines. I went back and grabbed hold of Ernie, who was half-sitting, half-lying on his bed. Putting his arm around my shoulder, I dragged him through the door and into the corridor.

Empty? Where was Khoragian? Or anyone else, for that matter? Surely everyone had heard the gunshot. Hadn't Khoragian called the cops?

I decided not to go back to find out. First order of the night was getting the hell out of this madhouse, where I couldn't tell the good guys from the bad guys, where a killer — whom I wouldn't have even recognized if I stumbled on him — might still have been roaming the premises.

Holding Ernie upright as best I could, I loped down the corridor, pushing doors open and hearing them click locked behind us. We ran like that for about ten minutes,

Sometimes You Get Killed

through four or five doors, until we found ourselves entering the same hallway on which Ernie's room could be found. We had run in a complete circle. I grabbed the door behind us before it could close, and pulled Ernie back into the stairwell from which we had just emerged.

Propping him up into a seated position, I released my grip on him. "Stay here," I cautioned. "I'm going back to get some keys."

"Hafta tell ya somethin'," Ernie slurred.

"Later," I told him, and left him there.

I guess I could've shot our way out of the building, so going back to try to get a key from Khoragian was just an excuse. I wanted to see if the police had been called, or were already there, or if the killer had been found. I'd been thinking of that the whole time I'd been running with Ernie: If the killer was still there, I'd rather be in a position to confront him than to be surprised while defensively fleeing. When we ended up practically where we'd started, I took it as a sign that running away had been a mistake.

When I got to the booth, Khoragian had been joined by Roger Samuels, Gregory Tessler and some blond kid I didn't recognize. Someone had discreetly draped a jacket over Rios' face and torso. There was an angry buzz of chatter in the room, which my entrance silenced.

"Did you call the cops?"

Khoragian nodded wordlessly, annoyed — at me, at the murder, at life, I didn't know.

I made a mental note of who was there, and who wasn't. "Check the patients," I instructed the room in general, under the misapprehension that anyone was even listening to me. "Two of you go and rouse everybody and wait for the cops."

I think the blond kid nodded.

"And what about you?" Khoragian demanded suddenly.

"Give me your key," I told Tessler. He held it out, but then hesitated. I grabbed it, and sprinted back to where

Sharon Carton

I'd left Ernie. I ignored Roger calling my name; nobody physically tried to stop me. I hadn't even realized that that was probably because I was still holding my gun in my right hand.

I found Ernie lying on the landing in the stairwell, face down. "Come on, Darwin," I said in irritation, kneeling beside him, "wake up."

Taking him by the shoulder, I rolled him over, and felt my stomach lurch. Ernie's white tee shirt was soaked red with blood, his throat, sliced open from his right ear to his Adam's apple, was dripping scarlet from the gaping wound onto the tiled floor of the stairwell. His eyes were slits of pain: He wasn't looking at me, or at anything else. I don't know what he saw. His breathing sounded ragged and labored, and his face was a mottled grey, perspiration beaded on his forehead.

My knees gave way and I sank onto the ground, my heart pounding, blood rushing in my ears. For about five seconds I knelt there frozen, unable to move. Ernie had begun to draw his knees in to his bloody chest in a fetal curl. Finally I put the gun on the floor alongside me and felt for his pulse in his wrist. His hand was ice-cold, clammy, and his pulse alarmingly weak, thready, erratic. With a soft insistence I spoke his name as I removed my jacket.

I had just placed it on Ernie's chest to keep him warm, when I heard a sound behind me. Half-turning, I was suddenly thrown off balance and knocked onto my back. On top of me was the bulky figure of a man I didn't recognize, a blood-stained switch-blade opened in his right hand, poised to strike. I grabbed his right hand with both of mine, as I rolled on top of him. Beneath me, he wrapped his legs around my left knee to flip me and regain his position of dominance. All the while we struggled for sole possession of the knife. I drove my right knee into his groin, and as his grip on the knife loosened momentarily I wrenched it away from him. Collapsing back into a sitting

Sometimes You Get Killed

position a few feet away from my attacker, I took a few deep breaths to regain my composure. Moving so fast that I barely knew what he was doing, the attacker twisted himself onto his belly and scrambled for my gun.

I didn't think. The knife was plunged deep in his back before I even realized I had moved. I must've picked up my gun soon after that, because it was held tight in my right hand when the police burst through the door a few seconds later.

Chapter Eight

"Police, drop it!"

I looked at the revolver clutched in my hand, then, with a mental effort, unclenched the fist and let the weapon fall. Instantly, two of four uniformed officers grabbed me, cuffing my hands behind my back with these weird, newfangled plastic jobs. One of the other cops kneeled over the body of the stranger with a knife in his back, looked at his partner and shook his head. Good, I thought viciously, then got my brain in gear enough to realize that maybe it wasn't so good. The fourth cop was between me and Ernie, blocking my view, but I guessed from the movement of his back and shoulders that he was performing CPR on Ernie. Oh, God. Dr. Khoragian pushed his way through the small crowd to help the cop with Ernie. The officers struggling to hold me, I tried to squirm free to go to Ernie, but couldn't budge.

It was only after the ambulance had taken Ernie away that I was able to explain to the cops' satisfaction what had happened, with absolutely no help from my good buddies of the Center. They vouched for me only as someone who had "claimed" to be the wounded man's brother-in-law, someone who had no business being there at that hour. With a gun. Khoragian chimed in that he had found me fleeing from the booth and Dr. Rios' body. Nobody had been shot, though, and the police seemed to reach a decision that they didn't have enough to hold me.

Roger had had a few words with the ranking officer who had arrived by that time, a Sergeant Brown or Black or something like that, but I got the feeling the police let me go despite, rather than because of, Roger's counsel. Brown/ Black evidently believed me; I've always been a credible

75

Sharon Carton

liar.

In the back of my mind, I knew that I had only bought myself some time. I had told the cops the truth about what happened, but everything else about my story was, of course, a fabrication. They would discover the whole truth soon enough, and I had no reason to think my situation would improve any with the inevitable revelations.

At the moment, though, my thoughts were concentrated elsewhere. I took my car to Broward County Hospital, knowing only that an hour and a half earlier Ernie had been alive when he was put into the ambulance. It took me nearly twenty minutes to learn where I could even find him; at first I thought I was getting a bureaucratic run-around. Gradually it became clear that the nurse at the station was genuinely confused about which room Ernie was in. Several phone calls later we learned to my surprise that Ernie was not in surgery. I took that as a good sign that his operation had been so brief.

The nurse sent me to a Intensive Care Unit on the second floor. I felt the blood drain from my face when I saw Ernie. His face was a pasty shade of grey, with a tube secured in his mouth by criss-crosses of white tape. The life support machinery showed a steady heartbeat, and I told myself not to panic, that Ernie had been in worse shape when he got shot last summer.

"Are you the brother-in-law?"

I spun around to face an attractive young woman apparently in her early twenties, wearing medical whites. Nodding, I asked her, "Are you his surgeon?"

"Oh, no," she smiled, then, catching herself, assumed a more somber expression. "I'm a nurse, Mary Dessimore. You need to speak to Dr. Grady. He's been waiting for you."

"Well, can you tell me what his condition is?"

"His condition?"

"I mean, I take it the surgery was successful, but-"

"Oh, no, we haven't even scheduled him yet."

Sometimes You Get Killed

"And I'll tell Jonah," Annie went on, in a measured tone. "He'll come, I know he will. We'll both be there on the next flight." She paused, and said into the silence, "Just hang on, Jack, all right?"

"You might call Jeff," was all I said. "Maybe he can do something. I don't know what."

"Do you want me to call Lieutenant Mendoza for you? At the very least, he can substantiate your claims."

"I don't know. Yeah, all right. Whatever you think."

"Jack?"

"Mm?"

"It wasn't your fault."

"I know," I lied.

"It wasn't."

"All right."

Three-thirty that afternoon I was released. Louise Fischman, the Center's therapist, was waiting for me.

"Why am I free?" I asked, trying to care. Maybe it matters, I told myself. Maybe it means something.

"Dr. Samuels corroborated your story. All they had on you were your fingerprints on the murder weapon. The only tricky part was getting the charge dismissed on our 'carry a gun, go to jail' statute."

"I have a permit," I said unemotionally.

"It's no good here," she replied.

"Where are you taking me?"

She turned to me in her car, a look of surprise on her face. "Back to your hotel."

"No," I insisted, "take me to the hospital."

"Why?"

I looked at her, and didn't say anything.

"You haven't been told, have you?" she asked quietly. "About Ernie?"

I cocked my head, and when she added, "He isn't at the hospital anymore," I understood. Of course; that's how they could charge me with three murders.

Sharon Carton

"It happened early this morning," she went on. "His heart failed. Twice. They, well, let's say that by the second time their efforts to revive him weren't exactly heroic. They'd had an idea about using him as an organ donor, but Florida law requires an autopsy for all homicide victims, so, well..,.."

"So," I echoed.

"I'm sorry. I really liked Ernie. His...he's been taken to the Medical Examiner's office...." Her voice trailed off, and when I didn't say anything, she began again. "You were close, weren't you?"

A shrug of the shoulders seemed my safest response.

"Had you worked together long?"

I stared. So they knew.

"The police filled us in," she explained. "At first, when they discovered you'd been operating down here under false pretenses, they became more suspicious. Then a Lieutenant McSherry confirmed that you'd spoken with him. They put two and two together and figured out the real story."

Finally I found my voice. It matters, Jack, I told myself, it makes a difference. "Who was this Eddie Velez?"

"A patient at the Center. He...we had no idea he was psychotic. It's our suspicion that he'd gotten hold of some drugs somehow. The autopsy will say for sure."

When she didn't seem to have anything else to say, I tried to think of a question to occupy her, to stop her from trying to read my face. I didn't feel like conversation, but even that was preferable to her silent appraisal of my reaction to Ernie's death. "Did Velez kill Santiago, too?"

I wasn't paying close attention, but I got the impression the theory of a connection between the murders was not new to her.

She hesitated, then shook her head. "I don't think so. Berto died of a drug overdose. That doesn't seem to have been Velez's style."

I winced, vividly remembering that style, then realized without much effort or surprise that she was lying. I tried to care why. "How well did you know him?"

"Ernie?" she said, startled.

"No, Velez."

"Oh, fairly well, I thought. After all those hours of counseling, I thought I understood the nature and scope of his, well, disorder. I had no idea...." She paused, then, without looking at me, "I blame myself."

Join the club, I thought.

She dropped me off at the hotel, giving me back my gun, saying goodbye and expressing regrets about Ernie. I tried to go back over what she had told me, read between the lines, remember anything that might have some significance. It took too much effort to get past the one thing eclipsing anything else she might've said.

Annie and Jonah had just arrived, and were sitting in the hotel lobby, waiting for me, not talking. We spent what was left of the day drinking at a bar on the Strip. Nobody had much to say. In the morning, we all left Florida to head home for New York.

Almost all of us, anyway.

I stayed in New York a little under a week, feeling sorry. On the fourth day I got in my car and began the drive south to Fort Lauderdale, to finish it.

Chapter Nine

1. Why did Eddie Velez kill Dr. Rios and Ernie, i.e., how did he choose those two as his victims? Was Rios his only intended victim, and Ernie only killed when Velez was attempting to escape?

2. Had Velez killed Berto? If so, is that why he killed Rios, i.e., because Rios had seen him? If so, why did Velez wait so long? And if Rios had seen the first murder, why didn't Rios tell the cops? Blackmail?

3. If Louise Fischman's story was true, where did Velez get the drugs he was on when he committed those two murders? Was it the same place Berto got the drugs he O.D.'d on?

4. What was Khoragian doing at the monitor booth the night Rios and Ernie were killed?

5. How did Velez get out of his room that night? He used Rios' key to get out of rooms after killing Rios, but how did he get out of his own room?

(I scratched out that last question, remembering that anyone could exit during the five-minute hourly breaks. Then I added another:)

5. Did Rios see Velez leave his room? Is that why Velez had to kill Rios? Was Rios the intended target, or just killed to eliminate a potential witness? Witness to what? What had Velez really planned for that night? To kill

83

Sharon Carton

Ernie?

 6. Where did Velez get the knife?

 7. Who the hell was Eddie Velez?

 8. What was Louise Fischman lying about? Something in her manner, and in Ernie's, had hinted at more than a professional relationship between her and Ernie. All jokes aside, should I take that as damning evidence against her?

 There had been a memorial service for Ernie in New York a few days before I left. Ernie's long estranged stepfather, Charlie Madison, showed up at the service. I counted that as a major victory.

 Over-sentimentality on my part. I'd also suspected Ernie had secretly longed for Charlie's approval, but for all I knew Ernie might have been pissed that Charlie picked that opportunity to patch things up.

 With as much delicacy as I could muster, I tried to sell Charlie on cremation. Ernie and I had once discussed it in drunken conversation, and he had proclaimed a desire to have his ashes scattered over Shea Stadium. Besides, I didn't know how good a job of reconstruction a mortician could do on his battered body. It was no use; Charlie stubbornly adhered to some unarticulated principle, and wouldn't be budged.

 So I got something of a surprise when it turned out that what was shipped home to New York wasn't a body, but only ashes. Those days I wasn't functioning too well, so Annie called the Fort Lauderdale medical examiner's office, where a clerk told her that cremation was *de rigeur* after autopsies. Annie seemed troubled by it, but I was trying too hard not to think about it.

 Charlie was an ex-cop who had been briefly married to Ernie's mother. When Ernie's mother died,

Sometimes You Get Killed

Charlie took over the job of raising him, or at least for those periods when he couldn't get out of it. He hadn't exactly been one of Ernie's biggest fans, but the grief he showed at his stepson's death seemed deep and heartfelt. Maybe it was regret at opportunities lost. Regret, or guilt.

He showed up alone at the service and didn't mingle with any of the others there. Annie made a point of spending some time with him; I tried to remember whether they had met before. I wondered whether she was consoling him as ineffectively as she had done me. She had the right words, and the right feelings — she and Ernie had been so close it had often made me jealous — but I wasn't too receptive.

Charlie and I hadn't spoken much over the years, but he got talkative when we all met over at my apartment for refreshments after the service. We both got pretty drunk. Charlie seemed to have some trouble holding his liquor, and before too long he was telling me about Ernie's natural parents.

Ernie's mother, Elizabeth, had fallen in love with a man whose name she would never reveal. He'd broken up with her when the illegitimate Ernie was an infant. Charlie met her while she was on the rebound, and won her hand, though he admitted to me that he was never sure she loved him.

"But God, she was beautiful, Jack, and there were times I just couldn't believe my luck, me, a street cop, married to this beauty. She was smart, sophisticated, real classy, like a model. But she couldn't keep faking it, pretending to love me, pretending to be happy."

I asked him, as delicately as I could, how she died.

"Booze and pills," he said shortly, as if he said it all the time. Maybe he did, to himself.

"Accidental overdose?"

He looked away a moment and shook his head, quickly, with short, rapid jerks.

Jesus. "Ernie never said."

Sharon Carton

"He never knew. He was just a baby when it happened."

"But when he got older? You never told him his mother killed herself?"

"What's the point, I figured. Bad enough I could hardly stand to see his face, to see her in his face, and kept shipping him off to her friends and my family. I knew it wasn't his fault, but I kept telling myself it wasn't mine, either."

"None of your relatives or Elizabeth's friends told him either?" I was incredulous that a secret of this magnitude had been kept for some thirty years.

"They didn't know," Charlie said. "My buddies on the force saw to that. Professional courtesy, you know?"

"Yeah, but something like that, how could you be sure it wasn't an accident?"

"Right," he said bitterly, "and she kept the suicide note on her nightstand just for emergencies."

I couldn't think of anything to say after that. After a few minutes of silence, he walked away. I went over to Annie's side and stayed there, her arm slipping comfortably into the crook of my elbow.

Those days were so jumbled. There was a part of me that felt it was fitting that Ernie, who, when alive, had told me of life's sadness and the guilt of personal responsibility, was now in death providing me with proof of both. A final lesson from the master of melancholy. Ernie would've appreciated the irony, the Zen orderliness he had never managed in life.

But another part of me said, stop it, don't try making sense of this. Ernie wouldn't have sought it, would've felt manipulated by it. Senselessness, anarchy, uncertainty, they were all states of existence unto themselves. They can be tolerated, they must be acknowledged and respected — "from a distance, if you're lucky, like you, Jack," Ernie had once said to me.

I hadn't liked that. All I wanted in life, what I did

Sometimes You Get Killed

for a living, militated against mystery, disorder, not-knowing. To me that was a temporary flaw or aberration, something to be corrected, something I was *charged* with correcting. I couldn't always prevent it; more often I was called in too late, and given only the chance of finding out what had gone wrong and, if I was particularly good, maybe why it had. This time that wouldn't make a difference. Everything that I did from here on was aftermath, useless trivia. It didn't seem worth it to restore order to the universe after the damage had been done. Nothing would change.

Annie talked me through it, counseling that it was part of my nature to need reasons for everything, that if I were to function I would require a logical environment, however engineered or artificial it might be. "It doesn't matter," she said, "whether the reality is an absence of order or sense or meaning. If there isn't, you have to create it."

"If it's not there already," I protested, "I mean, if it's not there and just hidden and my job is to find it, then it's not real. It's not reality, it's something else. Make believe. A semantic game."

"No, it really doesn't make a difference whether the sense is something you find or invent, Jack. *That* would be playing some specious word game. What's the difference whether it's always been there, known or unknown, or whether you're just the first to discover it? If it fits the pattern, it's reality, or as close as we're sapient enough to comprehend."

That had gotten a smile out of me. "Okay, but if I die and become more in touch with the truths of existence and find out you were wrong, I'm really gonna be pissed."

It's not that I was convinced by her reasoning. It was enough that Annie believed it. She was my oracle, and whether or not I always understood or was won over, the fact that Annie had considered my problem and deemed it less than apocalyptic was sufficient reassurance for me to go on.

Back in Florida, I had taken a room in the same

hotel on the Fort Lauderdale beach. I told myself it was just cheap and convenient, but Annie's look when I told her suggested there might've been a little more to it than that. My thought processes were a bit disarrayed just then. I was barely aware of being in Florida; I had some trouble focusing on exactly why. It had something to do with a list of questions. Annie had written them down after a marathon conversation with Jonah, Jeff and me. When she handed the list to me, I looked at her and asked why she had these questions. She looked right back at me and told me, with her typically cryptic style, and said they were my questions, but I just didn't have the psychic energy to ask them myself.

I figured she was right, more or less, and I guess that was why I returned to Fort Lauderdale. There was something here for me to do, but I couldn't get started. I didn't seem able to do much of anything. Instead, I sat in the hotel room, and felt much as I had the day Ernie died. I forced the time to pass in much the same way as I had done then, too.

The only volitional movement I was capable of was extracting cigarettes from the pack, lighting them, inhaling, exhaling, and then beginning the process all over again. I smoked one after the other, wheezing asthmatically, lighting the next cigarette by the embers of the butt-end of its predecessor. There was comfort in the rhythm, a safe mindlessness in the rote series of gestures. The carbon monoxide cloud in which I became enshrouded offered me distance from the grief.

I smoked, and, so I didn't have to think about anything else, I thought about smoking. I thought about why I kept up such a self-destructive habit. Sure, I smoked because I liked it, but also because when I had quit for a while, smoking became the most important thing in my life. During that brief period, a few years back, the significance of tobacco took on outsized proportions. I was never a chain-smoker, but suddenly cigarettes were all I thought about, from the moment I woke up in the morning until the

Sometimes You Get Killed

time I fell asleep each night. Time became elastic and unreal; thirty minutes were no longer thirty minutes, but a half hour I had gone without smoking. My days were measured by the yardstick of deprivation. I no longer had good experiences or bad experiences: There were only events that would've been more pleasurable, or less unpleasant, with a cigarette. I was experiencing a would-be life, a life that wasn't anything by itself but that would be something else if I were still smoking.

When I did quit back then, I did it cold turkey. Without hypnosis, acupuncture or nicotine gum, I beat out the physical addiction. Not so the psychological compulsion, the one that hangs on a bit longer, after the headaches, shakiness, nausea and the lump in your throat, had all been overcome. In the end, I had just reached across a coffee shop table to where Ernie was sitting, and I took one of his. As I remember, Ernie didn't comment. He understood all about addiction, about bad habits.

He had told me that he didn't worry about drugs being dangerous, that it would only be fitting if his bad habit should be his downfall. Bad habits, he told me, are the real life, modern day equivalent of the "fatal flaws" afflicting the characters in classical literature. It's the best we can do with the material we've been given, he said. "What's really obscene is when someone dies as a result of a good habit, like a runner dying of a heart attack while jogging, or a health food fanatic choking to death on a piece of broccoli. How can you justify something like that?"

Ernie was dogmatic about this point of view. Alice Morrissey, the woman on trial this summer in New York for murder, had been Ernie's lover during law school, when they had both been chiefly into sex, drugs and rock and roll. When they got reacquainted several months ago, Ernie's tastes hadn't changed, but Alice had moved on to more mainstream addictions, like the expensive material goods in her classy apartment on the Upper East Side.

Alice had told Ernie to grow up, that his bad habits

Sharon Carton

were a childish attempt to hold onto individuality by rebellion. Ernie complained to me that it felt like what the pod people kept telling Donald Sutherland in the remake of Invasion of the Body Snatchers, about how there's no pain in conforming, in becoming one of the body snatchers; just go to sleep and before you notice, the old things, like love, like freedom, don't matter anymore.

Ernie's principles weren't always easy to spot, but he knew what they were and he stuck to them. He didn't believe in too many things; outside of drugs and Elvis Costello, the Mets were Ernie's only religion. In deference, then, I kept the memorial service as secular as possible. He once categorized himself as an agnostic, or, as he put it, "an atheist without conviction." Another time he joked that he was "between religions," and that when he died, he wanted to be buried in an "agnostic church." I figured now he'd have to settle for adding a layer of debris to the Mets' playing field. Opening Day, next Spring. Part of the festivities.

I was ready to admit that an unhealthy portion of my grief was guilt. Could I swear that I hadn't forced him into this whole South Florida deal to satisfy my obsessive demand for tidiness? The same trait that made me so well-suited to my work made me impossible to live with. I needed everybody in their places, all of them with happy faces. Who was I to say Ernie hadn't been better off with his illicit coping mechanism?

Okay, let's be honest. Ernie hadn't been doing well. He had needed help. Is help the same as interference? I had certainly interfered, but getting Ernie killed hadn't exactly improved his lifestyle.

All I knew was that I felt miserable, and I wanted someone to blame. Someone other than myself.

And if I understood anything, if the questions prickling my subconscious told me anything, it was that Ernie's death had been no quirk of bad luck or bad timing. Someone had needed Ernie to die. Paralytic grief

Sometimes You Get Killed

notwithstanding, I figured I deserved to know who and why. It wasn't a lot to ask, and I wanted it enough to insist.

I was doing a lot of insisting lately. Annie had expressed some concern about my insisting on bringing my gun with me back to Florida.

"Last time, it saved my life," I said, just a bit defensively.

"And that's the only reason you're bringing it, right?"

"I think that's a pretty good reason."

"I just don't believe," she said, "that that's your real reason."

"But it *is* a pretty good one," I pointed out, sticking with my best argument.

"I might agree with you, Jack," she parried, "if the murderer were still alive. But you killed him."

"So what're you saying, I'm being irrational, I'm out for vengeance or-"

"Vengeance against whom?"

I consider it one of Annie's character flaws that she was able to keep a grip on good grammar when all about her were losing theirs. "You tell me, it's your scenario," I shot back, feeling my hold on logic slipping away.

"All right, then," she answered mildly, "vengeance against Ernie's killer?"

"Who happens to be dead," I said in triumph. It didn't last.

"That's precisely my point, Jack."

Oh.

"Whatever might have constituted a legitimate need for your gun on the last trip doesn't apply now."

"So what's your point, woman?" I said with as much derision as I could muster.

It was wasted. She smelled victory. "My point, you little charmer," she smiled, "is that you've become wedded — oh, sorry, I mustn't resort to profanity. Let me say instead that you've begun to feel incomplete without

Sharon Carton

that thing. It's as if you believe yourself helpless without it, and omnipotent with it."

"I go lots of places without it," I whined.

"Ordinarily, yes," she persisted. "It's just that since...all this happened, you feel particularly vulnerable, even perhaps-"

"Don't say it."

"-emasculated."

"I knew that was coming."

"Come on, Jack, you understand what I'm saying. I just don't want you to become dependent on that...object."

"I'm not."

"Good," she said, unconvinced.

"Good."

"So you won't take it with you?"

"I'll think about it."

She stared at me.

"No, I mean I'm going to give it serious thought. Some really serious thought."

My first clue that Annie's concern about my mental stability was justified had come when I approached a four-way stop sign in Fort Lauderdale, at the end of the seemingly endless return drive to Florida. When I pulled up to the intersection, there was one car, a yellow Volkswagen Rabbit, already sitting there, directly across from me. About five seconds — a full five seconds, at least — after I'd come to a halt, a white convertible BMW with the top down reached the corner to my immediate right. I watched approvingly as the Rabbit drove through the intersection, passing me on the left.

Then it happened. With complete confidence in the correct order of things in the universe, I lifted my right foot off the brake and placed it lightly on the gas pedal. Confusion changed to fury as the BMW charged ahead of me through the intersection. I barely managed to brake in time. Without even realizing what I was doing, I flipped on my left directional and turned through the intersection to follow the BMW.

The BMW turned right at the next corner; so did I. I'm not sure what my intentions were, but by the time the BMW and I made our next turn, I had taken my gun out of the glove compartment. It wasn't until I had pulled into the left lane and, now parallel with the BMW, I started to raise my right hand — holding the gun — until it was pointing at the BMW's driver, that I finally realized what I was doing. I briefly caught the look of horror on the motorist's face when I hit the gas and screeched away. I concentrated on getting the hell away from there as fast as possible, and, not familiar with the area, it took me some time to get my bearings again. It took me a little longer to stop trembling. It wasn't exactly my finest hour.

Chapter Ten

There was someone else, of course, who had lost somebody close to them in the Center's black hole. Annie had called Lieutenant Mendoza when I was arrested, but I phoned him again when I got to New York. He showed up at the memorial service; we didn't talk much there.

He had reacted well on the telephone. It wasn't a call I had wanted to make, even if I wasn't clear on why. Maybe I thought that he, unlike Annie, would be savvy enough to see my guilty part in Ernie's death. My friend Jeff was a cop, but he was still young and naive, and trusting enough to believe I could do no wrong. Jonah was neither naive nor trusting, but he was too loyal not to let sympathy override his better judgment. None of them blamed me — I knew it, I knew them well enough to be sure of it — but I was not so confident about Mendoza.

The Arlington cop surprised me. He made soft, kind noises of support and sorrow. He didn't ask for a report on his nephew's case. He didn't ask for any more details on Ernie's death than the bare essentials I had provided. He didn't ask why I was calling from New York, why I had left Florida without finding out the reason for what had happened, whether there was a connection between Ernie's death and Berto's, whether I had given up, whether in my mind it was all over.

Mendoza said nothing of any of that. He expressed regrets in a sincere, mournful tone, and said he would wait. "I'll wait, Jack," was all he said. I knew what he meant, though at the time I thought he was overestimating me. At that moment I felt capable of nothing, no conjecture, no resolution, no action. All I had were questions, and I was

Sharon Carton

too scattered just then even to recognize them as anything so structured, so aggressive as questions. At that moment I thought it would be like that forever.

Feelings had never seemed real to me; transitory, intangible, they couldn't compete with activity, movement, people, objects, even ideas, reasons, motives, beliefs. Alongside those things, emotion was amorphous, undefinable, fleeting, not to be dwelt or counted on. Now I had become mired in feelings so palpable as to have a physical shape, color, dimension. They seemed as real and permanent as a piece of furniture or the shade of Annie's eyes.

When the torpor lifted enough for me to return to Florida, it was with a suddenness that left me dazed and breathless, straining to recall with any accuracy the details of the dream from which I had only just awakened. I didn't feel so much better as different, and where I had so recently been frozen I now could move. It wasn't happiness, wasn't even a bad facsimile, but I recognized it as being enough, and the best I could muster just now.

From Florida, I sent Mendoza a bill for past expenses, waiving my fee based on what I told him in an accompanying note was "professional courtesy, and if you don't buy that, then because services were rendered in satisfaction of a preexisting debt, and because, at any rate, services rendered did not generate successful resolution of inquiry." I gave him my address and phone in Fort Lauderdale, hoping he would use the address to forward a check but wouldn't use the phone number.

I didn't especially want to talk to him. First, I didn't want to hear him blame me for, or try to absolve me of blame for, recent events. At the time, it didn't occur to me that Mendoza might feel himself responsible for Ernie's death; in view of my own role, Mendoza's part in things seemed too attenuated for guilt.

Second, I didn't want to fight over the bill, over its amount, over its implicit finality. Third, and most

Sometimes You Get Killed

problematic, I didn't want to grapple with the question of whether I'd returned to Florida to work on his case or on my own. I knew I had an agenda of sorts, but I wasn't sure how it jived with his. Mostly I didn't want to have to articulate that agenda; if forced to explain what I was doing here, I might have to confront the senselessness of my decision. Or the hopelessness.

Over and over I read through Annie's list. No matter how I approached the questions, they remained things I just didn't know yet, not things that belied the truth as I had been told it. Trying to come up with vulnerable points of attack, I looked for inconsistencies or inaccuracies. Everything had seemed to flow naturally from point A to point B to point C. Nothing had struck me as being illogical or out of sync. If there were something wrong, I hadn't seen it at the time. So why doubt now? Were my doubts genuine, warranted, or were they something else — camouflage, a diversion? If I could find a flaw in the reality of what had happened, in what had seemed to happen, maybe the worst part of what had happened wouldn't be real, either. So far everything made sense, things I didn't want to make sense, made sense. In a way I was fighting to destroy the verisimilitude; when I eventually put the pieces back together, maybe I'd come up with a different picture.

I considered the logic of the Center. Everything seemed appropriate there, nothing out of order. It was just what I expected the place to be. To the letter, it fit my preconceptions, even down to its warts. Maybe that meant something. The place was average, too average, maybe, too generic to be true.

Ernie had come to the Center with more experience; this was his second shot at rehab. What had he said about the place? Something about the place being like a movie set, no, like the scene in the film, The Sting, the scene at the betting office: As soon as Robert Shaw, the mark, left the room, the con men reverted to their real selves, and the room was no longer a betting office. Ernie

Sharon Carton

had said there was a similar feel to the Center. At the time I told him he was paranoid, wondering what the staff got up to when the patients were tucked in for the night. Now I was wondering, hoping that there was something more sinister to it than that.

It was absurd, of course, trying to infer abnormality from the very fact of normality. But I didn't think about logic. I thought, instead, about *The Human Factor,* a Graham Greene novel. It was a spy novel, I guess you'd say, in that its protagonist was a spy, but the book was less about espionage than about human nature. For much of the first half of the book we read about the mundane daily life of a British civil servant. His life is boring, routine, but we learn that he likes it that way, that he constructs it that way. It's only later that we learn why; it's the bland anonymity that gives him his security, his camouflage. He's not paranoid, he's not even dull; he's a spy who knows that it's only by appearing to be the same as everyone else that he would be above suspicion, and safe to conduct his clandestine activities.

Was the Center a shallow facade? More likely, it was as genuine as everything else, which meant equal parts honesty and deceit, the lies little ones to cover not evil but inadequacy, laziness, sloppiness, stupidity. I expected that, should I succeed in piercing the Center's cover, I would discover weakness and error behind the bravado. It was confidence gave them their strength; shatter it, and they'd be as vulnerable as I could hope.

The first person I got in touch with when I got back to Fort Lauderdale was Ernie's lawyer friend, Catherine Olwine. She had tried to reach me after news of Ernie's death hit the airwaves, but I hadn't returned her calls. I suppose I could've called her for legal help when I was arrested, but it hadn't occurred to me. Maybe she would've declined; maybe she would've thought it unseemly to represent the man accused of her friend's murder. Ernie had told me about her prosecutor's mentality, so maybe

Sometimes You Get Killed

she would've begged off on that ground.

The enthusiasm of her greeting took me aback. She'd struck me, both from our earlier meetings and from Ernie's comments, as being that anomalous yuppie combination of vibrant enthusiasm and chilly lack of emotionalism. But she seemed distinctly moved by Ernie's death.

"Have you filed suit against the hospital?"

"Excuse me?" So much for sentiment.

"I'm not soliciting," she went on in a business-like voice, "but I can recommend good local counsel if you're not represented yet."

"Wait," I broke in, confused, "are you talking about me suing the hospital where Ernie died? What for?"

"Well, presumably negligence. Gross negligence. I think you've got the basis of a cause of action, according to what I read in the papers. Didn't they allow him to die without a court order?"

"Did they need one?" I was puzzled, but felt excitement growing. Maybe there *was* someone else I could blame. "I mean, to be fair, he was already brain dead."

"Who said?"

I told her the doctor's name.

"All right, we have only Dr. Grady's word for it. Did he give a do-not-resuscitate order?"

"Huh? I don't know."

"Does the hospital have an ethics panel? How many doctors concurred in the order?"

"Look, I don't know any of that."

"Maybe you should."

"Hey-"

"All right, all right," she backed down. "I just think it's something we might want to look into."

"Look, I may be a little slow, but are you saying the hospital fucked up? In what way, exactly? I mean, are you saying that maybe he wasn't brain dead, and they killed him by discontinuing life support prematurely?"

Sharon Carton

"First of all," she said, in that way lawyers have of outlining their conversations, "they didn't just unplug him, from what I've been given to understand. He suffered a heart attack, and they didn't provide adequate care. That's what we'd argue, anyway. Second, even if their diagnosis was accurate, there are certain procedures which are mandated in this state. If they didn't follow them, they're subject to liability."

I sighed tiredly. "Okay. I'm just not sure...I mean, what's the point to all this."

Her frustration carried down the wire. "You're kidding, right? What kind of detective are you? Forget that: What kind of *friend* are you? Their negligence might've been responsible, at least partially, for Ernie's death. Don't you want to know that? Don't you want them to pay?"

"In dollars American?" I said wryly, unable to keep the note of defeat from my voice. "I just can't see pursuing a lawsuit at this point."

"You won't have to. That's what lawyers are for." She paused, then, plainly disappointed, added, "I can't believe you don't care about this."

I felt defensive. "I just don't want the money, not like this."

"Don't think of it as a reward, or a prize. Think of it in terms of accountability. If you win, you could give the money to some charity that would've pleased Ernie. Free hypos for drug addicts, I don't know. Better yet, don't think of the money at all, except as a means of measuring responsibility."

"If that were true,..." I began, then broke off.

She seemed to sense what I was thinking, and fell silent.

After a pause, I said, "I appreciate your concern. You're right. If the hospital is blameworthy, I mean, if they're responsible, even in some small measure, for Ernie's death, that's something I'd want to explore. You said you could recommend someone?"

Sometimes You Get Killed

"Listen, you just let me play with this on my end. All I needed was a go-ahead from you. Don't worry about a thing; just let me run with it for a while. I'll get back to you as soon as I get anything."

I thanked her, and gave her whatever details I could remember, including the name of the nurse, Mary Dessimore, I'd spoken to in Ernie's room. I felt embarrassed, and slightly ashamed, that Catherine was more zealous than I at pursuing all possible wrongdoers. Maybe it was just being caught off-balance, or maybe I just wasn't up to her energy level. It wasn't like me to ignore a lead. Why had I been so reluctant to latch onto a possible villain? How the hell was I going to accomplish anything down here if my brain still wasn't in gear?

After I hung up the phone, the wheels started to turn enough for a curious thought to occur to me. It began to strike me as a little too convenient that Ernie's body had been summarily cremated. If there had been some malfeasance on the part of the hospital, there were no longer any remains to be exhumed to enable us to prove it.

I decided it sounded too paranoid to be communicated to Cathy, especially since I had urged cremation to Charlie, so I just stored it away in the back of my mind for future reference. I didn't seriously believe Cathy would discover, much less be able to substantiate, anything actionable, but it didn't matter. It was Catherine's game to pursue now, not mine.

No longer on Mendoza's payroll, I had nothing but my obligation to the dead to spur me on. I lolled around, unable to mobilize myself, for three full days. Most of that time I spent on the beach, sitting idly by myself until the heat became oppressive, driving me into the ocean. Then I would swim with dogged ferocity to the point of exhaustion, at which time I would roll onto my back and float back to shore.

Some of that time I concentrated on not thinking,

Sharon Carton

but the rest of the time I gave in, allowing my thoughts to wander where they would. The anger fought with the depression to drive me out of my stupor. I couldn't face going back to the Center, confronting the false, oily heartiness of the Reverend or Khoragian's sly malice. A conversation with Louise Fischman wasn't such an unpleasant prospect, but what I remembered most about our chat was my feeling that she had been lying. I had no reason to think I could count on straight answers from her this time.

The list of questions wasn't much help. Whatever information I might've been able to get from them with Ernie undercover was now lost. Everyone concerned knew me to be a private investigator. For all they knew, I could be now investigating the possibility of legal action against them. For all I knew, that could be true. I considered asking Cathy whether we could name the Center as a defendant. Maybe court-supervised discovery proceedings could turn up more info than I could. Maybe I should hire a private investigator.

The only questions I had that could be answered by anyone not from the Center were about Nick DeBiasio, the friend who'd signed Berto into rehab, and claimed the body when he died. The whole mess about shipping Ernie's remains back to New York had provoked some questions about Berto. Why, for instance, had DeBiasio been called by the police, and not Berto's mother? I could understand the Center getting in touch with DeBiasio; he was the one who'd checked Berto in. But the police knew about Berto's mother from DeBiasio, so why had Berto's remains gone to DeBiasio? I know Berto's mother was eventually contacted, but almost as a perfunctory afterthought.

So, in the end, the first move I made to resume the investigation was to talk to the police. Which, if you think about it, was kind of funny, since at the time I'd been calling the telephone number the cops had given me for Nick DeBiasio. Oh, DeBiasio answered, all right, but it was the

Sometimes You Get Killed

way he answered that struck me as odd.

What he said was, "FLPD, Sergeant DeBiasio, can I help you?"

Chapter Eleven

Learning that Nick DeBiasio, the so-called bartender who had supposedly checked his friend Berto into the Center, was really a cop meant several things, but not others. It didn't mean I now knew how Berto died, or why Ernie did. It meant, on the other hand, that there had been that thing that warms the cockles of anyone who still shivers at the words, "grassy knoll": a cover- up. The Fort Lauderdale cops may not have been responsible for either death, or for Dr. Rios' either, for that matter, but when Nick DeBiasio answered that phone I knew that they had been hiding something from me. I just didn't know how much, not then.

Of course, the down side was that I had been wrong about DeBiasio. He really was Italian.

"You bastard." This was my way of breaking the ice. DeBiasio had agreed to see me at the station. I wasn't grateful, which is not to say I was exactly uninterested.

"Back off, Migliore. We're not gonna get anywhere with that attitude of yours," DeBiasio said, implacable as I remembered his being.

"My attitude? You're gonna see a lot more than my attitude if I don't get some answers from you."

"All right, all right. I'm here, aren't I, and I'm talking to you, aren't I? You probably have some questions, so why don't we start there."

I knew this tactic. "Sure, and this way you don't tell me more than I'm smart enough to ask about, right?"

"Don't be crazy, Migliore. I just don't know how much you've already figured out."

Sharon Carton

"Uh huh," I said, unconvinced. "So let's start with Berto. Did you even know him?"

"Not personally, no."

"But officially, yes?"

I got a nod, so I pressed on, wondering if I only got twenty questions. "Was he alive when you knew him?" I asked, slightly sarcastically.

Another nod.

"Did you really check him into the Center?"

"Of course."

"But you weren't friends. Was he a snitch of yours? Is that why you got him into rehab?"

"No."

"Look, could we speed this up a bit? Why did you get Berto into rehab? What was the connection between you?"

Pause. "Al was undercover."

My God. "He was a cop? Berto Santiago was a cop?"

"Yeah."

"Jesus. Jesus. But...nobody knew! His mother, his uncle...."

DeBiasio shrugged. "I don't know why he kept it secret. He wasn't tight with his family, that I know."

"And when he was killed in the line of duty, you didn't see fit to tell them? What gave you the right to-"

"It wasn't my decision, Migliore. The investigation was ongoing. The judgment was made that exposing Officer Santiago's cover could compromise our investigation."

"But what was he doing there in the first place? Why were you investigating the Center? I mean, obviously he didn't really have a drug problem, so why was he there?"

DeBiasio sighed. "We'd gotten complaints. From the neighbors."

"About what? About the Center?"

"There were two categories of complaints. One group was about drug addicts in the neighborhood. You

Sometimes You Get Killed

know the deal. Treat the sick, but not on my block. People made allegations about unsavory characters, drug dealing, you know."

"And the second type of complaint?"

"They said there was something suspicious about the way the Center operated. That these citizens had tried to get family members or friends admitted and were turned down. That no one they knew in the community had been able to get someone in there. So we looked into it."

"By putting a man in undercover."

"Not at first. We made inquiries, but they were fruitless. We kept running into brick walls. So we decided to put the kid inside."

"And?"

"And?" DeBiasio echoed.

"And what did he learn?"

"We never found out. We got reports from him, but he never learned anything significant."

"Then why was he killed?"

"Well," he temporized, "we never established conclusively that it was homicide."

"Oh come on!"

DeBiasio sighed. "All right. Yes, I suppose there's no point in denying it at this juncture."

"Was it even drugs?"

He shook his head.

"Don't tell me," I said. "He was hacked up, like Dr. Rios and Ernie, wasn't he?"

DeBiasio showed signs of deep inner turmoil, or at least that's what I inferred from the slight tightening of his lips. "We arranged with the Center to give out the O.D. story. They were only too happy to go along, lesser of two evils publicity-wise."

"Since when were you in cahoots with the Center? I thought you were investigating them."

"Officer Santiago's death changed all that. We called in the feds for help, and that's when we found out the

Sharon Carton

truth."

"The truth? About...?"

"About the Center," DeBiasio answered stingily.

"I knew it. It's not a rehab clinic at all, is it?"

"Well, of course it is. What did you think? The point is, it's just that, well, its government. The Center is run by the feds, of the feds, and for the feds."

"Wait," I said breathlessly, "let me get this straight. The staff and patients are all federal employees? What is that, some cosmic coincidence?"

"No, of course not," DeBiasio replied, not certain I was joking. "It's just that these were people, the patients, I mean, with high-level security clearance. The government couldn't risk letting them seek counseling and treatment at a civilian facility."

"Yeah, right. So you're trying to tell me that other than the fact that all these people got their paycheck from Bolling Air Force Base, there was nothing fishy going on at the Center?"

"That's-"

"So why the hell did three people get cut to pieces?"

"Eddie Velez," he said economically.

"Yeah. Eddie Velez. Where does he fit in all this?"

"He was just an outsider. A lunatic."

"A civilian? I thought you said-"

"There were a few at the Center; they were just carefully chosen."

"What, they had a quota of psychotics to fill?"

"Okay, bad choice of words. My point is that the Center decided to admit a select number of civilians to quiet some of the community complaints."

"Around the same time you sent Berto in?"

"Apparently."

"And you don't think it's a coincidence that the only two people murdered by this outsider were the only two sent in to investigate the place?"

Sometimes You Get Killed

"You're forgetting Dr. Rios."

"Fuck Dr. Rios, what about Ernie? Why would Velez want Ernie dead?"

"Velez only killed Darwin in the course of his attempted flight from the scene-"

"And Berto? And Dr. Rios? Why did he choose them as his victims?"

"Officer Santiago, I don't know. It could've been chance, it could've been Santiago learned something-"

"About what? About Velez? What could there've been to learn, since Velez had no connection with the operation of the place?"

"Our theory is that Velez learned something about one of the feds, patient or staff, we don't know, and might've been trying to blackmail them. Maybe Officer Santiago found out about it, and maybe Dr. Rios was killed because he had witnessed Officer Santiago's murder."

"Come on, that's pure conjecture. You're speculating without any evidence. Why don't you know more?"

In a mechanical voice, DeBiasio intoned, "The investigation is now under federal auspices."

"You mean the Center is now investigating itself? Fucking fantastic."

"In a manner of speaking. It's just not under our jurisdiction any longer."

"Lemme ask you something. Why are you so generous with the info all of a sudden? Aren't you afraid I'll compromise the federal investigation?"

"At this point it's strictly damage control. You stumbled on my identity, and we figured if we didn't inform you, you could only cause more damage with some more clumsy investigation. Besides, we looked into your background. Military intelligence. We're hoping you'll have some perspective on this, keep your priorities straight."

Sharon Carton

I did. I called Mendoza and tattled.

He took the news about his nephew pretty well. Of course, I omitted the more lurid details of the manner of death, focusing on the real reason Berto had been at the Center. If he was proud to find out his nephew had been a cop, he didn't say. He didn't say, "I told you so," either, but he didn't have to.

Instead, he thanked me, and told me I was still on his time clock. In return, I thanked him but rejected his offer. I was working for myself now, and he'd be welcome to anything I learned, as part of what he'd already paid for.

My next move was more directed, though nowhere near as gratifying. I set about trying to find out who Eddie Velez was, and what kind of government employees get their own private rehab clinic. I hadn't decided that DeBiasio was lying, but that didn't mean I bought wholesale into his story. What seemed more likely was that he was telling me only half the truth, the only half he knew. Maybe he was content to kick it upstairs to some feds, but he hadn't lost a partner. I made a mental note to speak to the Fort Lauderdale cop who had. It might not give me any insight into the murders, but I figured Mendoza deserved that much for his money.

There was so much that didn't make sense about DeBiasio's explanation. Something about the Center had aroused community and police suspicion. Something that predated Velez's entrance into the Center, since civilians weren't admitted until they were needed to assuage community suspicion. I made another mental note to get a list of the Center's chronology of admissions.

Anyway, since Velez had not been a fed, he had no connection to whatever was suspicious about the place. So what did Velez have to gain by killing the undercover cop? Did Velez have something in his past that Berto discovered? Or did Velez just kill Berto because he learned he was a cop, and wanted to prevent that secret from being discovered?

Sometimes You Get Killed

I wondered, too, whether Ernie's death was just the result of being in the wrong place at the wrong time, working for the wrong person. "I have something to tell you." Ernie's slurred last words to me. I hadn't forgotten them, but I still didn't know if they meant anything. He could've figured out who'd killed Berto, or maybe he just wanted to tell me he needed to take a leak. He might've been drugged or medicated or just sleepy. An autopsy would've given me some indication, but if they'd been able to fake Berto's cause of death, no doubt they'd done the same to Ernie. Now I knew the cremation had nothing to do with a lawsuit, and everything to do with the grassy knoll.

Cathy was in when I called her at home. Physically, anyway.

"Jack?"

"Yeah."

"Jack?"

"Yeah? Something wrong?"

"I can't begin to tell you."

"Well, try. Does it have anything to do with the case, the lawsuit thing?" It was back to twenty questions.

"Yes."

"Did you find out anything about Ernie's death?"

"No. Yes."

"Oh, well, at least we're getting somewhere."

"It's just that, I mean, I just don't know how...."

"Did you get in trouble because you're not supposed to solicit clients?"

"What? Well, no," she replied, on firmer ground, "I asked around about that, and it's no problem. First of all, I'm not doing this for a fee, so I'm not seeking pecuniary gain. Second, I could make the argument that we're close friends, which is an exception to the no-solicitation rule."

"Uh huh." She was getting more comfortable, more relaxed.

"There is something," she went on, "I hadn't

Sharon Carton

considered before, when I spoke to you, and that's standing."

"Standing where?"

"No, the doctrine of standing. It's a legal term. It limits those persons allowed to bring suit on an issue. You have to have a legally cognizable interest," then added, in layman's terms, "you know, like a stake in the outcome."

"So? I don't have a stake in Ernie's life?"

"Not in his death, you don't. At least, I don't think so. I might have to speak with Ernie's stepfather. He might be the only suitable plaintiff."

"Oh." I didn't know how Charlie would react to that bit of news, but that would have to wait. "Okay, so what's the other thing you wanted to tell me?"

"Oh, Jack...."

"No, don't start that again, just spit it out, don't stop to think."

"Those people you talked to in the hospital don't exist," she blurted out.

"What?"

"That Dr. Grady. There's no such person on staff. Nobody ever heard of him. And that nurse, Mary Dessimore, there's no one on record at the hospital of that name."

"How can that be?"

"I'm telling you. I asked at least a dozen doctors and nurses, and nobody knew these people."

"So what're you saying, I imagined it? Where's Zapruder when you need a guy with a movie camera?"

"What?"

"Never mind. All right, so I dreamed those people up. What did you find in Ernie's records?"

"Okay." She took a deep breath, then released it slowly. "There weren't any."

"Excuse me?"

She repeated it. "No records. Ernie was never there, according to the hospital files."

"All right, now we're getting weird." My mind

Sometimes You Get Killed

was shouting *grassy knoll, grassy knoll*. "You actually checked their little file cabinets, and Ernie's folder wasn't there?"

"It's computerized, but yes, Ernie wasn't there."

"Do they have any idea what happened to his records?" Somehow I knew what answer was coming.

"They never heard of him."

"Uh *huh*. Fine. Now, let me just see if I've got this straight. Ernie never was taken to Broward County Hospital. He wasn't put on life support there. He didn't die there. Did he die somewhere else, or is he still alive, playing poker somewhere with Elvis and Judge Crater?"

"What?"

"I mean, maybe I made this all up. Maybe it was all a practical joke. Maybe we should see if the coroner's even heard of him."

"Jack, this is all crazy."

"No," I said, "this is terrific, and you haven't heard the half of it."

I told her my news, and we tried to figure out what the two items meant.

"Look," Catherine said in her lawyer voice, "we know what you saw. Ernie was there, he was taken there by an ambulance — I'm sure we can find their records — and he died of heart failure. Somehow the people you met there disappeared, along with Ernie's file. How could that happen?"

"Forget how. How is easy. The feds are involved, they got how up the wazoo. I've read the book, I've seen the movie, I've got the tee shirt, I've even watched the committee hearings. What I want to know is why."

"To avoid liability?" she suggested.

"Maybe, but I think that's a stretch. Look, you have any friends in Washington?"

"D.C.? Did Ernie tell you I lived in the District for four years? Most of my friends are still-"

"No, not just friends. Connections, like high up in

the federal government. You know, networking and all that."

"Oh, well, I still have some former colleagues at the U.S. Attorney's Office, and one or two at Justice."

"Great. Good. Call them. Call them all. See if you can find out anything about the Center, about what was going on there."

"And what are you going to be doing in the meantime?"

In the meantime I had coffee with Berto Santiago's partner, Officer Rudy Grissom. He spoke slowly, quietly, with an understated intelligence that I found ingratiating. Grissom had large, expressive brown eyes, and a shy smile that was friendlier than any I'd yet encountered from the Fort Lauderdale Police Department.

Notwithstanding his cooperative attitude and patent sorrow over the loss of his friend and partner, Officer Grissom had little of substance to offer me. He and Berto had been patrolmen together, "you know, doin' the beach on Friday and Saturday nights, rousting the drunks and the druggies, occasionally busting the out of town gangs or the he/she hustlers.

"Then," Rudy noted, "Al gets pulled, because he's Latino, you want my opinion, to go undercover. No big shit, I think, but Al was psyched." Officer Grissom, despite the implicit criticism in his words, commented without rancor or apparent hostility.

"What was he supposed to be investigating at the clinic?"

"Community complaints, mostly."

"What kind of complaints?" I prodded, though I'd already heard this from DeBiasio.

"Well, two varieties. We'd had some complaints from people, or from their doctors really, who couldn't get their people into the clinic. Just complaints, filed but not especially suspicious. They were just annoyed, wanted us to look into the possibility of the place operating on

Sometimes You Get Killed

kickbacks."

"And did you?"

"Not enough evidence."

"What was the second kind of complaint?"

"Oh, that was the neighbors," Rudy said. "Didn't like having druggies and alkies in their backyard, so they made up stories about there being illegal narcotics on the premises."

"Any evidence to support *that*?" If anything, the fact that Grissom's version completely mirrored DeBiasio's raised more than it quelled my suspicions. I was finding Grissom credible, but I had to question any two people who could recite the identical stories. Reality, in my experience, has never been quite that reliably objective.

"It never got that far," Grissom was explaining. "A patrol was sent out to Davie to look into it-"

"Davy? Who...?"

"Davie, the town. West of Lauderdale. That's where the clinic is."

"I thought it was in Fort Lauderdale."

"Well, technically Davie. Border of the town. Anyway, patrol did a preliminary investigation, y'know, asked a coupla questions, looked around the buildings-"

"And?"

"Nothing, or not enough to go on. Except somebody wasn't satisfied — one of the complainants, one of the detectives, I don't know. So they decide to set up the undercover op and send in Al."

"Why him? He wasn't a detective, or an undercover cop."

"No, but like I said, he was Cuban."

"What does that have to do with anything?" I said, my knee jerk primed for action.

"Jeez, you must be new here," Rudy said, looking me up and down, as if first noticing my pale skin. "You want to advance here, you gotta have connections or a Latin

115

Sharon Carton

name.

"Funny thing was," Officer Grissom went on, softly, "Al wasn't big on his heritage. Never spoke Spanish, though I know he could. It was like he wanted to be Anglo, maybe because he figured that was the only way to advance, though it didn't work out that way. Kind of ironic. He didn't understand that you can think of yourself as American, you know, not just a hyphenated American, but you're not assimilated until others see you that way."

"And that didn't happen with Berto?"

"Not on the force. To the guys up top, Al was useful because he was 'Berto Santiago,' not some promising patrolman named Al. And of course, wanting to shed his Cuban image was one of the things that drove him away from family. Break with tradition, you know. To Al's mother, there's no such thing as a Cuban-American; you can only be one or the other, not both."

I thought about this for a moment, then said, "One thing I'm still having trouble with...."

"Yes?"

"...is how readily everyone accepted the overdose story. I mean, he was an undercover cop on assignment, and-"

"First of all," Rudy interrupted, "outside the Department, no one knew he was on assignment, and-"

"But what about within the Department?"

"Well, the Department didn't think it was overdose. They kept the investigation open."

"And? Who was put on this case? Did you ever hear of anything done on the case?"

"No, but...." Officer Grissom looked uncomfortable, his loyalties divided.

"What, Rudy? What do you know?"

He started slowly. "Al was...young. Single. You know?"

I nodded, but I didn't know. "Go on."

"There was talk around the Department that Al liked

Sometimes You Get Killed

to party."

Oh. "Did Al take drugs?"

"I don't know," he said, trying not to look at me.

"A joint now and then?"

"Maybe."

"Maybe," I echoed.

"There was just," Rudy went on tentatively, "some sentiment that this could've happened. A kid, kinda wild, moody, emotional. You know, the Latin stereotype. Maybe the pressure got to him. Even the fact that he'd been so eager to take the assignment, as if it was so dangerous that he might've had some kind of death wish...." Then Rudy looked at me, and added, "Well, it was just some people talking, you know? Not officially."

"And what did you think?

Rudy hesitated a moment, then said, with a trace of sarcasm in his soft voice, "I think even suicidal people get murdered."

I smiled grimly. "And even the paranoid get followed."

He searched my face, and allowed a shy smile to curl his lips. "You go get 'em, Mr. Migliore."

"I'll do that, Officer. I'll do exactly that."

And finally, I meant it.

Chapter Twelve

Ernie had provided me with a list of staff and patients at the Center, annotated with his handwritten comments about some of them and my own notes based on additional thoughts as he passed them on to me. I now revised it to indicate which people, according to DeBiasio, were government employees and which were civilian.

The return trip to the Center was weighing heavily on my mind; it was something I knew I had to do, but I kept putting it off. I rationalized that I needed more ammunition before I could accomplish anything there. In truth, the thought of walking those hallways again, encountering the ghosts I dreaded seeing, was more intimidating than I liked to admit.

When I finally got the information I'd been seeking, I could no longer delay the visit. It took three telephone calls to get it. First I tried my New York contingent, Jeff with his police computer and Jonah with his less conventional grapevine. Neither one panned out. Defeat being at least as informative as victory, I read a great deal into those failures. They should have given me what I needed. Even Catherine's D.C. resources tapped out, which she seemed to take as a personal affront.

My next attempt involved a young woman attorney Ernie used to work with at the Defense Department. Back then, Lucy Graham, whose slightly dithery personality belied a sharp intelligence, had been agreeable and cooperative in helping me access some not so accessible files at Defense in order to clear Ernie of the murder charge. This time she was not so obliging. What struck me as significant was the timing: Initially eager to get me what I

Sharon Carton

needed, especially when she learned the circumstances, she got back to me later in the day with a flat refusal. "More than my job's worth," was the way she put it. I wasn't sure how to read that, since a year ago she had disliked her job enough for me now to be surprised she was still there.

Pay dirt came from a last resort source. Last year, when Ernie went undercover at the Manhattan Law Center, we became acquainted with the school's debonair, enigmatic Dean, Laurence Summeridge. There had been a palpable air of mystery about Dean Summeridge, which, coupled with some tantalizing rumors and a few oblique comments by the Dean himself, gave me reason to think that he might be able to succeed where all else had failed. I was right.

"All of them?" I asked him.

"Oh, no," he said breezily. "You were told the truth as far as that was concerned." He listed the nonplayers.

"Make that a half truth," I replied, and told him the inconsistency between the lists.

"Well, I certainly understand the omission. Makes quite a difference, don't you think?"

I did, and told him so, thanking him for his help.

Never mind, he said.

I hung up, shaking my head in wonder, marveling at the ease with which this unusual man had just given me the precise piece of information I'd needed. For a moment I considered whether he or his information was to be trusted. Then I shook off the paranoia, deciding that, while the emotion was not out of place in this investigation, it could too easily get out of control.

Then I went back to the Center, to visit a ghost.

"Perhaps we should begin again." Roger Samuels was cordial, but his words weren't without a touch of arrogant disapproval.

"With introductions?" I managed to lift an eyebrow.

"I feel we're really strangers. So much deceit...."

Sometimes You Get Killed

"On both sides."

"As you say." This with a rueful shrug, and a brief, confessional nod of the head.

I tried to hide the distaste from my voice. "Am I safe in assuming we've at least got the names right?"

Dr. Samuels smiled. "Mr. Migliore. Jack. You aren't above reproach, you know. The service we offered your friend was genuine. It was you who were here under false pretenses. We did all we did in a sincere effort to provide therapeutic-"

"Yeah, and you worked wonders, didn't you? Look, none of that holier than me shit, Reverend. You guys aren't exactly what you seem, are you?"

"I thought that was all made clear to you, Jack." He seemed wounded. I wasn't really surprised that he'd been in touch with DeBiasio. "The fact that this facility is run primarily for the treatment of certain government employees who, by the nature of their rank and access to classified information, could not seek help elsewhere certainly does not vitiate the value of the care we afforded — to them or to Mr. Darwin.

"Not so long ago," he went on, "those government employees would have been booted out of their jobs because of their problems, when it was their high-pressured jobs that undoubtedly caused or contributed to those problems. Instead of finding fault, you should applaud the humanity of a program that-"

"Oh, shove your humanity up your ass, Reverend." I had had enough. "Do you even know how to tell the truth anymore?"

His mouth had dropped open. "How dare you-"

"And how dare you insult me by continuing to shovel the shit when four men, one a cop and one my partner, are dead? Don't you think it's time to give me some straight answers?"

"Mr. Migliore, if you think you know something-"

Sharon Carton

"I know which part of the government you work for." At the faint, almost — but not quite — imperceptible look of disbelief on Dr. Samuels' face, I added, "Oh, yeah, it's classified, but that doesn't mean it's not true."

"Well."

"Yeah, 'well.' At first I thought, even CIA spooks can need detox. That wasn't necessarily inconsistent with what I'd learned from DeBiasio."

"So? What is it that's troubling you?" Even now, he stayed in character, hearty, concerned, eager to make the connection.

"Eddie Velez."

"Yes," Roger nodded, lamenting. "A bad mistake on our part."

"At last some true words. Yeah, Velez was a poor choice, but not the way you mean it."

"What are you-"

"The mistake was hiring him. He wasn't just a civilian you sloppily decided to treat. He wasn't just some homicidal nut who slipped through your tight security. He was a Company man. He was one of you."

"Ah. Well."

"Yeah. Big surprise."

"Your sources are surprising, Jack, but not flawless. However, our own weren't exactly impeccable, either."

"You gonna try to tell me you didn't know Velez was CIA? Don't hand me that shit."

"No, the point is we thought he was, but we were in error."

"What? No, he-"

"He was a government employee, all right, " Dr. Samuels agreed, adding with relish, "it was just a different government."

I was speechless. It didn't last.

"Velez was a spy? I mean, a spy for the other side? FSK?"

Sometimes You Get Killed

Samuels nodded. The KGB is dead: Long live the FSK."

"And you didn't know?" I said. "What, until when, the night Ernie got killed? Before?"

"We suspected. We started to suspect we had been infiltrated. Well, even before that, our intelligence was that there might have been a possibility of compromise. That's why we felt compelled to admit civilians, to protect our cover."

"So you admit the Center is a cover? For what?"

"No, Jack, not the way you think. It's just what you've been told all along. The only difference is who we are, not what we're doing here."

"So why would the FSK be interested?" I felt slightly foolish, talking about Russian spies. Ernie would've been hysterical, rolling on the floor.

"Why would the other side be interested in debriefing our people?" It was a rhetorical question.

The other side. Suddenly I understood the comment Ernie had repeated to me: Friend of the bride or groom. Our side or their side. Who had asked Ernie that? I couldn't remember.

"So Velez killed Berto Santiago."

Samuels shrugged. "Possibly. We're still investigating."

"Why Berto? Why would FSK go after a local cop? Assuming he knew who Berto was."

"Oh, he knew. We all knew. That's why he, Berto, was allowed in. We didn't want to risk the exposure, so we decided to play along for the police."

"You still haven't answered my question," I persisted. "Why would FSK bother to kill a cop?"

"Maybe Berto discovered Velez' true affiliation."

"A rookie cop? When all of you boys couldn't? I find that hard to believe."

"As I said, we're still investigating."

"And Dr. Rios? And Ernie?"

Sharon Carton

Another shrug.

"I know, you're still investigating. Well," I said curtly, "so am I."

"All right then, I want you to feel free to-"

"Just a minute, Samuels, I'm not finished with you yet."

"What else can I tell you? I promise you, Jack, I'm not the enemy here."

"When the police finished questioning me the night of the murders, I went to the hospital. Broward County Hospital. That's where the ambulance had taken Ernie."

"Of course," Samuels said, oozing genteel sympathy.

"You admit it?"

"Of course," he repeated.

"The hospital now claims never to have had him there."

"Yes, that's-"

"So you *were* in charge of the cover-up!"

"Actually," Roger answered, "I was acting on a superior's directives, but yes, if you like. It wasn't as sinister as you may be thinking, though. In fact, you were the beneficiary of that particular scheme, though I'm not convinced that it wasn't more well-intentioned than advisable."

"What's that supposed to mean? You erased evidence of Ernie's death so I wouldn't be able to investigate?"

"Not you, Jack. It was feared that Eddie Velez' people might go after you, whether for revenge or for information you might be suspected of possessing, we couldn't know. It was just considered wiser to protect you by eliminating any evidence which could lead to you."

"What does that include?" I asked, not wholly convinced.

"Hospital records, police, ambulance reports. Our own records."

Sometimes You Get Killed

"Tidy."

"Cautious. Perhaps overly so," Samuels allowed.

"Let me get this straight. You're trying to protect me from Soviet agents."

Roger lifted his shoulders again, showing a trace of self-deprecatory amusement. "As I said, it might be overkill, but if Velez was FSK, we can't assume the threat ended with his death.

"And now," he said, standing abruptly, "I'm going to have to excuse myself. I have a great deal of work to get back to."

"I'm being dismissed?"

"For now, if you don't mind." It was clear that my agreement was not required. "You're welcome to speak to the rest of the staff-"

"And the patients?"

Roger put up an imploring hand. "Within reason, of course."

"Oh, I get it."

"We can hardly allow any of this to become known to the civilian patients."

"You're gonna trust me?" I said with a wicked grin.

"Given your background in intelligence, we have confidence in your ability to be circumspect."

"I'm touched." And so are you guys, I thought, if you believe that.

Reading my mind, "I hope our trust is not misplaced. The consequences could be, well, rather awkward."

"Look, I'm not here to...'compromise' your little set-up. But don't misunderstand me. My loyalties are not to your agency. If my interests conflict with yours, I'll sell you down the river. Don't underestimate me."

"I don't think I have, Jack. I think we understand each other just fine."

If I could've spit in his face without losing my dignity, I could've given him a reply that would've expressed

Sharon Carton

just how well I did understand him.

Instead, I had to settle for a glare that I hoped approached withering as I withdrew from Roger's office. Deep in the throes of paranoia, I thought I heard laughter as I closed the door behind me. My glare isn't what it used to be.

How much of all that did I believe? I thought the part at the beginning where he admitted having lied bore, what was that lawyer's phrase Ernie always used? Oh, yeah, intrinsic indicia of credibility. I figured the rest of Roger's information was equal parts fabrication and mendacity.

After the schmaltz of the deeply unctuous Dr. Samuels, Gregory Tessler was a charming breath of fresh air. Nattily attired in colorful vest and matching Argyle socks, Tessler displayed a breezy lack of concern for anything beyond a good host's desire that everyone within range be having a good time. His was a curious mix of gracious warmth and shallow fecklessness; one might not expect him to solve the world's problems, but I could understand his patients' willingness to talk to Tessler about their own. There was a disarming guilelessness about Tessler that seemed inconsistent with espionage.

"Oh, don't think of me as a spy. I'm just a shrink whose patients happen to be spies. There's a big difference."

"But you are CIA," I prodded.

"They sign my paychecks," Tessler admitted easily. "But don't be impressed, or put off, whichever is your inclination. My training came by way of medical school, not field work."

Tessler was an attractive man of average height, with a handsome face swathed in a mane of rich brownish-silver hair and matching beard. He spoke with a slight lisp that seemed, given his elegant styling, deportment and perfectly coiffed hair, less a speech impediment than an anachronistic throwback to the days of the 19th Century fop.

Sometimes You Get Killed

If you didn't look too carefully, you might mistake his demeanor as almost effeminate, but on closer examination Tessler turned out to be effete while exuding an aura of masculine sensuality. He wore his sexuality like a touch of expensive cologne; women were drawn to the scent, conscious of its rich and heavy allure, but the appeal managed to stop well short of being cloying.

"Was Velez one of your patients?"

"Yes, but I wouldn't count him as one of my successes. I had no idea he was deluding us so effectively."

"I gotta tell you, I'm having some trouble with that, too."

"You mean, how could someone professionally trained in reading people be so thoroughly conned?"

I nodded.

"You'd be surprised." Tessler didn't seem offended. "Patients con their shrinks all the time. This is not what you'd call an exact science. We're so concerned with working through their problems that it seldom occurs to us we're being misled.

"Oh," he went on, growing expansive, "spend enough time with the patient, and we'll be able to learn whether or to what extent we're being manipulated. But if someone deliberately sets out to fool us, if they've any skill at all, we haven't a chance. We're not mind-readers, after all."

"So you think Velez might've had some training?"

"You mean in how to fool us? I've considered the possibility."

"And?"

"It's likely. I was quite convinced that he was experiencing problems consistent with those normally suffered by the substance abuser."

"What kind of problems?"

"He manifested the classic symptoms of an addictive personality. I was so convinced that I medicated accordingly."

Sharon Carton

"You put him on drugs?"

"I prescribed for him to ease him off his — well, at least his self-described — cocaine abuse."

"But that was fake, too?"

"Truthfully?" Tessler asked. "All our tests substantiated the claimed addiction. It's my guess he abused cocaine prior to admission for just such a purpose."

"What did Velez tell you about his background?"

"I'm afraid I'm not much help there. Our sessions were principally in aid of regulating medication. His more in-depth counseling was with Louise Fischman. Our own sessions focused more on medical evaluation and monitoring his medication."

————————————

"I hold myself responsible."

"For anything in particular?" I asked Louise Fischman, smiling. I remembered she had said something similar when collecting me from jail. Despite my earlier suspicion that she had lied to me, I was finding it easy to be genial with this attractive, soft-spoken woman. Still, I couldn't shake the feeling that she and Ernie had had something going. She was a little gentler than Ernie usually was drawn to, but there had been times that my friend had shown good taste. Given Ernie's inability to resist temptation of any type, and the slight undercurrent in Louise's voice when she spoke of him, I was curious about the possibility.

"Why, for Eddie Velez," she answered. "For three murders, and for his own death."

"The way I remember, I'm the one who pulled the trigger on Eddie. And, unless I'm losing it altogether, Eddie wielded the knife on the other three." It wasn't easy for me to be that cavalier about any of those deaths, but I was hoping the glib routine would help her open up. I could tell I wasn't the only one seeing blood on their hands.

"Yes, but I was in the best position to see Eddie's

Sometimes You Get Killed

pain, and I did nothing about it."

Wait a minute. "His pain? Are you saying you were given the impression of genuine emotional problems? I thought he killed as a matter of professional responsibility, not because he was mentally ill."

"The two are not mutually exclusive," Louise said. "Eddie was deeply disturbed. I don't believe that was affected. If you tell me he was working for another government, that doesn't explain the anguish I saw in him. That kind of pain can't be faked."

"That's not what Gregory Tessler seems to think."

"I have the utmost respect for Greg, but he didn't see Eddie the way I did. That suffering was real."

"Even as a pro, you don't think he could've been putting it on for you?"

"Just look at the violence of the murders. My theory is entirely consistent with the brutality of his destructiveness. Eddie was so out of touch that, to him, love was synonymous with hate, sex with violence, sexual climax with death. The confusion over the two antinomies is not unusual, but in Eddie it was pathologically blurred, the distinction obscured to the point of nonexistence. They were not two sides to the same coin; they were the only side of his reality."

This wasn't something I wanted to talk about. The sadism evident in Velez' attack on Ernie had left a picture deeply and painfully etched in my mind. "All right, let me see if I understand you. You perceived Velez as so clearly demented that he couldn't have been faking. But you feel guilty because you didn't recognize how sick he was and do something to stop him."

"Well, yes, in essence."

"Don't you see some contradiction in that?"

"The way you articulate it, yes. I recognized he was deeply troubled, and in reevaluating it after the fact, I am convinced it was not an act. But I did not, at the time, correctly evaluate the severity of the problem. Because of

Sharon Carton

that, I hold myself accountable for the resulting mayhem."

"Mayhem," I repeated, then shook myself. "Lemme ask you something."

"Of course."

"You think Velez was nuts."

She smiled, and I thought, oh yeah, Ernie couldn't have resisted this. "Inelegantly put, but yes."

"And the reason you think that is, in part, because of the murders."

"Yes, well, because of my sessions with him, but the murders were of course the strongest evidence of what I gleaned from his therapy."

"No, wait, think about it. If you never learned about his killing anybody, would you have thought him crazy? I mean, to a dangerous degree?"

She hesitated, then said, "I suppose I would have to say no. After all, it was my failure to recognize his dangerousness that was my big mistake."

"Okay. Would you agree, then, that it was the murders that convinced you he was crazy, or unbalanced, or whatever?"

"Yes," she conceded, a bit reluctantly. Maybe she saw where I was going.

"So he killed because of some emotional or psychological defect. The murders were evidence of that to you, right?"

"Well, yes-"

"That's the part I can't buy. According to what I'm being told, Velez killed because he was required to, presumably to save his skin. He killed Berto because, or so the story goes, Berto found out who he was. He killed Dr. Rios because Rios was on monitor duty that night and saw the murder. Forget the fact that several weeks passed before Velez got around to eliminating his witness. Let's say Rios had kept his secret, but was now threatening to talk. Velez killed him, then killed Ernie while trying to escape."

130

Sometimes You Get Killed

"That's the prevalent theory," she agreed.

"So where's the psychotic bit come in? I mean, is it true what we think, that you don't have to be crazy to be a spy but it helps? Or was he just a spy who really loved his work?"

She sighed. "I don't know that I have an answer for you, Jack. Or for me."

Why was it that the people I liked down here had nothing to tell me, while the heavies had the whole case sewn up? The only people I felt any instinctive inclination to believe had doubts and confusion, which they willingly shared with me. The slimier the character down here, the clearer the case was to them. What was that Yeats poem Annie loved, the one about the best lacking any conviction? The way things were turning out, while I didn't especially like uncertainty as a character trait, it was something I could at least trust.

Chapter Thirteen

Louise Fischman seemed disinclined to end our conversation, so I persisted. "What can you tell me about Velez' background? Did he have a history of psychiatric disorders? Did his family? Did he leave any family behind? Do you-"

"Jack...."

"-have a copy of his personnel file here? More to the point, how can I get a copy? I assume you ran a check on him before he was admitted. What did you learn? Was any of it true? Did you do another search when...when he died? Is that when you learned he was FSK? Do you even *know* he was FSK, or is that just a theory? Can you-"

"Please, Jack." She put up a supplicating hand to stop me. "This isn't getting us anywhere."

"Okay, I'll go slower."

"No, that's not it." She seemed upset, and this time it wasn't guilt. "The questions you're asking...I can't give you that kind of information. It's all-"

"Classified? Privileged? But Velez is dead, so what does it matter?"

"I could ask you the same question, Jack. I could understand your desire for reprisal, but you've already gotten your revenge. You killed the man who killed Ernie. Why are you still pursuing this? What are you after?"

Sure, ask the tough ones. "Truth."

"You have that," she said reasonably.

"Information," I tried.

"That I can't give you."

"Well, I'm not leaving Florida without it."

"Jack," she smiled, "there's no need for

melodrama. We aren't keeping any secrets from you, at least nothing that has anything to do with you."

"Let me get this straight. I'm investigating the murder of Berto Santiago and my partner, not to mention your colleague, Paul Rios. I want to know something about the man I killed-"

"What more do you need to know than that he killed your friend? Do you feel remorse about shooting him? It was clearly self-defense, at least from what I-"

"Don't try to analyze me, okay?" I said, edgily. "I'm not your patient. I just want to know who the guy was."

"You already do. He was a double agent, working, we believe, for the Soviet government. More than that you don't need to know."

"Don't tell me what I need to know."

"I *can* tell you, Jack," she said, quietly but with a new firmness, "that we've already been inordinately forthcoming with you. Frankly, I'm surprised at the level of cooperation accorded you. Maybe it's because of your background in-"

"Intelligence, yeah, and maybe," I said heatedly, "it's because you guys were hoping the appearance of cooperation would placate me, that you'd give me enough to satisfy my curiosity and send me away happy."

"And maybe," a definite testiness in her voice now, "we overestimated your good sense."

"Or maybe just my gullibility."

From Kenneth Khoragian, who made only the most fleeting of pretenses that he felt anything but contempt for me, I got the hardest information. Of course. That might have made me suspicious, but for the obvious fact that Khoragian, an otherwise incisive intellect, was allowing his animosity to control his mouth. Unlike Iago, of whom he in many ways reminded me, hostility made Khoragian small-minded, and through the venom came words of unmistakable truth.

Sometimes You Get Killed

"I'm not here to answer your questions, Migliore."

"Your boss suggested otherwise."

"Roger?" he said, as if repulsed by the notion that the Reverend might be considered his superior.

"He is your boss?"

"Only in a technical sense," he conceded tightly, "in that he's in charge of the Center."

"Well, yes. So doesn't that make him your boss?"

Khoragian gave me his contemptuous glare.

"I mean," I tried again, "in what sense isn't he your boss?"

Khoragian spoke slowly, as if to an idiot, one he didn't much like, or need to suffer gladly. "Roger is an administrator. A person we hired to lie to everyone else, so we don't have to be bothered to do it ourselves. He flits from assignment to assignment, putting things into his concept of order, leaving his personal imprint, moving on when he, or more often some higher numbers, decide that he's achieved some ineffable level of success. He has very little to do with what goes on here."

"Gee, no kidding. He struck me as playing a more active role."

"Only in the disruptive sense. He has his finger in everything, but he understands very little. He's...he's an administrator, for God's sake," he said finally.

"What about Eddie Velez' case? Did Roger have a hand in that, too?"

"Oh, drop it, Migliore. That's got nothing to do with you."

"I don't see it that way," I said evenly. Somehow I felt no need to lash out at him. With uncharacteristic insight, I sensed that duplicity, that feigned equanimity, might give me the upper hand.

"I don't give a fuck how you see it, Migliore. You're way out of your depth, and I have no intention of humoring you."

"That will work out fine, Dr. Khoragian, since I

Sharon Carton

haven't come here to be humored. And I'm not asking you to divulge any company secrets, no pun intended. Maybe you can tell me about something else. Something that does have something to do with me. Like my partner."

Khoragian smiled thinly. "Let's be accurate, Migliore. Ernie Darwin was your, what, associate, or employee, or maybe even your friend. He wasn't your partner."

"I stand corrected." You bastard. "When did you learn all this?"

"Some of it," Khoragian gloated, clearly enjoying this part of it, "from the beginning. We conducted inquiries when the New York police made a phone call on your behalf. Roger decided it would be more dangerous to keep you out than to let you in. It was bad enough we had to let the FLPD in on our little secret. We certainly didn't want the New York police to start looking into this."

"So you knew Berto Santiago was a cop?"

"Oh, do give us some credit," Khoragian scorned. Professional pride, I guess.

"But you played along?"

"Roger hoped to convince Santiago and his people that there was nothing untoward going on here."

"Yeah. Didn't quite work out that way, did it?"

"Roger's plan," he dismissed.

"But when Berto died-"

"At that point, we had to apprise FLPD of the situation to keep them out of our jurisdiction. It was unavoidable."

"So you knew from the beginning...what? That I was a private investigator? That Ernie wasn't my brother-in-law?"

"Yes, of course," Khoragin was impatient, "all of that."

"And you weren't suspicious?"

"Roger took what he considered to be adequate precautions. He wasn't unaware of the possibilities."

Sometimes You Get Killed

"What, that we were really FSK agents?" I smiled even to say it. I mean, Ernie was — had been — something of a knee-jerk liberal, but working for the Eastern Bloc?

"That, and, on the other hand, that the rest of your story was legitimate. There was evidence to that effect — your associate's drug history was fairly well documented."

"But you weren't convinced."

"Anything can be faked."

Words to remember. "So what were these precautions you mentioned?"

"We...interrogated Darwin."

"What?" My eyes widened in amazement. "You tortured him? What did you — he never — why didn't he ever tell me?"

"He didn't know. And we didn't torture him, you cretin. Give us some credit. We used drug therapy. Sodium ambytal. What you would call truth serum. Oversimplification, but good enough for your purposes. Except that, as usual, Roger's method knew no finesse. Heavy-handed."

"What do you mean?" This news had taken me aback; I wasn't sure what to make of it.

"We had to cancel your visit, or don't you remember? Roger overdid it."

"Who conducted this...interrogation?"

"Roger."

"But he's no doctor. Who administered the drugs?"

Khoragian lifted, then dropped, his shoulders expressively. He didn't even have the conscience to be embarrassed. "I did, at Roger's so-called direction. He overdid it," he repeated. "There were no lasting side-effects, not after a day or two. By then, we'd found out everything we needed to know."

It took me a few minutes to find my voice. "One more thing. The night Ernie and Dr. Rios were killed."

"What about it?"

"Had Ernie been drugged?"

137

Sharon Carton

Khoragian had lost interest. "Only his regular medication."

"You're sure about that?"

"There'd be no point in drugging him. He was no longer of interest to us. He was just another addict, as far as we were concerned. Oh, we knew, or surmised, he had been given instructions by you as part of your little investigation, but that was meaningless, as far as we felt. There was no threat."

I thought about this sour little Ph.D.. He wasn't exactly Roger's ally, more of a bitter and humorless Iago whispering despairing and insidious thoughts to Roger's evangelical Othello. While Othello went about the clinic kingdom clobbering patients and staff with his heavy-handed optimism, Khoragian would slip him dark rumors of deceit and treachery among the rank and file. He seemed to relish his role so much that I wondered if he would feel called upon to create malevolence in his little universe even if none were to be found.

Khoragian's wife, Chrissy, was a petite, smiling, black-haired woman in her mid-thirties, not unattractive in a pixie-ish way. She functioned as a counselor, which seemed only to mean that she was sort of an ombudsman around the place, no credentials or degrees beyond college, but apparently something of a favorite of Roger's. The word from Ernie was that she lavished affection on her patients, and worked to engender the reciprocated outpouring of love for her, which, according to her reasoning, represented a return to mental health.

She and her husband never associated publicly at the Center, and I wondered whether their marriage improved at all behind closed doors. Based on Ernie's comments and my observation — of her and of her husband — I trusted her about as far as I could throw her. Nah, she was a lightweight, meaning I could throw her a bit farther than I could trust her, and meaning also that she probably

Sometimes You Get Killed

perceived herself as a lot more dangerous than she probably was. Her warm demeanor more than likely hid a more mean-spirited selfishness — being liked was too important to her for anyone else's well being — but she was mired in a level almost as petty as her husband's niggling carping. They were an unpleasant couple, and I had to wonder at Roger's hiring criteria.

I'd spent several weeks last Fall on that murder investigation at the small private law school in Manhattan. This place wasn't as erudite but it was as stuffy, airless and claustrophobic. It made me wonder if there was something about these small-scale, insular environments which tended to give its personalities an exaggerated sense of their own importance, fostering political infighting and futile bickering over mindless inanities. Something like inbreeding. From now on, I promised myself, it's the openness and anonymity of big city crowds for me. Much safer.

After spending some time with Chris Khoragian, I finished off the day with the receptionist, Debbie Galesseo. She wasn't able to contribute much to my investigation, but at least she avoided pissing me off, which was no small achievement given my frazzled mental state. Ms. Galesseo was a pleasant enough young lady, apparently in her very early twenties. Not especially attractive, she had a simple good nature which made the hour or so I spent with her rather agreeable. It also brought back memories of another world, where people actually said what they meant, and meant you no harm.

As soon as I got back to the hotel, I called Annie. I filled her in on my recent discoveries, then, embarrassed, I had to ruin the conversation by asking her to wire me money.

"I'll pay you back. When this is over I'll get a real job and I'll pay you back."

"It's all right, Jack."

139

Sharon Carton

"No, I mean, I know you didn't even think I should do this, and now I have to ask-"

"It's all *right,* Jack. Really. I'm just...you don't sound too good. When are you coming home?"

"Soon, pretty soon. I think things are going real well," I lied. "Any day now I should be able to wrap this all...."

"Wrap up what? Jack, from what you've told me, I don't understand why you're still there. What else are you hoping to learn?"

"I don't know. If I knew that," I said with impeccable logic, "I wouldn't still be here."

"Maybe I should come down there," she replied, a small note of panic in her voice.

"No, not when I'm not sure what's going on here. It could still be dangerous. You'll be safer up there."

"In New York?"

"You know what I mean. For all I know, the FSK could be after me."

"Does that sound as ludicrous to you as it does to me?"

It did. "Which part in particular?"

"The *FSK*, Jack? After *you*?"

"Why not?" For some reason, I was insulted.

"I mean," she went on, "the FSK? In Fort Lauderdale?"

"If the CIA can be here, why not the FSK?"

"You're really starting to worry me, Jack. Listen, I can be on the next flight out of JFK. Just say the word."

There was something about the way she said it that gave me pause, but I couldn't put my finger on it. "Don't get carried away. I'm fine. I just...maybe you're right about the KGB bit. There's an element to all this that doesn't ring true to me either. That's why I can't leave yet."

"That's pretty vague, Jack. Is that really why you're staying?"

I paused. "Annie, I'm not real sure what I'm doing.

140

Sometimes You Get Killed

I just know there's something more to this than I've been told. I can't leave 'til I'm satisfied I know the truth about what happened."

"All right," she gave in. "Just don't go crazy or anything."

It wasn't as touching a good-bye as "Take care of yourself because I love you," but I'm a practical man, and I'm used to taking what I can get.

After getting off the phone with Annie, I went for a walk on the Strip, feeling homesick and depressed. Nothing I had learned had changed anything, well, not anything significant. What was I doing messing with spies? Maybe Khoragian was right; I was in over my head.

Sitting in a bar called "The Off-Season", I thought of what the staff at the Center had been able, or willing, to tell me. The Center was an experimental operation, first of its kind in this country, where government employees with high level security clearances could go for counseling and treatment for substance abuse. Government employees? CIA. Spies? Not in so many words.

Security clearances.

When Ernie worked for the Defense Department, he was responsible for arguing in agency hearings against applicants for security clearances. Maybe Ernie was killed because he had denied clearance to Velez, or to someone Velez knew. Maybe there was a reason for Ernie's death, having nothing to do with Berto Santiago, or with me getting Ernie into the wrong place at the wrong time.

But no. Ernie's applicants for clearance were in the private sector, employed or seeking employment with government contractors. Not government employees. Not Velez.

FSK? I just couldn't swallow that. If I could accept CIA, why not FSK? I don't know, it just seemed cartoonish. Ernie told me that some of the people he'd worked with at Defense had seen Communists behind every bush. Maybe that's what this was. Did Roger have any proof Velez was a

Sharon Carton

Russian plant or a double agent who'd sold out? If so, he hadn't disclosed it to me. Was it just a paranoid suspicion of the CIA boys, or was it something they were disingenuously trying to palm off on me?

So, change the picture a bit. What if Velez wasn't FSK? He was a fed. Why would he kill Berto? Because Berto had learned something. Ergo, Velez had had something to hide. If he wasn't a foreign agent, what could've been his secret? If he had had a secret, did Roger and company know about it? What could Velez have wanted to keep quiet enough to kill for it, not once or even twice, but three times?

If I had been conducting an experimental top security government operation, and four people had been killed, one a cop and two of the other three feds, I would've judged the experiment a failure. Why hadn't the Center been shut down? Maybe shedding the light of publicity on things would accomplish that. Did I really want to go to the media? As a last resort, maybe, but I was afraid that by going public I would lose my only hope of getting any answers.

Maybe the Center was still in operation because there was something more important going on than providing TLC for some drugged out G-men. If that were true, would a fed kill a local cop to keep it secret? Even if so, that wouldn't explain why he would kill another fed. Unless, of course, Velez' secret wasn't one he shared with the rest of the Center.

Like working for the other side? Okay, that was one possibility, but it wasn't the only one. As the night wore on, the number of possibilities grew in coincidental proportion to the size of my bar tab. Eventually I got drunk enough not to be surprised at the coincidence.

Chapter Fourteen

I got back to the hotel, passably drunk, about one A.M. The alcohol hadn't answered any questions, but it made me feel less troubled by them. I had my key with me, so I didn't bother stopping at the front desk. If anyone had called me, I wasn't particularly anxious to find out. My friends and loved ones thought I was no longer working with a full deck, an appraisal I had heard with sufficient frequency so that I didn't need to hear it again at one in the morning, when I was too drunk to formulate a witty rejoinder. Anyone who might have something more positive to say could wait until I was hung over enough to need the pick-me-up.

When I got to my room, there were a few sober brain cells that happened to notice a light burning inside. I was pretty sure I hadn't left it on. Midnight room service? I put my ear to the door, and could hear water running. The tap in the bathroom sink; it was too hushed to be the shower. I gently unlocked the door, and every so slightly slid the door open a crack. The door to the bathroom, a few yards away, was closed, and the bathroom light was on, too.

I crept noiselessly into the room, shutting the door behind me. My gun was tucked into the waistband of my jeans, in the back. I left it there, mentally saluting Annie. See? I can be tough without it. Mostly I figured nobody, even if he's carrying, brings a gun into the toilet. Partly, in the back of my mind, I had this picture of Annie feeling guilty if my dead body was found with a gun I hadn't fired.

I stood with my hand poised on the wall light switch. After about five minutes, my arm beginning to go numb, I heard the intruder's hand on the doorknob inside

Sharon Carton

the bathroom. In the instant he opened the door and shut that light, I switched off the light in the bedroom, then took a running leap at the intruder. I'd caught a momentary glimpse of a young man, with a trim, compact body, several inches under six foot. Within seconds I was on top of him; within a few more seconds, I was under him, panting for air, his knees in my chest. My gun was no longer pressing into my back. I had no idea where it had fallen.

I went limp, then, with a sudden burst of effort, I threw him off me. He landed clumsily, on his back, legs splayed in the air. I slammed his legs onto the ground and sat on them. My eyes were straining to see in the dark and locate the gun, but I could only see shapes and shadows, not details. Holding my captive's hands down with my own, I pondered my next move, feeling as trapped by the position as he was. I didn't get a chance to think about it too long, because somehow he wriggled his hands loose and smacked me, how shall I put it, oh yes, upside my head. I went down on my side, and felt a short, powerful kick in my ribs. Nothing cracked so I rolled away, trying to get up. The kick followed me, twice in the kidneys. I stopped rolling so that I could more fully appreciate the pain. The kicking stopped, probably for the same reason.

Then the light went on. My visitor didn't even have the decency to be out of breath, but he did have my gun. He looked like he didn't know quite what to do with it; I decided not to place too much faith in appearances.

He couldn't have been more than twenty-four, twenty-five. From the look of him, he was completely unthreatening. Harmless. Friendly. *Nice.*

"Hey," he said. In a nice way. With a genial smile on his nice face.

It was a greeting.

I got slowly to my feet. I'd hurt my leg pretty badly last year, and although it had healed better than expected, rolling around on the floor was something I usually tried to avoid.

Sometimes You Get Killed

"Who the fuck are you, you little sonofabitch, and what the fuck" pant, pant "are you doing in my room?"

That was also a greeting.

My visitor's smile didn't dim, as he fingered open my revolver and emptied the load into his hand, then handed me back the gun. "Jonah Barnes sent me," he said by way of explanation.

The adrenaline was pumping, but the blood hadn't refueled my brain sufficiently for me to hear and recognize the name.

"What is that," I demanded, still huffing, "some kind of spy code?"

The young man shook his head, not in denial but in sorrow. "Jesus, you're even farther gone than Mr. Barnes feared."

"Huh?"

"Actually, he said you were 'round the twist,' but I knew what he meant."

I was starting to make the connection. "Jonah sent you? From New York?"

"Uh huh. Want me to describe him? Thick Cockney accent, about my height and weight, late twenties, straight black hair, fair complexion, cheeks are always red.... Okay?"

It matched Jonah, which is not to say it was making any sense to me. "Why would Jonah send you here?"

"To work with you."

"Sit down," I commanded.

He seated himself on the bed, grinning, then lazily lay his head back on the pillow, and crossed his knees on the bed.

While he was making himself at home, I went to the telephone and dialed Jonah's number. He answered on the third ring. He sounded wide awake. Fact is, I was surprised to find him home. Since he was, I had to assume my libidinous friend was not alone.

"Jonah? What the fuck are you playing at?"

Sharon Carton

"Jack? 'ow are ya, son?" He sounded cheerful, as always, and not the slightest bit defensive. Maybe he'd missed the subtle note of hostility in my voice. I tried harder.

"I've got some...*kid* in my room who says-"

"Oh, yeah? Kevin Draper, is it?"

I turned to the...kid. "Kevin Draper?"

He nodded, but luckily for him didn't offer to shake.

I turned back to the phone. "Jonah, what the hell is he doing here?"

Pause. " 'e still in the room?"

"Yeah, why?"

"Tell 'im to leave, so's we can talk, proper like."

I sighed. "Kevin? Jonah says to take a hike. Come back in ten minutes, if you've got a death wish."

"No sweat, Mr. Migliore."

When he'd gone, ambling confidently out the door, leaving my bullets on the nightstand — I didn't seem to intimidate anybody anymore — I spoke to Jonah. "Make it good."

"Well, it's only he's the answer to your prayers."

"I don't remember praying."

"Okay, the answer to all your problems, then."

"No, that would be vertical cuts across the insides of my wrists, about four inches in-"

"Nah," Jonah cut in, his grin coming through the line loud and clear, "don't be like that. See, Kevin's just this kid what comes to me for lessons, like."

"Yeah, yeah." Jonah ran his private security firm out of a loft on the Upper West Side, where he also gave classes in self-defense. Pretty vicious self-defense. Not for Jonah the spiritual niceties of Judo or Karate.

"And he's smart," Jonah went on, "but sorta useless, like, you know, knows a lot of stuff but can't do nuffin', you know, like one of them, whatchacallits, debutantes."

I frowned. "Dilettantes, you mean?"

Sometimes You Get Killed

"Yeah, awright, so 'is dad says to me, Jonah, old son, 'e says, do you 'appen to know of a trade for Kevin, somefink 'e might work up some interest in, and be useful at, like. So I get this idea-"

"-of me giving him a job, and wouldn't it be cute to give this kid a place to work while taking Ernie's place? Thanks but no thanks."

"But 'e'd be your apprentice."

"What do I need an apprentice for? I had one of those, remember."

"Yeah, and I'm not suggesting Kevin would be a substitute or nuffink for Ernie, but this bloke would pay, and you do need that-"

"Kevin?"

"No, 'is dad, what's rich, and connections," he went on, "what you also always say you need and what 'is dad also has."

I digested this. "How old is he, Kevin, I mean?"

"I dunno, twenty-five, twenty-six, I reckon. Coupla years younger 'n me, anyroad. Never done a day's graft in 'is life, just goes from one school to anuvver, droppin' out of this one, getting sent down from that one for aggro or bunkin' off. See, 'e's got a mouf on 'im."

"Sounds great."

"Well, let's say 'e's got...possibilities," Jonah said carefully.

"And money," I mused.

"And contacts."

"How much money?"

"Dad's got millions. I reckon you could charge, what, 'undred, 'undred fifty a week. Fair bit of knick."

I silently upped the sum. I would, after all, be giving the millionaire's kid a useful trade. "Just as long as you understand this is purely business."

"Do us a favor, Jack," Jonah said solemnly. Jonah had liked Ernie, and wasn't so much trying to use Kevin to replace one friend with a ready-made substitute, as trying

147

Sharon Carton

to give me the impetus — and financial wherewithal — to carry on. Transparent, but well-intentioned. And I could use the money.

"All right, then," I said finally. "I'll talk to him. The kid. Then I'll talk to his old man."

I knew what Jonah was thinking. Jack's depressed. Jack's lonely. Jack must've always been a little crazy, but Ernie — Ernie Darwin? — kept him balanced. Now, on his own, Jack's gone "round the twist."

But Jack's proud, and would never accept charity, or a new partner. So offer him something he's in no financial position to refuse.

It all seemed a little too convenient to be true. A bright young man who evidently knew how to handle himself — okay, big deal, I was drunk and about ten years older than him — whose daddy would pay me for the privilege of my company. I felt like a whore.

Okay. As long as I didn't end up babysitting him. I had other things on my mind. I decided to give him some chores tomorrow while I went back to the Center to interview some of the patients. I didn't want him tagging along for the interviews; it would be tough enough getting people to talk to me without having a volatile kid around. I was something of a familiar face at the Center, but the same couldn't be said for the kid.

So I'd give him something else to do. If he did it well, I'd call his old man and we'd negotiate. If not, I'd send him packing.

I'd been broke before. And alone.

When the kid returned to my hotel room, he just took it for granted that the matter had been straightened out to everyone's satisfaction. He'd already unpacked, obviously planning on sharing the room.

"I thought you had money," I said, a bit surly. My kidneys hadn't forgiven him, not yet, anyway. "Why can't you get your own room?"

Sometimes You Get Killed

"My dad has money," he clarified good-naturedly. "I'm just an unemployed grad student."

"Well, you're employed now."

"Not entirely correct, Mr. Migliore. In point of fact, you're the one on salary."

"Kid," I said, growing more testy by the minute, "the name is Jack. And get one thing straight. You are my employee, or assistant, or whatever. I don't work for you, and I don't work for your rich daddy."

The wise-ass smiled, and shrugged. He was finding me amusing. My new role in life, entertaining the idle rich.

Chapter Fifteen

The adrenalin rush of the night before had so effectively burned up the alcohol I had consumed that I woke up the next morning without a hangover. It was a little after nine, and the kid, Kevin Draper, was still asleep. Even asleep, he didn't look angelic. I studied him as he slept, trying to make a fair appraisal of my temporary new charge.

He was a good-looking kid, with finely chiseled, almost delicately pretty features. Long brown lashes shaded his closed eyes. He wore his straight dark hair parted in the middle, and an inch or two longer than I would've for a job interview. Even in repose, there was a smart-alecky curve to his lips, and I remembered the matching glint of distanced amusement in his brown eyes the night before. There was an impishness, a mischievous good humor about him which he probably knew how to turn to charm. I assumed his parents spoiled, or at least indulged, him; according to Jonah, he had been in school long enough to amass several degrees, and when the kid still had shown no interest or aptitude in pursuing a career using any of those, the old man was willing to sponsor this rather eccentric apprenticeship. Also according to what Jonah had told me, the kid had the brains to do most things well; he just didn't care enough about any one thing to bother. I figured that would probably make him just about useless as any investigator, where very often the only thing you have going for you is perseverance.

Ernie had once tried to persuade me that intellectual curiosity — Ernie's own variant on dedication — was an adequate substitute for the stubbornness that is generally my long suit. I never completely bought Ernie's

Sharon Carton

argument, mostly because of inconsistencies. There were times when it was only the obsessive, if abstract, need to solve a puzzle that drove me on, just as there were times that Ernie cared more about doing what he deemed right than about getting answers or vindicating some theory. The way I looked at it, we each leaned more in one direction than the other, but we had enough of both tendencies to ensure that cases were pursued to a finish. It was a neat bonus that most times we balanced each other's tendencies of that moment. Based on my possibly premature judgment of this kid, I had to wonder whether he had enough to make him a detective.

Which didn't mean I couldn't find his brand of smarts useful, even on a temporary basis. It also didn't mean that, if I accepted the job, I wouldn't give his old man his money's worth.

I showered and dressed without waking him, then left a note telling him I'd be down the block at the McDonald's, getting some breakfast. I was on my second cup of coffee when he showed up. Apparently he was a morning person. I nearly fired him then and there, on the basis of his being too cheerful before noon. I answered his comments and questions in monosyllables, missing Ernie's moodiness.

He didn't seem overly concerned with the complexity of the case, but that could've been because I left out one significant detail: Telling him only that the Center had surprisingly turned out to be government run for mostly government employees, I neglected to specify which particular agency within the federal government was involved. It wasn't a trick to see if he could figure it out on his own. I just hadn't determined how trustworthy he was.

Kevin demonstrated the appropriate sympathy when I came to the part about his predecessor, but I wasn't convinced as to its sincerity. I sensed this kid was too good at manipulation to be taken at face value.

At least he was asking relevant questions. He

Sometimes You Get Killed

seemed to be viewing the whole thing as a game. Suddenly I got a clue as to one strength — or at least useable trait — in his character: He liked to win. I got the feeling it had nothing to do with pleasing me, or even his father. He apparently got some gratification from succeeding, from learning to do something well. I don't know if it was competitiveness, or whether it was only himself that he was aiming to beat. It probably meant that, as soon as he'd satisfied himself that he'd mastered this new game, it would no longer have any fascination for him. That was okay as far as I was concerned; just don't fuck up this particular investigation and I don't care if you waste the rest of your life and your father's money.

He showed a ready grasp of information as I reviewed the status of the case. He showed, too, a funny habit of compartmentalizing, caring less about the big picture than in what his individual assignment was to be. That was fine; as long as he did his homework, I didn't give a shit about extra credit. Maybe I would've felt differently if I was considering this guy for an operative's job. Maybe then I would've quizzed him the way I had Ernie, judging his merit — or at least his potential — on areas like memory recall and reason for interest in the position. This kid meant only a source of cash to me, and, if I was lucky, someone to bounce ideas off of. Anything else he might contribute would be bonus. Straightening out his feckless nature was not my responsibility.

Annie understood, though she never spelled it out, that it was my sense of responsibility toward Ernie that was still hounding me. He had inspired an unwilling protective instinct that I wasn't used to. Because I'd so direly failed to protect him, I now felt I owed him something I could never pay. Annie knew that, if I let it, that debt could impair my judgment on this case, and, depending on its resolution, maybe for a lot longer than that.

I didn't know how to reassure her, because I felt the guilt more clearly than I saw it. The only way to treat

153

the pain was to give it a purpose, and so I allowed it to direct me, to propel me. I maintained some vague hope that it would be silenced eventually when, like the monster it had become, it was fully sated. The more answers I fed it, the less its hunger would need to consume me.

I was damned if I would substitute one hapless misfit for another.

"Where do I go?" he asked suddenly.

"Do you have a car?"

Kevin smiled wickedly. "Nah. I flew." Big shit. "You want me to rent one?"

"Ah, no. See, normally you can't function without one, even, to some extent, back home. But we're operating without a client, so we gotta keep expenses down." I felt a little embarrassed. Working for no pay wasn't something I liked doing, much less bragging about. Admitting it to people who knew me was dangerously suggestive of the emotional depths to which I had sunk; admitting it to a stranger, especially to a snot-nosed rich kid, could give an impression I didn't want to foster.

"I flew into Lauderdale, and took a cab here from the airport."

It sounded like a *non sequitur*, then I understood. "I'll reimburse you."

"Yeah? With whose money?" he demanded.

"Your father's," I rejoined. "Anyway, today you'll come with me. If it turns out you need your own car, we'll handle it then."

"It's walking distance, worst come to worst," he offered.

"You know where the Center is?"

"I've never noticed the place, but I know the area."

"Spent some time down here?" Oh, sure. I should've known.

He shrugged. "I've done the Spring Break number."

"I don't doubt it."

There was silence for about sixty seconds, as we

Sometimes You Get Killed

sat eyeing one another, each taking the other's measure. We both seemed content with our comfortable stereotypes: arrogant rich kid; obnoxious, ignorant street lout.

"So all I'm supposed to do," Kevin said, without much enthusiasm, "is talk to the receptionist."

"Debbie Galesseo, that's right. Just get her talking about the place. Maybe she has some dirt."

"Didn't you already talk to her?"

"Briefly, yeah. But-"

"So isn't it duplicating your efforts? It seems redundant."

I sighed. "It isn't, not necessarily. Two reasons," I began economically. "Any two times you hear a story, you generally end up with two stories. The variations are informative. Second, she's more your age. She might feel more comfortable with you, maybe open up-"

Kevin smirked. "You mean you want me to come on to her, because you'd feel like a dirty old man on the make if you pulled the same thing."

I couldn't help smiling. "Something like that."

"Okay, but how long can that take? You're gonna be spending the entire day talking to the patients there. How the hell am I supposed to kill time while you're occupied?"

"Walk back to the hotel," I muttered under my breath.

"Excuse me?"

"I'm thinking. Well, I suppose you can try something else. You see, there is something that's been bothering me. I'm having trouble buying the attitude of the police on this."

"They seem pretty cooperative now, on the whole."

"Yeah, too damned cooperative, that's just it. They're willing to concede jurisdiction to the feds in a cop killing. That's unbelievable."

"Literally."

"Yeah," I nodded. "I don't know, maybe it's a regional thing, but no New York cop would roll over when

Sharon Carton

one of their brothers gets blown away."

"Well, there may be some rednecks around here, but that doesn't mean the cops don't care about their own."

"That's what I would've thought. So how come all of a sudden the FLPD are willing to play dead on this?"

"You think maybe they aren't?"

"It's occured to me, yeah. Like maybe they're still involved. If they put another man in there after Berto Santiago was killed, it's possible they didn't trust me enough to tell me."

"Okay," he said, giving it some thought, "but why didn't this second undercover cop surface when your friend got wasted? I mean, what kinda cop stands by and watches that happen without identifying himself and helping you?"

"Maybe by the time he, or she for that matter, got to the scene from his bedroom, it was too late to help. Nothing to gain from blowing his cover."

"Mm. Maybe. So what is it you want me to do?"

"Well, I'm gonna try to determine which of the patients arrived after Berto's death, but I'm not sure how forthcoming they'll be. Maybe you can ask the young Ms. Galesseo about dates of admission. But be subtle about it," I cautioned. "I don't know how smart, or suspicious, she really is. As far as I know, she's just a receptionist, not an-" I stopped myself. I was about to say "agent", but changed it to "-expert at interrogation techniques. I don't want to give anything away."

"No sweat," he said confidently. "Is that it?"

"Just do that and I'll be happy."

"How are you going to introduce me?"

"With tremendous pride."

"No," he said, rolling his eyes, "how will I be identified to these people?"

"Yeah, I know. I don't know. An operative of mine from New York. I don't want to get them nervous by telling them this is your first case." I didn't mention the fact that, given these people's resources, it probably wouldn't be long

Sometimes You Get Killed

before they knew the truth.

      As I drove to the Center, with Kevin sitting placidly beside me, I found myself thinking of crossword puzzles. A while back, Annie had tried to get me interested in them. It was a frustrating experience for both of us. Annie had an adventurous, childlike way of approaching the puzzles: She would fill in as many words as she knew without regard for how the answers would intersect. My own attitude was more plodding: Every time I got one answer filled in, I would work around it, down and across, to try to use the one answer I'd gotten to help me answer as many of the surrounding questions as possible. Used to piss Annie off; she'd call me obsessive compulsive, or anal retentive, or some other, similar term of endearment. She would accuse me of being unable to work — or play — without a game plan; I would counter by charging that she didn't know how to make use of acquired information to build on it and establish a pattern. My criticism of her wasn't as justified as hers of me; that is to say, she was accurate, even though I don't see it as a fault.

      I was thinking about crosswords because I knew, going back to the Center, that I wouldn't go in without a theory: What was I looking for? What was I trying to prove? It's acceptable to begin a case without a premise, but by this point I had accumulated enough raw material to start identifying the inconsistencies, the gaps in logic, the weak points in the tissue of lies I had been handed.

      My theory, which I tried to resurrect from the night of boozing, focused on Velez, and determining his motive for three murders. By talking to the patients, I hoped to get their perspective on the killer, to see whether the homicides were inexorable product of disturbed mind, or the acts of a calculating professional. If Velez was just a murderous maniac, I could accept the arbitrariness in his selection of victims — in fact, only Berto need have been a random choice, Rios then killed to eliminate a witness, and Ernie

Sharon Carton

during his attempted flight. It was the only explanation that made any sense at all. What became maddeningly nonsensical was the FSK angle. If that was the true explanation, the only thing that made less sense than the FSK selecting a local cop as the target over any of the CIA agents was the idea of some CIA shrink destroying all records of Ernie to protect a clueless New York p.i. from the FSK in Fort Lauderdale.

Chapter Sixteen

After making some brief and probably unpersuasive introductions, I left Kevin with the Reverend, who promised with characteristic expansiveness to bring him by for a chat with the receptionist, Debbie Galesseo. I explained off-handedly that I didn't plan on staying long today, and that, if no one minded, I'd appreciate their letting my assistant hang out in the reception area until I was ready to leave. It was, I explained further, simply to make it easier for me to have him wait here instead of my having to stop and collect him from the hotel when I was through. I didn't delude myself that anyone was buying my story, but I couldn't believe it would make any difference. If they were suspicious, fine, let them be on guard: Maybe they'd trip themselves up.

Remembering, with fond if blurring nostalgia, how nervous Ernie had been on his first assignment, I was a little disappointed to note how unaffected Kevin was. Determined not to let him distract me, I concentrated instead on meeting the patients Ernie had told me about. Since Ernie, of course, had known nothing about the government connection, he hadn't differentiated between the patients whom I now knew to be CIA and those who weren't.

If the FSK saga was true, I couldn't expect to learn much from the civilian patients, but I wouldn't neglect them entirely. There was no reason to assume Velez had kept himself apart from them, although, being at least nominally CIA, he would've known them to be outsiders. Equally as important was the possibility that, if Velez wasn't FSK — or, illogically, if Louise Fischman was right in suspecting

159

Sharon Carton

that the murders weren't necessarily the result of his being FSK — the civilians would have as much to contribute as the feds.

I began my inquiries with the patient whom Ernie had found most likeable, a young man named Davy Rittenby. He turned out to be the blond kid I'd seen the night of Ernie's murder. Now I tried to remember anything Ernie had mentioned to me about him, while trying to reconcile all that with the one thing Ernie had not known about him: Rittenby was a spy.

"He's, I don't know," Ernie had guessed, "maybe mid-to-upper twenties, but he acts ancient, older than you even."

I hadn't liked that comment, but I don't think Ernie had noticed.

"It's not just that he's so intense. I mean, he has a great sense of humor, but it's like nothing's trivial to him. Weight of the world, you know? Anyway, maybe it's because he feels he's let his family down. His father's rich, old Yankee rich, you know, New England patrician, came over on the fucking Mayflower, that kind of thing. His mother's Cuban, but from what I understand, her side of the family was pretty heavy duty, pre-Castro rich, powerful politically. Davy himself went the whole deal, prep school, Yale, but you'd never know it." From Ernie, that was a compliment.

"He got into coke big time in college, then gradually made his way down here. I didn't ask, not outright, but I gather he's mostly living off a trust fund. If he works, he hasn't mentioned it. I thought it was rude to just come out and ask."

My partner, the detective.

"We've talked a little about Mendoza's nephew, the murder, you know. Davy seemed to like him, but didn't seem surprised by the death. When I asked Davy how he thought Berto could've gotten the drugs, he kinda shrugged it off, not as if he didn't care but as though it was no great mystery.

Sometimes You Get Killed

"No," Ernie had amended, "that's not quite right. More as though it were too big a mystery. Beyond comprehension, or resolution. If he weren't such a pragmatist, I'd almost say he seemed embarrassed by Berto's death, as though it were his own private failure."

Ernie added, "I didn't know whether he felt it wasn't appropriate for him to speculate, or whether he just didn't want *me* to speculate. Because I'm a newcomer, and didn't know Berto, do you think? Or maybe he didn't think much of my capabilities."

Or maybe Davy Rittenby figured Ernie had no need to know.

A tall, even gangly young man, Rittenby had to be at least 6'4" or 5", with waves of sandy blond hair that fell over pale blue eyes. A wide mouth and long, sharp aristocratic nose, together with a too high forehead, saved the face from being completely appealing. Rittenby had folded his long legs and lean frame into a chair in his room as we talked. He had a deep, bass voice but was soft-spoken, almost taciturn, as if to foster the impression of guarded intellect.

"I was really sorry about what happened to Ernie," he was saying.

I think I believed him. "Well, I appreciate that."

"He was one of the good guys. What happened that night was just incredible."

"How well did you know Eddie Velez?"

"I didn't see this coming, if that's what you mean. Far as I know, nobody did. But it's not as if I knew him long."

"Were you in therapy together?"

"Sure. But he didn't have any dramatic catharsis in which he revealed some homicidal fantasies."

"Or FSK affiliations?"

Rittenby smiled slightly. "All right. I keep forgetting you've been told. No, I didn't pick up on anything. I've been wracking my brains since it all happened, trying

161

Sharon Carton

to figure out how I could've been so sloppy. Maybe it's because of this place, you know, that it made me let down my guard. Maybe it's just...." His voice trailed off, and I wondered if he was blaming his drug habit for clouding his vision.

"Do you have any doubts?" I asked, interrupting his thoughts.

"About what?"

"About whether Velez was FSK?"

"Jesus, you're kidding, right?"

I shook my head.

He started to answer, then paused. "Okay, so I never overheard Cyrillic syllables, and I never caught him in the act of passing secrets to some Russian contact. But do I believe he was really working for them? Yeah, I do."

"Why? Because that's what you were told?"

He shrugged. "In part, yes. In part because it explains a lot. In part because-" He stopped and looked at me.

Oh. "I get it. Classified information."

"Look, Jack, it's not what you think. I'm not using some national security bugaboo to avoid telling you the truth."

"Funny, that's exactly how it looks to me."

"I know," he said, uncomfortable. "That bothers me. I liked Ernie. I enjoyed his company. There aren't many people I can talk to here. You were in intelligence, you know what I mean."

"So?"

"So if I felt there was something you should know, something about his death, I would tell you."

Did I believe him? Ernie did, but that didn't mean much. If Ernie liked someone, he usually trusted them; he had trouble distinguishing the two.

"Even if it were classified?"

Rittenby took a deep breath, then exhaled slowly. "I wouldn't necessarily divulge classified information. I...I'm

Sometimes You Get Killed

not sure that would ever be justified, and I'm not sure it would ever be necessary. There would be some other way, I would have to believe I'd find some other way."

"Would you?" I pressed. "Could I count on that?"

Rittenby's discomfort seemed to be growing. "Look, Jack, I told you I liked Ernie. I'm sure his death was a blow to you; it upset me, too, I can tell you that. I wouldn't want the person responsible to get away with it. If I thought that was happening, I'd take steps to correct it. I think you and I would be on the same side on that one.

"But," he went on, "you should know something. I'm not just some nice, easy-going guy you can assume would back any play you come up with. In fact, I'm not really a nice guy at all."

I couldn't tell if he was apologizing or threatening. Slouched sloppily in his chair, Rittenby didn't seem particularly intimidating. Maybe he had a problem with that; maybe spies resent it when they don't inspire fear. "That's not what I heard from Ernie," I said mildly.

That got a sudden laugh. "Come on, are you trying to suggest Ernie had any kind of insight into people's characters? The guy had brains but couldn't tell the players even with a scorecard. No criticism, it's just the way he was."

"You think it got him killed?"

Rittenby fixed me with a penetrating stare. "Ernie was no more inadequate than the rest of us, as far as that went. None of us saw through Velez. Ernie got killed because of where he was.

"Or maybe," he said, with an unpleasant edge to his voice, "that's not what you meant. If you're wondering whether Ernie was only killed because he was here, and he was only here because the person he misread was you, well, I guess you're the only one who can answer that."

It was nasty, and calculated enough to take my breath away. How much had Ernie, who for such a guileless person had a remarkable proficiency in keeping secrets,

Sharon Carton

revealed to this man? More likely, Rittenby was as lethally perspicacious as I'd always imagined spooks to be. Had Rittenby read all that in Ernie, or in me?

I spent nearly two hours with Rittenby, longer than I had planned. More than once he repeated his remark. "I'm not a nice guy." While I was finding him engaging, I've learned to listen to people, to know when a warning should be heeded. Ernie used to lambaste himself, saying "I'm not a very good person," but that was different. Ernie didn't like himself because he was holding himself up to some liberal ideal of morality, self-sacrifice and altruism that no one could live up to. It meant he was always disappointed in himself, but it meant he was always trying. In fact, being "nice" came naturally to him; it was the way most people described him, but even if he would've acknowledged that as one of his character traits, I don't think he would've equated that with being a "good" person.

When Rittenby, on the other hand, said he wasn't an especially nice person, he said it in a way that suggested I should believe it, even without any supporting evidence. My gut instincts about people were good enough that they sometimes ignored the report of my senses: He acted, sounded, seemed like a nice enough guy, but I had a feeling he knew what he was talking about when he denied it. There was some hope for this guy — not being nice apparently bothered him enough that he would warn me about it — but reform and pledged reform are two different things, and they're both worlds apart from acknowledged need for reform. For the present, I was dealing with someone of whom I should beware.

When Rittenby talked about not being "nice", I could only guess that he was speaking on a pragmatic level, that he wasn't "nice" because he'd done some not-nice things. I figured he should know. I figured I should listen, as one not-nice person to another.

Because talking with Davy Rittenby took so long,

Sometimes You Get Killed

I ended up having lunch at the Center. Roger extended the invitation when we ran into each other as I was leaving Rittenby to look for my next victim. He had Kevin in tow, and as they approached I saw Roger gesturing animatedly, while Kevin kept his gaze straight ahead, a bored, long-suffering look on his face.

The cafeteria set-up was a few steps above standard institutional facilities, with fare to match. Sitting at a table with Kevin, Roger, Khoragian, Rittenby and another patient, Walt Coleman, I had a plateful of baked stuffed flounder with broccoli in front of me. I took a bite, then told Roger to pass along my compliments to the chef.

The Reverend beamed. "We do well with the funds allotted us."

I knew Coleman wasn't CIA, so I was surprised at the carelessness of the remark, and of Rittenby's, "Don't tell the taxpayers how well we eat. They'd raise holy hell at the extravagance."

"I'm really impressed," I said, "but I bet Ernie wasn't."

Coleman emitted a coarse laugh. He was a short man with a compact, apparently muscular body. I guessed he was in his mid-forties; his black, neatly trimmed hair, slightly long in the back, was streaked with gray, and his mustache was pure silver.

Roger looked puzzled, and mildly affronted. "We serve well-balanced, healthful meals, prepared with care and taste, and a minimum of salt, oil and cholesterol."

"Exactly," I said between mouthfuls of flounder. "You put in everything Ernie hated, and left out all the good stuff like grease and fat and calories."

"Don't worry about it," Rittenby drawled. "Ernie never ate here. He used to bribe Debbie to go down the road to the Mickey Dee's on Federal Highway during her lunch hour."

"I should've known. No wonder he never mentioned the food. But what did he do for dinner?"

Sharon Carton

"Debbie'd bring back a half dozen cheeseburgers and some bags of fries at noon. Whatever Ernie didn't eat for lunch he ate cold for dinner."

Roger turned to Davy, perplexed. "But we have a microwave."

"Ernie and machinery didn't mix," I answered. "He's never used a microwave in his life."

Rittenby laughed in recognition, but when he finished there was an uncomfortable silence. It was finally broken by Walt Coleman's nasal Midwestern twang. "Jack, how are you finding South Florida?"

Deadly, I thought. "I haven't gotten to see much of it," I said without really thinking.

"Oh, really?" he replied. "How are you spending your time down here?"

Oh, shit. What was my story with these guys? There were so many layers of deceit to this case that I had lost track of how much this guy knew, how much I was supposed to know, and how much he was supposed to know I knew. "Oh, mostly tying up some loose ends."

"From when you were here before?"

"That's right."

"What sort of loose ends?"

I shrugged. "Murder can be a messy business," I said, trying to keep a light tone to my voice.

Roger seemed to be listening attentively, but Khoragian simply ate stolidly, determined not to let me spoil his meal. Kevin looked restless, impatient with the enforced nonactivity. Rittenby just played with his food.

"Not to put too fine a point to it," Coleman went on, unperturbed, "but I would've thought everything was wrapped up with a rather violent finality the night Ernie Darwin was killed. I mean, it's not as if there were a trial to hang around for."

Accurate, if tasteless. "What do you do for a living, Mr. Coleman?"

"I'm a businessman, Jack, and it's Walt."

Sometimes You Get Killed

"You must be doing well," I said, aiming to match the level of tastelessness, "to afford a place like this." I hadn't missed the expensive tailoring of Coleman's suit, or the diamond in his pinky ring.

Rittenby laughed, flashing Coleman a derisive glance. "It's that old chestnut, Jack: Don't do the drugs if you can't afford the rehab."

Coleman smiled tightly. "Davy's joking, of course. My problem's alcohol, unwise but legal."

"Every good reactionary's drug of choice," Davy snapped.

Suddenly Kevin spoke. "I know you."

I looked up to see the object of his accusation. It was Coleman, who colored slightly. "I don't see how."

"Give me a minute," Kevin replied, concentrating. "You spend any time in Manhattan?"

Coleman grew fidgety under Kevin's stare. "A few days a year, business meetings, conventions-"

"That's a Chicago accent, isn't it?" I said, interrupting, wondering if Kevin had put his foot in it. Coleman turned to me in gratitude. "Yes, born and raised there. My firm's main headquarters is in the Loop-"

"That's it," Kevin announced in triumph. "You know my father, Nathan Draper. Draper Industries, Draper Electronics, Draper Exports? You know my father, right?" he repeated.

"Oh. Oh, of course," Coleman acknowledged reluctantly. "Nate Draper. Good man."

Kevin smiled, glee moving him to rare enthusiasm. "I knew it." He turned to me. "I'm good with faces."

"Do we...have we ever met?" Coleman asked Kevin.

"Mm hmm." Kevin squinted. "Once. Lincoln Center. *Turandot*. Nineteen...eighty-four. December?"

"Yes, of course," Coleman said, clearly not remembering. Then he laughed nervously. "I'm sure your discretion can be trusted, young man."

Sharon Carton

Kevin answered with a straight face. "Oh, don't worry. Alcohol abuse is being viewed more and more these days as a disease rather than a sign of weak character."

I laughed. I couldn't help it: Kevin's feigned solemnity, Roger's pompous disapproval, Coleman's barely repressed anger. It was all just such a ridiculous picture.

Rittenby seemed to enjoy my hilarity, but Kevin didn't know how to take it. Khoragian, who had had his fill of us, got up and silently removed his tray and winning personality from the table.

At another table, Khoragian's wife Chris was attacking a salad while engaging in lively chatter with two men I didn't know. I assumed they were patients. One, a sun-bleached blond, seemed to be in his mid- to late twenties. The other appeared to be a few years older, with thinning brown hair and the results of a haphazard shaving job on his jowls. He had the nervous gesture of running his fingers through his hair tenderly, fondly, the way many balding men do, as if memorizing every last strand. There were deep circles under his eyes, but believable smile wrinkles around those eyes and a pleasant smile on his face. Khoragian walked past their table without pause or comment.

A young Latin man, who couldn't have been too far out of his teens, was seated at a third table, smoking and nodding as he listened to Louise Fischman, who was calmly speaking in a voice too soft for me to overhear. At the last occupied table, Gregory Tessler and Sofia Cisneros, whom I had met briefly during my first visit, had both finished their meals and were chatting amiably over coffee.

There were two empty tables. The population at the Center had taken a sharp downward turn recently: Berto Santiago, Dr. Paul Rios, Eddie Velez, and, of course, Ernie. I wondered whether there would be any additions made to make up the difference.

I turned back to my table. Kevin, gloating insufferably, kept shooting furtive glances at Coleman.

Sometimes You Get Killed

Coleman looked like he wanted to strangle the kid. Davy was maintaining a conversation with Roger, whose glazed expression belied the warmth of his smile. I sighed, suddenly eager to be away from here. What the hell was I doing here? I had solved Mendoza's case, his nephew didn't overdose, hadn't even been on drugs. I knew who had killed him. If I was here because of Ernie, that was equally pointless. He was dead, and so was the man who had killed him. What was I doing here? I lit another cigarette, ignoring the no-smoking sign, and tried to will myself back to New York, to Annie and the bookstores, Shea Stadium, my friends and my apartment. Ray's Pizza. The Village. The Park. David's Cookies. Foreign films. Dirt. The subway. Cops who'd beat you up but never lie to you. New York.

I stayed at the Center for another couple of hours, talking with Sofia Cisneros, Jaime Oyola (the Hispanic young man who'd been sitting with Louise Fischman), the aging beach bum Dennis Wixtead, and Gary Nicholas, he of the receding hairline, an agreeable man about my age whose chief interests in life seemed to be *film noir* and alcohol. Wixtead was a vacuous, bleached out, burned out native Floridian. What he lacked in intellect he made up for in crudity.

My conversation with Nicholas was more enjoyable, but no more informative. I grew fascinated by his speech pattern: clear articulation, slow, with lengthy pauses and frequent repetition, as if he, having already forgotten his last remark, assumed his audience was under a similar disability.

Jaime Oyola was Venezuelan-born, charming but slightly antagonistic. He seemed to have something of a chip on his shoulder, but he was at pains to conceal it. I found him an interesting, potentially explosive personality, but I didn't know what difference it made. Oyola and Cisneros were CIA; Wixtead and Nicholas weren't. So what. At that point I had lost sight of what I was trying to prove.

Sharon Carton

Tired and depressed, I wanted to be alone with a bottle of Scotch and a carton of cigarettes. I stopped by Reception, collected Kevin and headed back to the hotel.

Chapter Seventeen

On the drive back to the hotel, the kid didn't say anything for the first mile or so, then could contain himself no longer.

"Do you want to know what I got, or not? I mean, was this just a joke, or did you really want that information?"

"Look, Kevin, I'm kinda tired. Let's get a drink, then you can-"

"Because I got the list of dates of admissions and discharges. It's a computer print-out, but it's letter quality and very legible."

"Uh, excuse me. From what computer did you print this out?"

"Debbie had a terminal and printer in Reception."

"And she let you use it?"

"She went to the ladies' room."

"How'd you get into the system?" I asked, frankly curious.

"No sweat. I had a minor in Computer Sciences."

"That wouldn't give you an access code."

"Debbie," Kevin said, with a worldly-wise air, "isn't the most circumspect person in the world."

"She told you?"

He shrugged. "Recidivism."

"That was the access code?"

"No," he said, and looked faintly repulsed by my ignorance. "Forget the code. I'm trying to say that I noted a high rate of recidivism among the Center's patients."

"Oh, really?" I replied, without much interest. "Well, hold that thought. We'll take a look at the print-out after I've had a couple of drinks."

Sharon Carton

Disappointed or frustrated, Kevin intoned, "I would've thought the Center would've put you off alcohol."

"Fuck you," I said wearily.

After a few minutes, "Oh," the kid said, off-handedly, "and I don't know whom these guys are lying to, you or the government, but if these people have any psychiatric training, then I'm Sigmund Freud."

Too tired to get into it, I had to force myself to reply. "What're you saying, they're quacks? Unqualified?"

"No. I'm not saying they're not good shrinks; I'm trying to tell you they're not shrinks, period."

I stared. Now I was interested, and fully awake. "How do you know?"

"Are you kidding? My old man had me in deep analysis when I was ten. I have a minor in Psychology. Psychobabble is my second language."

"They're frauds?"

"Oh good, I'm not going too fast for you. I mean, I pulled up your friend's record when I was at Debbie's terminal-"

"You what?"

Extra credit.

Kevin acted nonchalant, but he had to read my reaction in my face, not to mention my body language: I practically jumped out of my seat. "I wanted to see their treatment." He paused. "Okay, and maybe I was a little curious about this guy. From what Mr. Barnes said about him, he sounded like an interesting case study."

I wasn't crazy about his opinion, or his motive, but that seemed unimportant right now. "You found Ernie's record?"

"Well, yeah. I mean, the guy's dead, right, so I didn't think privacy was a concern anymore." He saw I was agitated, but didn't know why.

"His record was erased," I said. "You couldn't have found it in the computer."

"Want me to tell you his mother's maiden name

Sometimes You Get Killed

or something? It's there, all right. Anyway, that's not my point. The point is they were medicating him as if he were a chronic depressive, not a manic depressive."

"What-"

"These guys don't know their elavil from their lithium. I figure they were just medicating everyone the same."

"Maybe," my mind was reeling, "maybe they had diagnosed him as a chronic depressive."

"Nah. Their entry diagnosis was manic depressive, probably just based on your friend's having told them that's what he'd been diagnosed as in the past. My guess is they just medicated everyone the same," he repeated. "I pulled up a coupla other patients' files and those guys were getting the same thing, regardless of their different diagnoses. Besides, I wouldn't be surprised if they were just handing out placebos. Since these so-called shrinks had no medical knowledge, they must've just familiarized themselves with some of the jargon, but I don't see them actually prescribing."

I thought for a minute. "Can you be really sure they aren't genuine?"

"The staff? Well, yeah," he seemed offended. "We can check with their respective professional associations, find out which schools they supposedly attended, stuff like that. But if they're any good at all, they could've covered their asses. It's not all that difficult."

I believed him. He didn't even know just how practiced these guys were at deception. It was time he did. He hadn't done anything to prove himself trustworthy, especially, but I was starting to see that the more he knew, the more help he could prove. What the hell, he had just broken the case wide open.

I told him the whole story, or rather, the whole story as I knew it.

"So let me get this straight," he finally said. "First they lied to you that this was a regular rehab clinic. Then

Sharon Carton

they lied to you that this was just a government sponsored clinic. Then they lied to you that this was a CIA clinic. But it isn't a clinic at all. But it is something. I mean, it's *here*. So there must be something else going on other than rehabilitation."

"No shit, Sherlock. Question is what."

"And why they lied to you," Kevin added.

"No need to know," I said sarcastically. I didn't know which revelation was more astounding, or more significant: the fact that Ernie's record had not been destroyed, contrary to what I'd been told; or the fact that, according to Kevin's conviction, none of the staff of the Center was legitimate.

What was really going on at the Center? If they were CIA— and at this point I had my doubts about even that — the possibilities were virtually limitless. I did have some corroboration to the effect that the staff was CIA, courtesy of MLC's Dean Laurence Summeridge, but I couldn't overlook anything, not now. I had to know for sure if Kevin's conclusion was correct; if it was, then it meant the CIA was engaged in some kind of top secret clandestine operation. Had Berto found out about it? Had Ernie? Is that why they died? I was jaded enough to believe that it wasn't inconsistent with the CIA's ethical code to kill two civilians to protect their secret, but that wouldn't explain why one fed would kill another.

The stakes must've been pretty high, probably an illicit operation of some kind. Maybe I was missing something: How did I know Velez had killed Paul Rios?

All right, wait. Let's say the feds were truthful, and correct, about Velez being FSK; he'd just infiltrated a CIA operation of a different nature to the one I'd been told about. It was still credible, then, that he'd killed Ernie and Santiago for discovering his identity, and Rios for witnessing the murder of Santiago.

That required two great leaps of faith, neither of which I was willing to make: first, that a young,

Sometimes You Get Killed

inexperienced patrolman had been savvy enough to catch a FSK agent while the CIA could not; second, that my naive and gullible partner had seen through a Russian spy's cover. I wasn't sure Ernie ever even believed there was any such thing as an honest-to-goodness Communist. From the political discussions I'd had with him, I got the impression Ernie remained unconvinced that communists were anything but a figment of paranoid right-wing fanatics' imagination.

So I had a hard time buying into the FSK in Fort Lauderdale scenario. That meant that, if indeed Velez was the murderer of Berto and Rios, there had to be some other motive. Money? I didn't see how. Sex? Not noticeably. Vengeance? Maybe, if there was some history between Velez and Rios, but I didn't think there was one with Berto, and I knew Ernie had only met Velez at the Center.

Ambition? Was Rios standing in Velez' career path at the Company? And what did that have to do with my two *naifs*? Okay, maybe I didn't know enough about Berto to be skeptical, but Ernie? Ernie Darwin? Get real.

It didn't scan, none of it. Unless Berto was killed just because he was a cop, Ernie just because he was in the corridor, and Velez killed Rios because...because...oh hell, I didn't have any idea why he Velez had killed Rios. If he had.

He had shown me some aptitude with the knife. Okay, so he did kill Rios. And I know he killed Ernie. But maybe not Berto. Then who had?

Oh, fuck. There was something else, something I was missing.

All right, moving right along. I had no problem with Ernie's records still being on file, but what I couldn't figure out is why they'd bother to lie about it. It had to mean something. They didn't want me to see those records? Did it have anything to do with the medication Ernie had been prescribed? If only I could get hold of the autopsy report, it should tell me about what drugs had been in his bloodstream. Maybe I'd try again; I'd call Berto's partner.

175

Sharon Carton

Medical experimentation. I've read about stuff like that. Had the Center performed experimental drug testing on the Center's patients? But then wouldn't they have employed medically-trained personnel? Is that why Ernie's body had been cremated? I'd have to check on Berto's autopsy; had his remains been cremated, too?

The more I thought about it, the more confused I grew.

"Why would they leave Ernie's record in the computer bank?" I asked aloud. It didn't seem to make sense.

This smirking kid didn't seem to care about sense. Knowledge, and the acquisition of it, were all he concerned himself with. "Why didn't Nixon destroy the tapes?" he asked rhetorically.

"What could you possibly know about Watergate? You weren't even a fetus at the time."

"I minored in American History."

Great, my life was now in the history books. "When did you graduate high school, when you were twelve?"

"Fifteen," he said seriously, then went on to list his other degrees. "Finished college when I was eighteen, then got my first Master's in...."

I soon stopped listening to Kevin's academic credentials, but I did notice he made no mention of the schools he'd flunked or been kicked out of. Since I've never known Jonah Barnes to be anything less than honest — sometimes brutally so — or accurate, I had to believe Kevin's version of reality was not entirely to be trusted.

But for the moment my thoughts were elsewhere. All right, so they weren't concerned with someone infiltrating the Center and learning my identity or my connection with Ernie. Did that mean they knew Velez had no co-conspirators, no FSK colleagues to hunt me down? If so, then that seemed to give the lie to their explanation for sanitizing the hospital records on Ernie. I started to get

Sometimes You Get Killed

excited. Forgetting myself, I asked the kid, "Do you have any idea what this means?"

He shrugged, which seemed to suggest that he neither knew nor cared. "Maybe," he said, unemotionally, "it's got something to do with that lawsuit your friend's lawyer friend wants to bring."

"So what're you saying, the CIA assassinated that doctor and nurse to safeguard the hospital from liability for negligence in their treatment of Ernie? Too weird."

"Too weird for the CIA?" he asked, dubious.

I raised my eyebrows, and smiled.

"Look," he went on, "it's just some scam, you ask me. I spent a total of a few hours with these guys and could tell they were passing. They never bothered to get the records of your friend's previous treatment. He goes to the hospital, and kicks when he's there. The people who treated him there disappear. Ernie's record there disappears. Ernie's dead body becomes ashtray dirt." He paused, and I waited. When he didn't seem inclined to go on, I prodded him.

"So? What does it all mean? What's the connection between all those lies?"

He gave me a noncommittal shrug. "How should I know? Why should the CIA authorize payment of a death benefit to the mother of a FSK agent? I mean, not everything in-"

"Wait, stop," I interrupted him. "What was that about a death benefit?"

"Velez' mother. A widow, lives in Venezuela. I saw a letter on Debbie Galesseo's computer disk, authorizing the payment of Velez' government pension, lump sum benefit to her. His mother, that is, not Debbie Galesseo."

My God. "This may sound like a dumb question, but this was dated after Velez' death?"

"Sure," Kevin said, nonplussed. "It was dated three days ago. I remember being kinda surprised that the feds

177

Sharon Carton

had acted so quickly for once."

"Oh? Did it occur to you that this might suggest Eddie Velez wasn't FSK, that the Center people *knew* he wasn't FSK, that-"

"Well, no, not at the time. I mean, at the time, I wasn't aware of the 'FSK in Fort Lauderdale' scenario," he mimicked.

"All right, so you know now. That's it," I said. "That's it," I said again, in case he'd missed it. I paused for effect.

"All right," he said finally, humoring me. "That's what?"

"Proof. A verified fact. Velez wasn't FSK. He was as much CIA as the other Center people." Then I fell silent for a few minutes.

Kevin didn't speak. Maybe he'd fallen asleep.

Then I went on. "Unfortunately, that raises as many questions as it answers."

"Are you calling my old man tonight?" Kevin asked suddenly.

"What?"

"My father. You said you'd call him tonight."

"Oh. Yeah, sure." How could he be thinking of that when all hell was breaking loose?

"What're you gonna tell him?"

"About the CIA?" I teased.

"No, about...you know."

"I don't know. What do you want me to tell him?"

"It's not up to me, is it?"

I was surprised to detect vulnerability in his face.

"Well," I said carefully, "I think you're working out. In fact, I'd have to say you've already exceeded my expectations."

"Such as they were," he said pointedly.

I smiled. "Such as they were. No, you did great, kid. I'd really like you to stay on, and I'll tell your father that. That okay with you?"

Sometimes You Get Killed

He smiled back. "I guess."

I took that for an enthusiastic expression of commitment and appreciation, and let the subject drop. Besides, I had too many other things to think about to press the matter.

Later that evening, I waited for Kevin to leave the hotel for some unarticulated solitary pursuit, then placed a long-distance call to his father. It inspired as much curiosity about Draper senior as about my new protégé. Nathan Draper, according to Jonah, was a self-made millionaire, first generation loaded, all drive and no class. Both from what Jonah had told me, and from what I learned in my conversation, I liked Draper; he reminded me of a more successful version of myself, at least as hungry for the acceptance and education possessed by the wealthy as for their more tangible acquisitions.

Under no delusions as to his flaws, or the good fortune which let him amass a few million dollars despite them, Draper expressed a chief concern that his youngest son, Kevin, had inherited the weaknesses as surely as he would someday inherit his share of the money.

"I'm a reprobate, Jack. I don't mind admitting it. I don't even mind being a reprobate."

"You just don't want your son to be one," I volunteered.

"That's it. You got me. Kevin's smart, he's very smart. Smarter than me. No question. He's got no drive, that's different from me, too, but that's okay. I pushed hard enough so he don't have to."

"Then it doesn't bother you that he has no particular ambition, or goal."

"It bothers me that he doesn't care about anything. I don't care what. I don't care that he's not like his brothers. He tell you about his brothers?"

"No," I admitted. "I didn't even know-"

"Well, that's all right, they don't get along, not with

Sharon Carton

him. They do well for themselves, very well. Kevin doesn't have to make money. Whatever he needs I can give him, and he don't seem to need much."

"So what exactly is it that-"

"I want him to find something that matters to him. I want him to learn about good and bad, I want-"

"You want me to teach him how to be a private investigator so he can learn about morality? From me?" Jesus, I thought, what did Jonah tell this guy about me?

"I worry that...he keeps himself at a distance from things, from people. He's a good kid. Oh, sure, he's gotten himself kicked out of a lot of schools. They tell me he cheats, he steals, he lies, but I know he's a good kid. I think he does all these things, if he does all these things, because maybe he can't tell the difference between what's right and wrong."

Or, I wondered silently, to hurt his father? "You think he's amoral? But you also think he's good?"

"I think he's basically good," Nathan Draper said slowly, choosing his words with care. "But I think he don't know why he should bother being good, why he shouldn't do certain things. It don't matter to him."

"Mr. Draper," I began.

"Nathan. Nate."

"Nate, your son is bright, he's clever. I think he's got potential. I just don't know if you're asking too much of this whole arrangement."

"No," he insisted. "The Cockney told me about you."

"What did he tell you exactly?"

"He says, and half the time I can't understand what the hell he says, he mangles the language so bad. But he says you care more about doing the right thing than about anything else."

Me, I thought? That sounded more like Ernie, the late great crusader. All I cared about was getting by. "He may've exaggerated a little."

Sometimes You Get Killed

"No," Draper said firmly. "He said you've got standards, and you've got rules, and when they clash you give priority to the standards. I like that."

"But-"

"And he said half the time you don't even know this, that you think you're choosing doing what you want instead of what's right because you don't even know that doing what's right is what you want."

I was impressed — with Jonah's having spent so much time deliberating on my character, with Draper's remembering it, and with myself for being such an admirable human being.

Draper interpreted my silence as acquiescence. "So I'll send you a check for this month, right?"

Penury and pragmatism fought with my noted set of ethics. "Look, I don't know if your son should be mixed up in what I'm working on right now. My partner got killed on this case-"

"Yeah, yeah, I know, but the guy who did him is dead, Jonah told me. And Kevin's tough, Kevin knows how to take care of himself."

"Yeah, that I've seen, but-"

"Whatever you may think, Kevin hasn't led a sheltered life. He's been around, that kid."

"Still, it might be better if he goes back to New York, and, when I get back there we could-"

"No. You don't understand. He's interested now. We wait, he loses interest."

Oh, great, I thought, another one with an Ernie Darwin five-minute attention span.

"I got your address down there, Jack," Draper concluded, "and I'll mail you the check."

"Let's wait until I get back to New York."

"I'll mail you the check," he repeated.

"Mail me the check," I said with resignation. No sense in both of us being stubborn. Since I had no idea how I was going to pay my hotel bill except by exceeding the

Sharon Carton

credit limit on my American Express card, I decided on a compromise. "Let's take it month by month. No guarantees. Anytime he wants out, or I want him out, the deal's over."

"I'll mail you the check."

I don't know whether he even heard me, but I felt better for having at least articulated the terms of our arrangement. I decided that it might be a good idea to do the same with Kevin, but the rest of the telephone conversation I would keep between his father and me. Ethics, you know.

Chapter Eighteen

Whether you're talking fact or fiction, knowledge improperly possessed can be as accurate a reflection of deceit as can be an inappropriate ignorance. An imposter fails to recognize an old childhood friend, a German spy in a war movie can't identify the third baseman for the Brooklyn Dodgers. Someone blurts out, "I'm not the one who shot Louie," when no one had yet mentioned how Louie died.

In my experience, suspects are rarely clumsy enough to err in either way. I tend to have to rely on hostility for my clues. Ernie regarded secretiveness as an inalienable American birthright, but to me it always signaled guilt of one kind or another. Surrounded by the CIA, I was suffering an embarrassment of riches. I hardly knew whom to accuse first. Suspicion grew exponentially with the discovery of each new level of deceit, and yet the truth still eluded me. The police, who I thought would be allies, seemed to owe allegiance elsewhere.

Early the next morning, I drove to Broward Boulevard and presented myself to Sergeant DeBiasio in the office of the Homicide Division. I don't know what I was thinking. I don't usually give the local cops an opportunity to solve my case before I got a chance to do so. Even Jeff Fenton, a good friend for several years, only got my confidential information when I needed his help, and if that's the reasoning that impelled me to share my goodies with DeBiasio, it was only part of it.

Yes, I was hoping to be rewarded with police cooperation, but I also had less grasping motives. Feeling my own sense of loss, maybe I thought the Fort Lauderdale police were as bereaved; I guess I chose DeBiasio because I

Sharon Carton

thought that he who unwittingly sent Berto to his death might have as sharp a need as I to put matters right, or as right as they could ever be.

I misjudged my reception. Greedy for my own information, he proved disappointingly stingy when it came to reciprocating. All I really wanted from him was the police report of investigation for the murders of Santiago, Rios and Ernie. I didn't expect major breakthroughs. At this point I didn't have any significant hope that they were holding out on me; rather, my conversation with DeBiasio had me convinced I had learned far more than they had. I didn't know whether they had genuinely abandoned the investigation, consistent with federal directive, or whether they were struggling to carry on surreptitious inquiries but were proving unequal to the task.

So what did I want from the ROI? Two things. First, figured I could learn something from seeing what the official Department posture was. I didn't expect it was closer to the truth than what I currently knew; in fact, it was from the lies that I hoped to learn. What kind of statements had the Center people given the cops? How much did the cops buy? Where were the gaps between the story they told the cops, the story they had — at various stages — told me, and the story as I now knew it to be? I thought it might prove illuminating. Triangulation: Locate various points on a three-dimensional field, and the picture would gain shape and clarity.

I said there were two things I wanted from DeBiasio. The second was one particular element or document within the ROI: the Medical Examiner's reports on the autopsies of Velez' victims, specifically, Mendoza's nephew and Ernie. I at least knew the cause of Ernie's death; I couldn't say as much for Berto's. I didn't even know how Velez had killed Berto. Which of the two stories fed me was true? Were there drugs involved, or had Velez really done to Berto what he did to Rios and Ernie? Here again, at least as important as the truth was what the police recorded. I

184

Sometimes You Get Killed

needed to know not only what happened but who knew what happened.

I knew more, of course, of what Velez had done to Ernie, but I still wanted to see the official write-up. There was an additional consideration: What I didn't know was what happened to Ernie in the hospital. I'm not saying I was seriously contemplating the lawsuit Catherine had been suggesting, but I couldn't overlook the possibility that there was something sinister in the disappearance of Ernie's record, doctor and nurse. If the fact that Ernie's records at the Center hadn't been erased meant that the hospital record hadn't been destroyed to protect me, there had to be some other reason for the cover-up.

DeBiasio was unyielding. "It's an ongoing investigation, Migliore. You know what that means."

"Yeah, but I thought you guys had let the feds take over."

"Just because we're not actively pursuing the case doesn't mean it's closed. Ongoing investigation," he chanted accurately, "no public access to the ROI."

"It's a public document," I tried lamely.

"Not until and unless the ROI has been offered into evidence by the state's attorney."

"What're you talking about? The killer is dead. Who's the state's attorney gonna prosecute?"

"Don't give me any ideas, Migliore."

"Yeah, right. Drop dead, Sergeant."

"Why don't you get outa here, Migliore? In fact, why don't you go back to New York?"

"So does that mean I don't get the Report?"

"You catch on quick, Migliore. Stop wasting my time."

"I know. You've got a case to investigate."

"Fuck you, asshole. You don't know what you're talking about."

It wouldn't be the first time, I thought. "So why don't you enlighten me, Sergeant? I'm only here to learn."

Sharon Carton

And learn I did, but not from anything DeBiasio gave me. Like I said, secrecy and hostility are educational. DeBiasio was right about the letter of the law; he was authorized to withhold the Report from a member of the public, at least until it became evidence in a trial. But Jeff got them for me all the time. And, in light of all the information I gave to DeBiasio, I would've thought he could've coughed up one autopsy report, especially that of my dead partner, if it meant helping me determine the truth about the death of one of their cops.

Unfortunately for me, Berto's partner, Rudy Grissom, gave me no more than DeBiasio. As before, he seemed more willing, but lamented plaintively that even he had been denied access to the files on the Center murders.

Unfortunately for the bad guys, my dead partner had been a lawyer. A non-practicing lawyer the last few years, but a lawyer. Ernie had once told me morosely that a lawyer is a lawyer for life. Like alcoholics, he had said, they can be in a state of recovery, but they're marked until they die. It's a way of thinking, a way of speaking, and Ernie, who had loved the law but not being a lawyer, was as sick as they come.

I had caught a little of it from him. As soon as I left the police station, I went back to the hotel and called Mendoza. Recalcitrant at first for the same reasons I had expressed myself, Mendoza at last agreed.

Then I called Cathy.

"Jack, I'm so glad to hear from you. Look, Richard and I want to know if you'd like to check out of the hotel and come stay with us. We've got plenty of room, and-"

"Thanks, but I need to stay in Fort Lauderdale. That's not why I called," I went on brusquely. I was too impatient for good manners. "I want you to file suit against the hospital."

"Really?" She seemed pleased but surprised, and maybe a little skeptical. "I've been doing some research, but I thought it was still premature."

Sometimes You Get Killed

"That doesn't matter. Draw up a complaint. Draw up two. One with Charlie, that's Charles Madison, and one for Luis Mendoza. Charlie's against the hospital, and Mendoza's against the Center. You can-"

"The Center?" she exclaimed. "So you want me to sue the federal government? Do I name the Director personally, too? And what's the basis of the cause of action? What're we alleging they did, or didn't do?"

"Wrongful death, conspiracy, fraud, negligence, I don't care." I told her everything about the case that she needed to know, including the CIA connection, but told her to keep that out of the pleadings. "You've got all the facts. Turn it into a lawsuit, two lawsuits."

"Jack, drafting a complaint that'll stand up in court isn't as casual an-"

"I don't care if it stands up in court. I don't care about winning the case. I just want the suits instituted."

"Why? For harassment purposes? Jack, I'm willing to go out on a limb to penalize whoever's responsible, but I stop short of filing harassment suits."

"It's not for harassment," I said calmly. "It's for discovery," and then I explained the law to a lawyer, what Jonah would call "teaching my grandmother to suck eggs." I learned a fair bit of English slang from Jonah, just as I'd learned some law from Ernie, and from Tom Wriggley, a lawyer in a midtown Manhattan firm for whom I often did some investigative work.

A police ROI isn't available as a matter of public record, but it is discoverable in a lawsuit. In other words, it's a document which a party to a lawsuit can be compelled to turn over to the other side as part of the pretrial investigation, called the discovery process, conducted by both attorneys.

"Jack," Cathy replied, a new, uncertain note in her voice, "I'm not sure what party would be compelled to provide the ROI. Would it be within the control of the hospital? The Center? The police?"

Sharon Carton

"I don't know, Cathy. The police are the ones who have it, but as for whom we can force to provide it, that's your specialty, not mine. Find out," I ordered her, "and draw up the papers. As soon as possible. Call me if you need any more information, or when you've got the papers read to be signed."

I hung up. I loved the law, too.

I spent the rest of the day poring over the computer print-out Kevin had obtained from the Center. It listed the dates of admission to, and discharge from, the Center. Kevin had gotten the records as far back as May of this year, a month before Berto Santiago died. Mendoza's nephew had been undercover at the Center about two weeks when he was killed.

There was a pattern, I knew there was a pattern. I just couldn't figure out what it was, or what it meant. The problem wasn't that I mistrusted the data; if anything, the opposite was true.

Documents aren't my long suit. I do people better. Papers confuse me; not figuring them out — though I'm better at people on that score, too — but trusting them. Like most uneducated slobs, I'm impressed and a little intimidated by official-looking papers. I have an embarrassing tendency to believe the written words when I would instinctively distrust the same words if spoken. When it's not just written but actually printed, it's what Ernie would call "well nigh unassailable." Maybe I imagine scores of editors weeding out the untruths; maybe it's the thought of people being willing to lie orally but cowed into integrity when their lies would be committed to writing for posterity. Maybe it's just my nature to trust ideas and institutions, *things*, more than people. Ernie, predictably, was the opposite.

I found my mind wandering, as I started to wonder whether Ernie had ever become aware of the information printed on these pages. I started to feel there was a secret here, maybe the same secret that had cost Berto Santiago

Sometimes You Get Killed

his life.

Because somehow, at that moment, I had settled on the theory that Berto's death had been tied to the secret of the Center, but Ernie's had been an accident of timing. Paul Rios' death I believed to be inextricably tied to his being in the control booth when Berto was killed.

So what did the papers tell me?

"I told you," Kevin said. "Recidivism."

"Yeah, you keep saying that, but what does it mean?"

"Recidivism means the rate of relapse, usually into crime, but in this context it relates to the rate of failed recovery among the Center's patients."

"I know what the word means, kid. I meant what's so significant about it?"

"Oh. Well, I don't know the figure nationally, but the rate at the Center seems significantly disproportionate. Or disproportionately high," he clarified. "Didn't you tell me Dr. Samuels had said it was somewhere in the seventieth percentile? Well, it's not even close to that."

"Well," I said thoughtfully, "let's remember what we're talking about. If you're right about the staff being phony, it's not surprising no one ever got cured."

Kevin rolled his eyes in disgust. "Look, you're not getting this, are you?"

His superior tone rankled, but I wasn't oblivious to the fact that he at least seemed to be getting caught up in the case. "All right, all right," I said. "If there was no real rehab staff, it's probably an indication not that the staff was defrauding the patients, but that the real purpose of the Center had nothing to do with drugs or alcohol." A bell went off in my head.

"Right," Kevin said appreciatively. "It's all some CIA scam. The question becomes, first, were the patients in on it, too. And second — are you listening?"

"Mm hmm," I said, distracted.

"It's just you have this funny look on your face."

Sharon Carton

"Go on, I just remembered something."

"Well, I was saying that the second question is why the same patients, with a few variations, kept coming back. I don't think we can answer either question without learning exactly what the CIA was up to down here."

"I might be able to answer that one."

"Huh? You mean you know what the secret operation was?"

"Well, maybe I exaggerated. But I think I've been overlooking something. I learned from several people, the police and the Center people, that the cops started investigating in part because neighbors were complaining about suspicious, drug-dealing types hanging around."

"So?"

"So what does that mean?"

"Probably just some paranoid rednecks getting nervous. I mean, I've never seen any drug smugglers hanging around the Center, have you?"

"You've only been there once."

"You haven't," he countered. "Did you ever see any scuzzos lurking about the grounds?"

"No," I had to admit. "But that doesn't mean they were all in the neighbors' imaginations. Maybe we should speak to some of those neighbors."

"I guess," he said, without much enthusiasm.

"What, you don't think it's worthwhile?"

He shrugged, then said awkwardly, "I'm not so good with strangers."

I smiled. "Kid, you're not so good with people who know you, either."

He grinned back, embarrassed. "So what's so important about these neighbors, anyway?"

"Well, what if they were right? I've only spent a total of maybe fifteen, twenty hours at the Center. What about the rest of the time? What if the Center were really a front for drug dealing?"

"The CIA?" he said, dubious. "I mean, the federal

Sometimes You Get Killed

government?"

"When were you born?"

"Why?"

"Just trying to figure out if you're old enough to know better."

"Oh, I'm sorry, what is this, some cynical liberal conspiracy trip?"

Ernie would've cracked up to hear me described as a liberal. "I'm just saying it's not beyond the realm of possibility that the Central Intelligence Agency engaged in illegal covert activity on the domestic front."

"Yeah, I know, I watch tv, I've read the papers. I just find it a bit ludicrous that the CIA would set up this whole operation just so it could score some dope."

"Yeah. But what if it was on a really big scale? Or what if that's just a small by-product of their operation?"

"I don't know," he shook his head, "this is all just speculation and conjecture. How do you substantiate any of it? We're no better off now than we were before."

"Don't underestimate the value of speculation and conjecture. We are better off. We just don't know why."

"That makes no sense."

"Maybe."

I made a mental list of chores. Talk to the neighbors. Review the print-out (again). Check out the credentials of the Center's staff. Go back to original list of questions from Annie. My brain fried from all the useful speculation and conjecture, I decided to avoid the items that would require any analytical ability.

"I don't like the world much anymore."

I knew how she felt. Standing on the front stoop of a house belonging to a Mrs. Hanley, slapping off the mosquitos, my shirt glued to my back, I wasn't too crazy about life, either. But Mrs. Hanley was talking about the global situation.

"War and hunger, revolutions and terrorism-"

"Mm hmm," I nodded, wondering what I'd have to

Sharon Carton

do to gain entrance to the house, out of the humidity, while suspecting vaguely that I might be better off outside.

"—new diseases, I mean, what was wrong with the old ones, and of course things aren't any better at home, what with the murderers and rapists and the kids with their drinking and taking drugs-"

"Yes," I jumped in, "that's what I wanted to talk to you about. You lodged some complaints with the police about the Center?"

"Oh, yes," she lowered her voice conspiratorially, "down the road. *Them*."

"What exactly was the problem?"

She hesitated, looking me up and down. "Are you working on the case?"

She obviously meant was I with the police, but it's not my fault if people can't speak more clearly. "That's right."

"Well, it's about time. It's been weeks, and nobody's done anything. That place is an outrage. I warned you people, but you ignored me, and what happens?"

"I don't know, what happens?"

"People die," she said mysteriously. "First one boy takes too many pills, and then, on one night, five people die! A big shoot-out! A massacre! You should've seen it — cops, ambulance, tv reporters—"

Even with the embellishment, she had to be talking about the night Velez attacked Rios and Ernie. I hadn't been aware of any press presence; maybe they arrived after I went to the hospital. Maybe not.

"Did the— did anyone from the Department come to talk to you after all that happened?"

"Nobody," she said emphatically. "And it's all connected, I could've told your people that. If anyone saw fit to ask me."

"I'm asking you, Mrs. Hanley. Why did you contact the police in the first place?" I thought I had gotten lucky; the first neighbor, the closest geographically to the Center,

Sometimes You Get Killed

had been one of the complainants.

"Late at night, and not once, I can tell you that, there'd be cars behind the Center, people coming and going. Very suspicious, real shady characters."

"What was suspicious about them?" This is a waste of time, I was now thinking. Of course there were shady characters: These people are spies, for God's sake.

"Oh, you know," she answered, waving a hand dismissively. "I mean, they didn't belong there. After a while you get to know the faces of the people who work there or the inmates."

"Your house is several yards from the grounds."

"I have eyes, don't I?"

I got the impression Mrs. Hanley used those eyes to keep tabs on all her neighbors. "Could you describe any of these visitors?"

"Describe? You mean what they look like?"

Oh, great, another student of the Ernie Darwin School of Observation.

"I don't think I can say exactly what each of them separately, by themselves, looked like. You know, their faces, or how tall, or like what color their hair was. It was dark, you know? Nighttime?"

"Right," I agreed, "like after the sun went down."

"That's it."

"But you could tell they weren't any of the people who belonged."

"Well, of course. One thing has nothing to do with the other."

"Uh, right. Maybe they were former patients?"

"No, I knew all the old inmates. Besides, they always end up coming back. Old habits die hard," she pronounced knowingly.

"Delivery men?"

"At night? Don't be silly."

She was right, I was being silly. This woman figured drug dealers because strangers arrived in the middle of the

Sharon Carton

night, and because she'd seen too much Miami Vice. She hadn't a clue as to what was going on at the Center. That made two of us.

Or more like five or six. I spoke with the other neighbors, finding several more who had complained. It turned out most of them had based their complaints on what Mrs. Hanley had told them. I didn't need them to tell me there was something going on at the Center. The only question was what. The neighbors didn't have the answer, and neither did the police.

Chapter Nineteen

For three nights I sat stakeout a few dozen yards down the road from the Center, not far from Mrs. Hanley's house. Kevin sat alongside me, asleep most of the time, reading when he wasn't dozing. It was a sharp reminder of the hours spent on stakeout with Ernie, engaging in pointless bickering and time-wasting word games of Desert Island Discs, me making bad jokes about Elvis "Abbott and" Costello, Ernie deriding The Boss, or as he referred to him, "Loose Bedsprings." I kept trying to start conversations with Kevin, but I seemed to bore him.

"How can you see in the dark?"

"Moon," he answered briefly.

"You want me to drop my pants? Your dad's not paying me enough."

No reply. Several minutes passed.

"Is my smoking bothering you? I mean, I've seen you smoke, but you haven't lit up in the car, so I was wondering if you might've given it up."

He shook his head.

"No you haven't given it up, or no my smoking isn't bothering you? Of course, the two alternatives aren't mutually exclusive, so it's possible you meant no to both."

Silence.

"So which was it? Was it no you haven't given it up, no my smoking isn't bothering you, both of the above, neither of-"

"Mr. Migliore, do you have a problem with my reading? You obviously are bored, and are trying to annoy me into dialogue, but I'm not bored. I have a pleasant way of passing time. So fuck off, okay," he finished genially.

Sharon Carton

I wasn't insulted. "You've got it all wrong, kid. This is part of your tutorial. You can't read when you're on stakeout, not when you're alone, anyway."

"But I'm not alone, am I?" His eyes had never left the pages of his book.

"You don't have to sound so disappointed. My point is that you have to learn how to pass time while remaining alert and observant."

"And you're going to teach me that."

"Yup."

He finally looked up. "Mr. Migliore, this is the third night we've sat out here doing nothing, and the only thing I've learned from you is how not to do surveillance."

"Oh?" I said coolly. "And what exactly am I doing wrong?"

"Well, it hasn't been productive, has it?"

"Not yet, but it's not a waste of time. Or," I amended, "if it was, it was a necessary waste of time."

"No, that's my point, it wasn't necessary at all. You didn't make effective use of your research."

"Excuse me?"

"The computer print-out."

"Yeah?"

"If you'd studied it carefully, you would've noticed a pattern emerging."

"Yeah, I know, recidivism."

He sighed. "There's an odd little schedule, didn't you notice? They've got it programmed in such a way that every week one patient leaves and another arrives. It's a rotation that's so arranged to avoid ever losing a patient, or agent, or whatever."

"Except by murder."

"What? Oh, yes, well, that's neither here nor there. The point is it's always the same people. They leave one week and come back the next. There's approximately a one-week turnaround, which is probably why you've never noticed anyone missing. Sometimes it's less than a week,

196

Sometimes You Get Killed

sometimes more. By looking at the past record of arrivals and departures, it's possible to predict, with a margin of error of two days, one in either direction, the next day of rotation."

"And you're saying that this rotation is when the agents are going out on assignment, or whatever they're doing?"

"Or out in the field, yes, that's my theory."

"And may I ask when you were planning to share this theory with me?"

"Well," he said, slightly embarrassed, "it's only a theory. I wanted to see if it was correct."

"Yeah, and you wanted to see whether I was able to pick up on it, didn't you? Kid, this isn't a contest. You're here to learn and to help. Your idea makes sense. Next time you come up with something, tell me."

He wasn't sure whether he was being praised or criticized, so he said nothing.

"So when is this margin?"

"Tomorrow, Thursday and Friday."

So we *had* wasted three nights. "All right, but these three nights haven't been wasted."

"How do you figure?"

"If something does happen in the next three nights, we'll be so familiar with the normal scene that we'll be able to recognize the abnormal."

He raised one eyebrow and squinted, an impressive combination. "Is that so?"

"That certainly is," I lied.

"If you say so," he said, unconvinced, but apparently reluctant to argue with his elder. Or maybe he just wanted to get back to his book.

To prove my point, I stubbornly stayed put until daybreak, at which time I calmly and ceremoniously turned the key in the ignition, shifted gears, and drove us back to the hotel. Kevin didn't utter another word until the next morning. For my part, I passed the remaining hours debating

Sharon Carton

whether the kid was as useful as he seemed, or as useless as he felt.

His margin of error hadn't been necessary. It was two nights later, the precise day he had predicted, when the stakeout finally paid off. I was feeling rested and healthy, having spent the last several days on the beach, swimming, lying in the sun, running along the shore. I'd been catching a few hours sleep right after stakeout and a few more just before, and I felt healthier than I had in a long time. The heat no longer bothered me, though I couldn't say as much for the stickiness. I got my complexion from my Italian father, so I was tanning a nice golden brown.

I don't know how Kevin was spending his days. Every few hours he reappeared on the beach, either to tell me he was still alive or to see if I was. The rest of the time he went off on his own. He'd been down here before, so I figured he might've been catching up with old friends, or making new ones. For all I knew, he could've been sitting on the same beach a few yards away. I didn't much care. I had nothing to talk about with him. Once I had decided to stake out the Center, I became too focused to begin anything else. Zen-like single-mindedness, Ernie once called it, although another time he called it pig-headed myopia.

On the night the stakeout bore fruit, Kevin had brought yet another book with him. Every night he had a different book. Either he finished each one during the succeeding day, got bored and gave up on each one, or was doing it just to throw me off track. This time he didn't get too far into it when things started happening.

I saw two figures leave the Center and walk through the parking lot between the main building and the dormitory. I recognized Davy Rittenby first by his slouched, loping gait. A moment later, I identified the other as Jaime Oyola, the diminutive Venezuelan patient Davy had introduced me to a few days earlier. They emerged from the main building together, exchanged a few words, then their paths diverged

Sometimes You Get Killed

as they got into separate cars.

"Get out," I said suddenly.

"What?" Kevin was startled. I think he'd been falling asleep.

"Get out of the car."

"Here? Now? How will I get back to the hotel? Where are *you* going?"

"Take a bus, take a cab, jog back to the fucking hotel, I don't care, just *go*," I said, getting more insistent as Rittenby pulled out of the parking lot, Oyola a few yards behind him.

"How am I going to get-"

"I don't give a fuck, just get the fuck out of the car now before I throw you out!"

"All right, all right," he muttered, scrambling out the door, clearly convinced I'd lost my mind. I figured I'd tell him my reason — or some reason — later. To his credit, he shut the car door without slamming it. I started to pull away, then stopped short, keeping my eyes on the two cars driving away from me, heading east on State Road 84.

My window rolled down, I called out to Kevin, "If I'm not back by morning, go to the cops. Sergeant DeBiasio," then hit the gas. If I wasn't back by morning, I'd probably be dead by the time he got to the cops, but I didn't know what else to suggest. As it turned out, Kevin came up with an idea of his own, and he didn't wait until morning.

Oyola and Rittenby led me down 84 several miles to U.S. 1, turning right onto Federal Highway, headed south. My biggest problem in tailing them was keeping a few cars between us on the relatively unpopulated highway. It was a novel problem for a New York detective. I began to pine for the Long Island Expressway, the longest parking lot in the world.

Our little procession made a right at the airport exit on Federal Highway, but my quarry ahead of me made another right before the airport. At first all I saw were car

Sharon Carton

rental places. We drove around, in what seemed like circles but must've been spirals, for about fifteen minutes. The car rental shops disappeared, leaving deserted fields in their wake. I was having greater trouble staying far enough back to avoid being spotted. I extended the distance between us, hoping the curving road was concealing me.

Finally, the journey ended as Rittenby, then Oyola, pulled into what initially appeared to be just another empty field. Then I saw the small aircraft clustered on the ground. Rittenby and Oyola drove up to what was apparently the airfield's office. I got as close as I dared, and watched as they both left their cars and walked toward the building. Davy said something to Oyola, who answered briefly, explosively, then returned to his car. He leaned against the passenger side, facing the office, his arms crossed. Davy in the meanwhile had entered the building. When he emerged a few minutes later, he was carrying a briefcase. He joined Oyola, and both men conferred as they walked several yards to one of the airplanes. I cursed myself for lost opportunities as I watched, wondering if I'd missed my only chance to see what if anything was on the plane. Silly, since I'd had no reason to guess which aircraft they'd be taking, unless you count the fact that two men had just finished fueling only one of the three planes sitting in the field.

Davy and Oyola looked inside the plane, but didn't board. Then they gave me my second chance. They both headed back toward the office; I didn't wait to be asked. I jumped out of my car and half-crawled, half-ran to the plane, taking care to keep out of sight of the office and the two maintenance men who'd followed my two CIA buddies into the office.

I climbed into the plane, and fought the rising, claustrophobic fear that under normal circumstances kept me as far as possible from airplanes. A quick glimpse into the cargo area of the plane showed it to be only half-filled with boxes. At the time I didn't know whether it was in the

Sometimes You Get Killed

process of being loaded or emptied; I only knew I hadn't much time.

I ripped open one of the boxes, and caught my breath. Stacks upon stacks of bricks of white powder. I slit open one of the bags, and touched a finger to the powder, then tasted: cocaine. Or Johnson's baby powder — I couldn't be sure. I switched around the packages of cocaine to conceal the one with the hole in it, then closed up the box as best I could. I crept back to the cabin, and looked briefly at the flight plan, trying to make some sense of it, or at least commit it to memory. Then I scrambled out of the plane, and raced back to my car.

Confession. When I got on the plane, it occurred to me that stowing away might be the best way to find out what was going on at the Center. I just couldn't do it. I chickened out. Lost my bottle, as Jonah would say. The terror at the thought of being trapped aboard an airplane was too much. Another minute and I would've started screaming.

I suppose it was for the best, because I barely made it back to the car before six men, including Rittenby, Oyola and the maintenance men, emerged from the office and approached the plane, On the back of a piece of paper with the address of the Center, I wrote down the information I had gotten from the charts in the cockpit. For the next half hour the six men transferred the remaining boxes from the plane into the trunks of Oyola's and Rittenby's cars. When they finished, the did the same with three boxes taken from the office.

All six men then returned to the office. A few minutes later Davy and Oyola came out with the other two men, the two who'd evidently arrived on the plane, pilot and co-pilot or passenger, I guessed. One of these two men now held Davy's briefcase, and everyone but Oyola was smiling.

Davy said something to Oyola, who nodded without speaking, then both returned to their cars. When

Sharon Carton

they drove away, I followed them, as much to find out where they were taking the drugs as to let them lead me out of the maze.

Where they led me was to a warehouse deep in the heart of Davie, past signs for an upcoming rodeo, gun dealerships, stables and bridle trails. I definitely wasn't in Kansas anymore, or even the twentieth century. Apparently South Florida is cosmopolitan only in patches; I had a feeling the people who owned all these cars with Dixie bumper-stickers would be only too willing to remind an Irish-Italian New Yorker just how far south I was.

I waited, parked in the shadows, for Rittenby and Oyola to unload the cocaine from their trunks into the warehouse. Then I waited another ten minutes for good measure before getting out of my car. My gun tucked securely into the back waistband of my jeans, I stole into a spot under the bushes beneath one of a series of smoked glass windows to the building. I couldn't see into the warehouse, and I couldn't hear a thing through the walls.

Then I did something stupid. Maybe I wouldn't have done it if I didn't feel embarrassed at having copped out on the plane ride, or if I didn't feel my gun pressed against the small of my back. Then again, if I'd played it safe, I probably wouldn't have found out just how far the CIA was willing to go to keep their secret safe.

Scooting around to the rear of the building, I looked unsuccessfully for an unlocked window. What I did find was another door. It wasn't open, but that wasn't a permanent condition. I stopped congratulating myself on my lock-picking abilities just long enough to slip inside, so far still undetected.

Now I could hear Davy and Oyola talking quietly. Even with the acoustics in the building, I couldn't make out their words. I crept closer, hidden among stacks of boxes, until I was able to catch pieces of the conversation.

"...kilos short...."

"...counted money...."

Sometimes You Get Killed

"...last week...."

"...next shipment...."

This was getting me nowhere. Under the time-honored doctrine that we hear better when we see better, I attempted to slide some of the cartons to one side to afford me a view of the speakers.

In one sense, I was successful; I now had a clear, if narrow view of Davy and Oyola as they were looking into an opened box, assaying the contents. If the two agents had heard me, or could see me, they gave no sign of it.

The one hitch in my maneuvering was that it required concentration. I've already acknowledged my inability to walk and chew gum at the same time if I was expending any mental effort on either operation. So I failed to notice the other two men in the building, the two who crept up behind me, until they made their presence known, one by simultaneously sticking a gun in my back and removing the Colt from my jeans, and the other by announcing, "Get them hands up," to me, and "We got company, boys," to his colleagues.

Oh, fuck. "Now that's not fair," I said, turning to face my hosts with my arms in the air, "now I've got none and you've got two."

The man who had spoken smirked, and raised his own gun in my direction, as if to correct my math.

Rittenby and Oyola had joined us, Oyola looking happy for the first time since I'd known him, Davy looking distinctly uncomfortable. At the time I thought it was embarrassment at being caught out (even though I wasn't sure at what). Later I would realize it was bemusement as much as it was reluctance; he was going to have to act, to commit himself, and I would come to realize it was something he had not done often enough to have gotten good at it, or to have developed any taste for it.

Oyola had his own gun out — that made four for them and none for me, if you're counting — but Davy walked over to the man with the gun who was holding mine.

Sharon Carton

The latter handed it over without a word of protest.

"Wow," Davy mused admiringly, and looked up at me. "I've always liked the Python."

I smiled back. "I can make you a good deal on it."

Davy emptied the cylinder and, pocketing the bullets, handed it back to me, much as Kevin had a few days earlier. "Why don't you hang on to it? The way you're going, I have a feeling you'll need it more than I will."

This was my first indication that I might get out of this alive. The others had apparently gotten the same impression, but they weren't as gratified by it as I was.

Oyola machine-gunned something in Spanish, and the two I didn't know chimed in, evidently agreeing with him. Oh, great, I thought; when even the rednecks speak Spanish, I knew I was in trouble. Rittenby responded by mumbling in Spanish, and I remembered Ernie telling me Davy's mother was Cuban.

Rittenby must've won the argument. The others in the room treated him with some respect, almost deference, as if he was a person to be reckoned with, if not necessarily obeyed. I'd noticed the others in the Center, patients and staff alike, showing him similar courtesy. I remembered the night Velez killed Rios, and how Davy had been treated in the control booth crowd.

Oyola wasn't for letting me go, though out of sheer bad temper or part of a larger scheme, I couldn't tell. The other two were without personality or definition, or, as far as I could detect, emotion. Since they seemed on Oyola's side, I could only guess it was because they had found me and resented losing their spoils.

"C'mon, Jack," Davy said, taking the initiative, and my arm, to lead me out of there, "let me buy you a cup of coffee. We have to talk."

I didn't think that was an appropriate time to complain that coffee at that hour would keep me up all night. By all appearances he had just saved my life, which is not to say I was convinced he and I were on the same side. His

Sometimes You Get Killed

warning ("I'm not a nice guy") echoed in my head, and I remained on guard, waiting to see if this move of his was proof of his assertion or just anomalous behavior.

His large bony hand was still firmly wrapped around my forearm as he steered me to my car. He opened the door of the driver's side, and practically shoved me inside. Leaning over me, he said, "You know Lester's?"

"That diner on 84? I've passed it a couple times."

"Follow me there."

He shut my door.

I rolled down the window. "Aren't you afraid I'll just escape?"

He threw back his head and laughed. "You mean am I afraid I'll actually get rid of you?"

"Oh, what is that," I sneered, "spy sarcasm?"

"Jack, let's just get out of here while the getting's good." With that, he strode off to his own car, still laughing.

The waitress set before us two bowl-sized cups of coffee. "Wanna share some fries?" Davy asked me, sounding more like the twenty-four year old juvenile he was than a spy. Which he also was.

"No."

"Their chili is great," he suggested hopefully.

"I'm not hungry, Davy," I said, between deep drags on a cigarette. I'd been chain-smoking since returning to my car from the warehouse.

"Really?" He ordered chili for himself and, as the waitress turned to leave, he grabbed her arm and added an order of fries. She frowned and walked away without verbal comment. Then Davy looked at me expectantly. "Well?"

"You're asking me? You're the one with the answers. At least," I added, letting a slight threatening note enter my voice, "you better have some answers."

"Okay, so try me," he replied pleasantly, "ask me a question."

"Let me make it easy. One question. What the

205

Sharon Carton

hell is going on? What were you doing with all those drugs? Where did they come from, and where do they go from the warehouse?"

"Whoa, wait, that's four questions." He paused. "Jack, how do I know I can trust you?"

"Oh, don't give me that shit," I said impatiently. "You've already decided you don't have a choice, or you would've let Oyola kill me."

"That doesn't mean I've decided to give you more ammunition to get yourself, or someone else, killed."

Low blow. "You know I'm not going away until I know the truth."

"I know," he smiled. "It's your least appealing trait. Anyway, I am curious as to why. You solved your mystery, you know how and why Berto Santiago was killed, so what're you looking for? The guy who did it is dead. It's over, as far as you're concerned."

"But not as far as you're concerned? Maybe I know who killed Berto, but I still don't buy the why. Every line of bullshit I've been fed has made just enough sense to satisfy me temporarily. Then I find the flaw, continue to investigate, and get handed another lie."

"Jack, you've been told only as much as necessary. The more you interfere, the more you jeopardize what we're doing."

"I think I've earned the truth."

"You haven't earned anything. All you've done is make trouble from the very beginning," he said, not bothering to hide his disgust. "Amateurs."

"Fuck you, Rittenby. None of this would've happened if you'd been straight with me from the start."

"Oh, yeah, some New York private detective shows up, lying to us while he investigates us, and we just tell him, 'Oh, glad you're here, let's open up about our covert operation and we'd really appreciate it if you don't tell too many people.' Why didn't we think of that?"

"Well, we're really past that now, don't you think?

Sometimes You Get Killed

You can either tell me what's really going on, or you can kill me."

"What were my choices again?" he asked, and smiled, the tension gone for the moment.

I smiled back coldly, waiting.

"And if I tell you the truth...?"

"You mean, do I plan on keeping your little secret? That depends on how dirty you guys are."

" 'Dirty'? It's not an illegal operation, if that's what you mean. But, yeah, what're your plans?"

"After I tell the *Washington Post*, I'm not sure. Listen, all I want to do is get the hell out of Florida. You tell me what I need to wrap this all up, and I'm gone. I'm not some crusading hotshot out to expose you. I don't give a fuck what game the government wants to play; I'm not interested in stopping you. I just want the truth."

Rittenby had listened to me, but I don't know how much he believed. As I had told him, his decision had been made in the warehouse. "How much do you know about the drug cartels in Colombia?"

Chapter Twenty

"Cartels?" I said, surprised, then went on, "Nothing, I guess."

"A cartel is a syndicate of a sort, like the Mafia, but their primary business is narcotics. And murder, too," he added. "Narcoterrorism, some call it, and it's immense, beyond your wildest imagination."

"It? One in particular?"

He nodded. "The Medellin Cartel, named for a city in Colombia, the second largest city in the country, in fact. There are more than one, cartels that is, but Medellin is the headquarters of what's generally regarded to be the world's largest cocaine smuggling ring. It's huge, vicious, and impossibly successful, on a terrifying scale. The Medellin Cartel is considered responsible for about 80% of the cocaine imported into this country."

"This is fascinating, but what's it got to do with what I saw tonight?"

"What you saw tonight is cartel cocaine being stored for destruction. We've, well, it's taken a long time, but we've infiltrated the cartel. We've been buying drugs from them for several months now. We pay them, take the cocaine off the market, and destroy it. In the process, we've been gathering enough evidence against the players to lead us to the big guys. We've already indicted some of the major players, but our ultimate goal is to sabotage them from within."

"To destroy them, rather than to bring them to justice."

"In essence, yes. Initially we had hoped the legal route would work, but we no sooner eliminate one player

Sharon Carton

than another leader springs up in his place. Well, that's an oversimplification of the operation, but you get the general idea."

"And the Center is the headquarters for this operation?"

"Oh, hell, no, it's just one of several locations, mostly but not exclusively in South Florida. It's all being coordinated through Washington, of course."

"And everyone at the Center is in on this?"

"Except for the few civilians you already know about."

I thought about it. "You're telling me Roger goes down to the mountains of Colombia to deal drugs? Somehow I can't picture it."

Davy smiled. "Neither could I. No, the staff at the Center are just paper pushers, the administrators. The 'patients,' like me and Jaime, are the field agents. Although," he amended, "Greg Tessler's not in Roger's class. Greg was one of the best in the Company until he got promoted out of the field. Well, you know the government, too many chiefs, too few Indians."

"All right, so far, so good. How did Velez fit into this deal?"

Rittenby sighed. "Typical. He got greedy. I guess it's like working at Treasury and having to watch all that old cash getting burned. He couldn't stand to see all this good dope going to waste, started skimming off the top and selling it locally."

"And Berto found out about it? Before any of you did?"

A wave of the hand. "It doesn't really matter whether he did, or whether Eddie just thought he did, or felt threatened by having an undercover cop around. The end result was the same."

"And Dr. Rios?"

"Much as you suspected. Paul must've seen something the night of that first murder."

210

Sometimes You Get Killed

"You know he'd agreed to meet with me the night he was murdered?"

"Paul Rios did?" Rittenby acted surprised, but I didn't believe it. I had told this to the cops, and I had to assume the info had found its way to the Center. "For what, did he say?"

"I didn't speak to him. Ernie set it up. When I got there, Rios was already dead."

"And Eddie? Where was he?"

I shrugged. "Hiding, I guess. On his way back to his room, maybe, or on his way to kill Ernie."

"You believe that." It wasn't a question.

"I don't know," I admitted. "I've gone over it in my mind, again and again and again. The timing, the motive, and I still don't know if he was really after Ernie or if Ernie just got in the way of his escape."

"Does it matter?"

I was silent for a few minutes.

Davy interrupted my reverie. "Look, whether it does or doesn't, Jack, I don't think we'll ever know. You may have to live with not knowing."

Finally, I nodded. "Then that's it? That's all of it?"

"I'm sorry we couldn't tell you sooner, Jack. That's just not the way we work."

"Did you know Berto was a cop?"

"Yes, almost from the beginning."

"But nobody told him this was going on?"

"That's not-"

"-the way you work, yeah, I know. It could've saved his life."

"Monday morning quarterbacking," Davy said simply. "We had no reason to think his life was in jeopardy, but we knew that other lives would be if our security was compromised."

"By telling a cop?"

"By telling a cop. We just decided to try to convince him, and through him the rest of local law

Sharon Carton

enforcement, that there was nothing here to investigate. Of course, it all backfired because we hadn't counted on a traitor in our midst's."

"You don't mean that literally, do you? I mean, Velez wasn't really FSK?"

"Nah," he said, a small smile curling his lips. "Eddie's motivation was financial, not political. I never liked that FSK story. So comic-book, to a civilian. In reality, it's not so far-fetched, but outsiders have trouble conceptualizing a Russian spy lurking among the palm trees of Fort La-di-da."

"So that's why nobody bothered excising Ernie from the records at the Center."

He looked puzzled. "How did you...?" Then he broke into a grin. "We keep underestimating you, Jack. Yeah, we didn't have to worry about reprisals from avenging Russians."

"But why were the hospital records sanitized, then?"

"They weren't under our control, Jack. It was one thing to leave the data in our secure computer, quite another to leave it in an unprotected civilian system."

"What would it matter if anyone found out?"

"Probably wouldn't, but Roger didn't want to take a chance."

"He won't be happy about me knowing the truth," I predicted.

"You're reading my mind," he agreed, rueful. "Can't be helped."

"Which, your telling me or your telling him?"

He smiled. "Both, I guess. But even if I didn't tell him, Jaime would."

"You two aren't exactly on the same wavelength."

"Who, me and Roger or me and Jaime?"

"Both, I guess," I mimicked him.

"Yeah," he smiled again, "right on both counts. You really messed up our timetable tonight, you know? But

Sometimes You Get Killed

don't worry about it. I'll straighten things out on my end. And you?"

"I guess there's nothing keeping me here anymore."

"I'm sorry it all had to go down this way, Jack." He seemed sincere. "What're you gonna tell Berto's uncle?"

A bell went off. "Lt. Mendoza?" I asked mildly. "He already knows Berto was a cop. I figure anything more would hurt."

"Yeah," he agreed. "And that kid you brought here that other day?"

"Kevin?" Kid? They were the same age, but I could understand the attitude; Rittenby did seem older, even older than I was. "He's just an apprentice," I said dismissively.

"Uh huh."

"A rich apprentice."

Davy smiled. "Don't hold it against him," he said knowingly, "it's not his fault."

Chapter Twenty-One

Driving back to the hotel, I thought about what Rittenby had told me, about the drug cartels and Colombia traffickers. Ernie wouldn't have known what to make of it. Drugs were personal to him, not political. They were, to him, a private remedy for his ills, a way to correct his flawed nature to fit the world, in such a way that the world could tolerate him...and vice versa.

It would have seemed the ultimate obscenity for drugs to be the basis of a national economy, the underpinnings of a national government. He didn't use drugs to rebel — he needed them because he was too defeated to fight — but the societal institutionalization of a mainstream drug culture would have seemed to him absurd. He depended on drugs to gloss over his inability to cope with society, or reality, which are really two words for what was to him the same foreign concept. What was the point of aligning drugs with reality, he would've wondered, since if you've got one, by definition you wouldn't need or understand the other. Ernie never did understand the principle of an export economy; abstract theories of economics wherein a country could base its financial health on a product it got rid of were too devious, too *insincere,* for him to digest. Besides, numbers were involved, and as he'd told me more than once, if he'd understood numbers, he wouldn't have had to become a lawyer.

Somewhere in the middle of these thoughts I wondered belatedly whether Kevin had made it back in one piece. I still had the bruises to prove the kid could take care of himself, but one-on-one combat isn't the same as street sense. I'd had to lecture Ernie about his tendency,

Sharon Carton

during his good moods, to walk down the streets of Manhattan with a smile on his face. People in New York get assaulted for that; muggers resent people happier than they.

Why hadn't I allowed him to come along? Two reasons, and I couldn't swear to which one had predominated: Once the stakeout became interesting, I got an attack of caution, worrying about exposing some novice to what might be a dangerous situation. The other reason was less generous. I have this thing about coincidences, and not trusting them. The conversation between Kevin and the civilian patient, Walt Coleman, had not gone unnoticed by me. It probably proved nothing but what a small world this is, or even how useful it would be to a have a kid with his rich father's contacts, but there was a part of me that was suspicious.

Then again, if it was at all sinister, wouldn't Kevin have tried to conceal it? I didn't know; maybe he had wanted to bring it out in the open on the theory that I might find out anyway, and it'll look better coming from him.

Thinking about muggers made me homesick. I imagined myself returning to the hotel, telling the desk clerk to prepare my bill for an early check-out tomorrow morning, leaving a wake-up call, packing most of my stuff tonight, and heading north on I-95 after a big breakfast and a final dip in the ocean. I'd call Annie and tell her I was on my way, and if Kevin and I took turns driving I could be home, with any luck, by....

Why was Davy so anxious for me to leave? A bell had gone off in my head when he became so insistent: If only he hadn't been so patently concerned with whether he'd convinced me the case was closed, I might've been convinced. Even without any real questions remaining, I had to wonder why it was so important to him that I leave town. Since I did believe what he'd told me tonight — it was the first time what I'd seen jived with what I was told — it occurred to me that he might not be acting out of a

Sometimes You Get Killed

desire to protect his secret as much as out of a desire to protect *me*, but from what? Or whom? Velez was dead; who wasn't?

Of course there was a logical explanation. Just because Davy had decided it was safe for me to know the truth didn't mean Oyola, or Roger either, for that matter, would be equally confident. Davy had said I'd thrown off their timetable: Did that mean he and Oyola would not be leaving the country on assignment?

Of course the logical explanation didn't satisfy me. When a private investigator doesn't have any answers, or even meaningful questions, sometimes all he can rely on is doubt.

If I'd been allowed to return to my hotel room and sleep on those doubts, chances are my eagerness to go home to Annie and the muggers would've prevailed. Just goes to show you I'm not the only one who made some bad mistakes that year.

When I pulled into the hotel parking lot, I turned off the ignition and pulled my empty gun from the glove compartment, where I'd stashed it after Davy returned it to me at the warehouse. I also removed a baggie filled with .38 caliber slugs, and systematically reloaded each chamber. Ah, I thought, doesn't that feel better?

Then I replaced the baggie and got out of the car, the gun still in my hand. Standing facing the car, I reached behind my back to tuck in the Python, but never made it. Pain split my head as something hard made contact, and the gun slipped from my flaccid hand as I felt myself go down, surrounded by an enveloping blackness. My last thought, right after "Ow" and "oh, fuck", was that here was someone who knew what they were doing; instead of just getting confused and a headache, I was actually losing consciousness.

At least that's what I started to think. I don't remember finishing the thought, and I don't remember

Sharon Carton

hitting the ground. Nausea and fear, which don't take as long to crystallize as thoughts, were all I felt for the eternity it took me to reach the ground.

When I woke up, my face was under water. I couldn't tell if I was already dead or just on my way to getting there. I decided to assume for the sake of argument that I was still alive, because that gave me more incentive to fight back.

A few seconds later the hand that had been holding my face under water, tightened its grip on the nape of my neck, and lifted me out of the water. Blackness still engulfed me, and for an agonizing moment I thought the concussion had left me blind. Then I realized my eyes had been blindfolded with some rough piece of cloth, bound tightly around my head, and now dripping salt water down my face and into my mouth. I didn't think I'd been crying, so I figured I'd been taken to the beach.

I hadn't realized this was to be a recurring process, so when the hand pushed me back into the ocean I hadn't thought to fill my lungs with air. I held my breath desperately as long as I could, cursing every cigarette I'd ever smoked, but it wasn't long enough. My mouth opened up in spite of me and water flooded in, choking me. I started coughing and sputtering, and the hand jerked me up. Gasping and gulping in as much oxygen as my lungs would hold, I tried to shake myself free but someone — the person who belonged to the hand with the stranglehold on my neck — had my hands tied tightly behind my back, and was straddling me, his legs on either side of my waist. I couldn't budge.

Then I was plunged into the ocean again, the water now feeling warm but not welcoming. I hadn't sensed it coming so again my lungs weren't filled with air. I tried to stay calm but my heart was racing and my head felt like it was going to explode. I couldn't help it; even with my mouth clenched shut, my nose gave in and breathed. The salty water burned down my throat and my mouth popped open

Sometimes You Get Killed

to cough, my throat opening and closing spasmodically, my chest heaving in convulsions.

The hand lifted me again and I wheezed, struggling to take in something my lungs could handle. In between gulps of air, I finally managed to cry out, "You're drowning me!"

Now, never let it be said I've normally felt it necessary to say the obvious, but this time there was a reason. See, I figured this guy wasn't trying to drown me, otherwise he wouldn't have kept pulling me out of the water. Instead, it had dawned on me that he was trying to bring me to consciousness, and had just picked a particularly unpleasant way of doing it.

"He talks," came a deep voice I didn't recognize, and with that I was pulled upright and dragged, stumbling and coughing, out of the ocean onto the beach.

"Are you awake?" said another voice, high-pitched, nasal and whining, and belonging to a person who also had no trouble recognizing the obvious.

I spit out the salty tasting water. "Can't put anything past you, can I?"

For that I got a sharp, vicious jab in my kidneys. My knees buckled and folded beneath me, and the hand that had gripped me let go, letting me fall forward onto my face, my mouth in the sand. A second later a kick in my left side made me expel the air in my lungs, and I instinctively drew my knees in to protect my stomach, and other vital parts in that vicinity. A kick in my right temple made my hands strain at whatever was biting into my wrists, in an automatic attempt to shield my face, but the ties held fast.

The kick left me dazed, and worse, scared. The belief that I was in for a beating left me hopeful that I was not about to die; if these two guys meant to kill me, there are a lot quicker and quieter, not to mention less demanding, ways of going about it. The blindfold had me convinced. The kick to the head, which is never guaranteed to leave any survivors, suddenly panicked me that these guys had

Sharon Carton

lost sight of the game plan.

After that I didn't think about much of anything but pain. The kicks came fast and furious from then on, punctuated only by grunting and moaning, most of which I'm pretty sure came from me. Towards the end I heard the nasal one say, "If that doesn't make him homesick, nothing will," which I thought was ironic, and which I also thought meant they were finished.

I was wrong. It wasn't until I felt something inside me crack, and felt the sweet, warm taste of blood streaming from my mouth that the blows abruptly stopped. I felt them watching me, and concentrated dizzily on remaining motionless, hoping they would go away.

Eventually they did, and I passed out again, but I have no way of knowing which came first.

I remember dreaming of the Center, but all my New York friends were there. Tied to a cross (sorry, pain makes me religious), I was being subjected to a series of methodically delivered karate kicks by Kevin, while Jonah was coaching, "Don't bend your knees!" and Annie, holding my gun with a limp-wristed distaste, tsk-tsked me, chiding, "See how foolish this is?" and Davy shook his head sadly while telling a sorrowful Roger, "I told him I wasn't a nice guy." A few feet away Cathy stood by, attentively making notes in a legal pad, saying, "This is actionable, this is actionable." I heard Kevin's voice saying, "Shouldn't we take the blindfold off?" but the me on the cross wasn't wearing one, and I realized I was no longer dreaming.

I thought I answered him, but I didn't hear my voice. Instead, someone I quickly recognized as Walt Coleman said, "All in good time." I felt someone poking and prodding me, looking for a pulse. A hand probed, not so gently, the side of my head, and I felt myself blacking out again. From a great distance, I heard my dear friend Kevin say, "Hey, watch that!" with some anger, as Coleman responded forcefully, "Just grab his legs." With that I felt two arms I

Sometimes You Get Killed

assumed were Coleman's reach under my arms, still bound behind my back, and, attempting to lift me, squeeze my ribs. I screamed from the sudden pain, but still no sound came out. The last thing I heard before losing consciousness again was the stalwart Kevin saying, with preppie understatement, "Hey, I think you're hurting him." If Coleman responded in any way, it was too late for me to notice.

Chapter Twenty-Two

I woke up in Broward County Hospital several hours later, feeling like a butch but battered Dorothy in the Wizard of Oz. Gathering around the bed in the next few hours was a parade of concerned and reassuring faces, faces which gave me the dazed impression of belonging in two worlds, one reality and one just a bad dream. Were these people really spies, or were they just patients and staff at a rehab center? The reality seemed so — what had Davy called it? — *comic-book*, that it seemed that was the dream, and not the other way around.

In between my steady stream of visitors, I focused on trying to piece together the events of the night before. All I knew for sure was that I had lost my gun, probably for good. It unsettled me to realize how deeply I felt that loss, knowing that the vulnerability was disproportionate, disconcertingly so. Ernie would've psychoanalyzed my reaction, while Annie — if I were asinine enough to talk to her about it, which I probably was — would be dismayed and softly condescending. I stuck to worrying about whether it was a loss I could write off, and where I'd get the cash to replace it, not to mention how soon I could manage the latter.

Roger stopped by for a few minutes, vaguely disapproving but not entirely unsympathetic. The conversation was kept light, generic sick-bed stuff, and I was feeling too lousy to make anything of it. The doctor, whose name I didn't even note, was reassuring about my prospects, while expressing mild concern about the possibility of my having re-injured my leg. Concussion, broken ribs, evidence of some internal bleeding that had

223

Sharon Carton

stopped: nothing major, which is not to say that I felt as though I'd ever be well enough to walk out of the hospital under my own powers. Every significant region of my body ached in protest and, prognosis to the contrary notwithstanding, I felt terminal. The only injury that even came close was to my wrists, which it turned out had been bound with some kind of wire. My struggling during the beating had made the wire slice into the flesh. The bandages made it impossible to tell how deep the wounds were, but the throbbing gave me a pretty good indication.

Cathy was my first visitor, apparently because she powered her way into seeing me before visiting hours. She got the amenities out of the way with perfunctory haste. It made me remember Ernie's telling me that she was a loyal, caring friend who just showed it by doing, rather than saying. I thought he might've been overly generous, the way he was with people, but Cathy kept me guessing.

She told me that the papers for the lawsuits were ready for filing. Her briefcase on her lap, she seemed to want to show them to me now, but restrained herself. I didn't have the energy to tell her otherwise. Maybe, too, it still wasn't clear to me whether I had decided to pursue any of this anymore. "Leave the papers," I told her wearily, "and I'll look through them as soon as I get a chance."

She had to content herself with that, just as I had to promise myself I'd spend some time trying to remember why I'd wanted the police reports in the first place.

Kevin showed up, looking faintly ill at ease. At first I put it down to normal hospitalities, then I developed a vague impression that he was hiding something.

"What made you call Coleman?"

At the mention of the name, Kevin's discomfort became acute, as did my suspicions about coincidences.

"You mean," he stalled, in a distinctly Darwinesque touch, "why did I call someone, or why was it Coleman I called?"

"Knock yourself out, tell me both."

Sometimes You Get Killed

"Oh. Well, around midnight I started to wonder what the hell was taking you so long, I mean, I'd been back forever. Did I tell you what happened to me on the way back to the hotel?"

"No, and I appreciate it," I said curtly. "Go on. It was about midnight...."

"Yes, and I decided to go downstairs and wait for you outside."

"Why? Didn't you figure I might try calling you?"

"Huh? Oh, I don't know. It made sense at the time. Anyway, that's when I noticed your car was in the parking lot. That didn't make sense, unless you had come back and gone for a walk or something. I went back inside and checked out the lobby, and then tried some of the nearby bars, you know the way you drink. When I couldn't find you, that's when I called Coleman at the Center."

"Why him?" I could still feel the tenderness from where Coleman had grabbed me under my arms.

Kevin shrugged, but there was a studied air to his casualness. "He was the only person I knew. I mean, I knew him from before, from outside. It was like, with all the pretense, he was the only real person I knew. And he wasn't CIA, we knew that, so I figured he couldn't be in on any of it. You know?"

"I guess. What did he say when you called?"

"That I was probably being silly, but I insisted. I mean, I was pretty convinced something was wrong. So finally he said — oh, no, wait, that's not right. First he said no, and wouldn't give in. That's when I called the cops, and-"

"You called the cops, too?"

"Yeah, and they-"

"What did you tell them? Who'd you speak to? Did you dial 911 or-"

"No, I didn't see this as an emergency, not necessarily, anyway. I called Information and got the number; I didn't remember the name of the cop you'd told

Sharon Carton

me about. All I told them was that you were a private investigator and that you were missing."

"I bet they all lost sleep over that."

He smiled. "They could barely contain their anxiety. They told me I had to wait 72 hours."

"Uh huh." I only wondered if DeBiasio would've been any more solicitous.

"Yeah," Kevin went on, "and I was about to try to hot-wire your car and try to find you myself."

"Hot-wire my car?" I was impressed. Apparently Draper Senior hadn't been lying when he said he hadn't sheltered his kid.

"Don't ask. But no sooner did I hang up from the police than Coleman called back. He said he'd thought about it, and given all the craziness at the Center lately, you know, the killings, maybe I was right. He came and picked me up, and we started cruising around, looking for you."

I thought about this. "So how'd you know where to look?"

"Well," Kevin began, looking confused, "we just sorta drove around."

"Yeah, but where? How long did it take to find me?"

"I don't know, not long. Maybe ten, fifteen minutes. We drove along A1A-"

"The beach road?"

"Yeah. We headed south and-"

"Wait a second, what had you told him?"

"Some."

" 'Some'? Can you be more specific, or at least more articulate?"

Kevin avoided my eyes. "I told him we were investigating your friend's death, and that you'd been on stakeout, and, well, from there on it was pretty much the truth."

"Did the word 'CIA' come into this conversation?"

"No, of course not," he blustered, still looking at

Sometimes You Get Killed

everything in the room but my face. I couldn't tell whether he was lying or just embarrassed. Normally, I would've assumed the former, but this time I was tempted to believe the latter; if the kid was as practiced at deceit as his father believed, he should've been better at lying than this clumsy effort indicated.

"Uh huh," I said. "All right, so go ahead."

"Where was I?"

"Driving south along the beach."

"Oh yeah. Well," he began, "the street wasn't too crowded. From what I remember about traffic on the Strip, we were lucky it was a week night. Coleman said we should stick to that area because you couldn't have gone far from the hotel, since that's where you'd left your car. So he kept his eyes on the beach and I looked for you on the other side of the street.

"We did that for a few minutes," Kevin continued, "up to Bahia Mar, at one end of the Strip, then Coleman turned around and we headed north until Sunrise Boulevard. This time I checked out the beach, but we still didn't see you."

Kevin paused for a breath, then went on. "Well, at Sunrise I said maybe we should try someplace else, you know, that maybe you'd been kidnapped and taken somewhere. He looked at me kinda weird, like it was a dumb suggestion, and he just turned around and went back up the beach. This time he spotted you." Kevin stopped and smiled. "You know, I don't know how he saw you. Even when he called out I could barely see you. But there you were."

"On the beach."

"Yeah, south of the hotel. Not far off, really."

"So then you and Coleman took me to the hospital."

"Uh, not exactly."

"Well?"

"We picked you up and carried you to the side of

Sharon Carton

the road, and-"

"Didn't anyone ever tell you not to move an injured man?"

"Oh," he said, nonplussed. "Well, Coleman just started to lift you, and told me to help, so, well, I wasn't thinking, I guess."

This time I was sure; he was lying. "All right, so now I'm on the side of the road."

"Yeah, and that's when this FLPD cruiser spotted us and pulled over. They radioed for an ambulance, and, well, that was it. Except I still don't know what had happened to you. What did you find out? Who beat you up?"

I told him everything that had happened. He was lying to me about something, but seeing as how he had come to my rescue, I was relatively secure in my conviction that he was on my team. The only thing I did leave out was the reason I had abandoned my hasty plan to stow away on the airplane.

"And those numbers?" he finally asked.

"What numbers?"

"There was a piece of paper in your jeans pocket, with some weird figures on them."

"You went through my pants pockets? Kid, I don't even let the woman I love do that."

He looked embarrassed. "The nurse did. She gave me the stuff in an envelope. You know you only had seventeen dollars in your wallet?"

I didn't hear him; I was remembering the envelope I'd gotten with Ernie's personal effects. He had never carried a wallet. Just some bills, a few coins, a Bic lighter. His reading glasses. Driver's license. Organ donor card.

"How well do you know Walt Coleman?" I asked abruptly.

Kevin seemed unhappy about my return to an inexplicably touchy subject, but he forged bravely on. "Not well at all, or just enough to recognize his face at the Center that day."

Sometimes You Get Killed

"Uh huh." Then I let silence fill up the room, until it made Kevin claustrophobic enough to speak.

"So I called my father, just to talk mostly but then I figured, I have him on the phone so what the hell, you know?" He looked at me expectantly, but I let the silence keep doing its job.

"Well," he went on, "all my dad knew about him was he was self-made, like dad, but on the opposite side of the political fence. My dad likes to say he's not political, but he's been giving money to the Democratic machine since before he had it to give."

"And Coleman?"

"GOP all the way, after a brief fling with the Democrats, and the right wing of the party at that, which is saying something. Like there's a left wing?" he asked rhetorically. "Anyway, my old man says he's always suspected Coleman went Republican because they were more likely to protect his financial investments rather than out of any ideological affinity. Does any of this matter?"

"Probably not," I said mildly. "What about you?"

"What about me?"

"You have any politics?"

He shrugged. "Some of it is...interesting, on a cerebral level, but I can't say it goes beyond the abstract."

I smiled to myself. Great, from a partner who's a semi- socialist social misfit to an amoral, apolitical apprentice. I must be paying for one hell of a sin in my past life.

"So you don't have any idea who grabbed you?" Kevin was saying. "Or why?"

"No to both," I admitted. "I haven't had much time to work it through."

"Oh." He sounded disappointed. "So is that it? You're only supposed to be here 'til tomorrow. In the hospital, I mean. Were you telling Rittenby the truth?"

"About going home? Why, you got an appointment in New York you gotta keep?"

Sharon Carton

His face clouded over, and I wondered suddenly what home meant for him. I didn't even know if he still lived with his parents. Even if he didn't, I got the impression family — or at least his father — was a strong and not always welcome presence wherever he was.

When he didn't answer, I said, "Lemme think about it. I'll let you know when I'm discharged tomorrow."

At that, his expression brightened. "I'll pick you up, okay?" There was an eagerness in his voice that surprised me. Maybe my getting beaten up had been a bright spot in his life.

"How," I said dryly, "by hot-wiring my car?"

"Nah," he grinned, "the nurse gave me your keys."

"Watch out for her."

Chris Khoragian had just left my hospital room, passing Davy Rittenby on her way out and his way in. It had been an unexpected and confusing visit. I hadn't spent much time with her during my visits to the Center. I don't know why; maybe she seemed too flighty to be taken seriously. Too superficial to be threatening or attractive to me, Mrs. Khoragian just hadn't generated   much interest on my part. Ernie had referred occasionally to her catholic sexual preferences (which, taking as some kind of religious slur, I had made him explain), but he too had dismissed her as a suspect in Berto's death.

Her visit had unsettled me, then, but there'd been no revelations. She had displayed sympathy and, in thinly veiled innuendos, offered solace, but there was nothing to suggest previously unnoticed substance.

"Why, is she dangerous?" I asked Davy, in response to his warning.

"Not in and of herself," he hedged.

"In and of whom, then?"

"She has Roger's ear," he said, not bothering to hide his disdain, then added, "and she never misses an

Sometimes You Get Killed

opportunity to pour poison in it."

"Hamlet's stepfather," I said, catching the reference.

"Or maybe the allusion's too good for her. She's more like Roger's loyal puppy dog. I guess she's grateful for her position, so she repays him by cozying up to his charges and bringing their dirt back to her master."

"You sound like you speak from experience."

He shrugged. Maybe. "What did you tell her?"

"I told her my ribs hurt too much to have sex with her."

He raised an eyebrow, but declined to ask. "Anyway, just be on guard."

"Always," I said amiably. "So I don't suppose you know who's responsible for my being here?"

"Other than God?" he smiled. "No, but I have my suspicions."

He eyed me carefully, curiosity fighting with discretion. Discretion won. "What're your plans now?"

"Oh, I don't know. I'm being discharged tomorrow."

"And then what?" he pressed. "Home?"

My turn. I shrugged. Maybe.

He sighed. "Ernie said you were a stubborn asshole," he said, shaking his head. "I'm not even gonna try."

"Anymore, you mean?"

"Huh?"

"I mean, after last night."

He looked at me, cocking his head.

"After you already tried to talk me into leaving. Last night. At the diner."

"Oh. Yeah." He was still suspicious.

That was okay. So was I.

All things considered, I didn't really think Davy had sicced those thugs on me. Sure, he had wanted me out of Fort Lauderdale, and he hadn't determined to his

231

Sharon Carton

satisfaction that I'd been convinced. So maybe he'd taken out some insurance.

But I hadn't ruled out some other possibilities, most notably Jaime Oyola, who'd been obviously dissatisfied by Davy's appeasement policy at the warehouse.

Davy's warning — "I'm not a nice guy" — notwithstanding, the brutality of the beating seemed out of character. It didn't seem inconsistent with Oyola's, or what little I had seen of it.

There was also a small idea growing in my mind: Just because Velez had been in it for profit rather than politics, did that guarantee he'd been working alone? If he'd had confederates in the CIA, those confederates would be highly motivated to keep me out of their affairs, and preferably out of their state. That didn't point me in the direction of Oyola over Rittenby, or Rittenby over Oyola, or eliminate any of the other people at the Center.

When visiting hours ended, I finally managed to drift off to sleep, until a nurse woke me for dinner. She shook me awake and raised my bed, depositing the dinner tray without a word.

She had almost left the room when I could take it no longer. "You're the third nurse I've seen today, and not a goddamn one of you has looked me in the face or said one word. What the hell is going on? Am I dying or something, and you just don't want to get too attached to me?"

She turned and faced me, anger mixing with fear on her young, rather homely features. "I've got half a mind to tell you...."

"Tell me what? What have I done to piss everyone off?"

"It's not you," she said, her ferocity crumbling suddenly. "It's because of your friend."

"Who, the lawyer?" I asked, thinking of Cathy. "Look, I know she comes off pushy, but she was just anxious

Sometimes You Get Killed

to talk-"

"No," she shook her head vigorously, "not her. The man, the one who died."

"Ernie?" I said, stunned.

"That's right, that was his name, Ernie Darwin. It's all because of him-"

"Wait, are you telling me you admit he was here?"

"Of course, and I don't care if I do say it. My friend Mary did nothing more than she was told to, what she's paid to do, and the next thing I know she practically drops off the face of the earth, and the hospital, and her, are being named in a lawsuit."

"What do you mean? What happened to her?" She had to be talking about Mary Dessimore, the nurse I had met in the Intensive Care Unit.

"She was *transferred*," she answered, in a voice that suggested doom, "along with Dr. Grady. Mary and I were good friends, but now she won't tell me where she's been sent, and she doesn't answer my calls, and I'm not the only one who's scared," she answered defensively.

"Scared of me?"

"Of what'll happen if we talk to you, of what happened to our friends, of being sued, or even worse."

"What...why do you think something bad happened to your friends? What happened here after my friend Mr. Darwin died?"

She hesitated a moment, then let her reluctance be overcome by indignation. "I could tell you a thing or two about that, too."

"Oh?" I held my breath, afraid she'd change her mind.

"Mary told me, that very day, before she was transferred. There was no heart attack, no myocardial infarction. It wasn't Dr. Grady's decision, or the hospital's, not to resuscitate. It was *his* decision, his instruction to take Mr. Darwin off life-support-"

"Whose? Whose decision?" I burst out, able to

Sharon Carton

restrain myself no longer.

"That...that pompous man, the one who looks like Howdy Doody, no, like Orville Redenbacker's grandson in those TV commercials. You know, with a gap between his two front teeth?"

Very carefully, I said, "Was that man here today?"

"Oh, sure, he came to see you. In a camel colored suit."

Roger Samuels.

She went on, "That's how we remembered who you were, you know, when you'd been here for Mr. Darwin."

I swallowed. Suddenly I was having trouble catching my breath. "Tell me — don't leave anything out — what exactly happened to my friend."

"Well," she said thoughtfully, "the first thing Mary or anyone else knew, was when he was brought here by EMS. By then," she said, taking some care to be delicate, "he was already brain-dead. He was maintained on life support, but we knew, well, we were told, that that was in the hopes of using some of his organs for...well, for transplants."

She looked at me solicitously, knowing she was talking about my friend. I nodded, encouraging her to go on.

"Well, some of us thought it was also because of some flack the hospital had gotten three years ago, when a patient's daughter had him taken off support. He'd been comatose for-"

"Yes, yes," I broke in, "please, tell me about Mr. Darwin."

"I'm sorry. Anyway, the next day, this man, the one who was here today-"

"Mr. Samuels."

"All right, Mr. Samuels, well, he showed up and pulled some strings or something, we didn't know, except that Dr. Grady had his life support disconnected and your friend's body was removed from the hospital. The day after that, Dr. Grady and Mary weren't there. Word was they

Sometimes You Get Killed

were transferred, but no one knew where to, or why, except we knew why when we found out about the lawsuit. When it was that *man's* doing, not theirs or the hospital's!"

My head was swimming. Of course. Everything made sense now: the disappearance of Ernie's records; the cremation of his remains; my inability to get access to his autopsy report. Roger had killed Ernie. Had Ernie even been brain dead? Probably not.

Why had Roger needed Ernie dead? The answer was obvious: Ernie had posed a threat to Roger, who couldn't risk Ernie's regaining consciousness. That meant only one thing — that Ernie had had knowledge Roger feared, and that could only have been information linking Roger to Velez. That's what Ernie had found out — from Rios? — and had tried to tell me. When Velez' homicidal attack on Ernie was interrupted by me, Roger came to the hospital and used his government authority to finish the job.

You bastard. You're finished now, I thought grimly, and I was thinking about his life, not his career. The legal system was fine, to a point: When there's doubt, let a jury hash it out. But this was different, because I *knew*. Fuck reasonable doubt. I would kill Samuels, and I'd find a way of making him suffer before it was finished. Suddenly I knew there'd been a reason I hadn't left Florida yet; this was what I'd been kept here for.

Even medicated, I didn't sleep that night. I didn't mind. It was a good night, better than any I'd spent in about a month. I had a lot to think about, and it's surprising how much pleasure planning a murder can give.

Chapter Twenty-Three

But it wasn't over yet.

The next afternoon, Kevin showed up to collect me from the hospital. He had something on his mind, but he was trying to be nonchalant about it.

"Oh, spit it out, kid," I finally said.

"What you told me?"

"Yeah?"

"Davy's story? About Colombia?"

"Yeah, yeah?"

"I...I think he was lying."

I had been buttoning my shirt, and I stopped, startled. "Lying."

"Uh huh."

"About what, in particular?"

"Those numbers. On the piece of paper. The numbers you got from that airplane."

"Yes," I said, impatient.

"They were coordinates, presumably of the plane's destination. Except they weren't in Colombia. I checked a map. They were in Panama. Not Colombia," he repeated. "Panama."

I hesitated. "Should that mean something?"

"Well," he exploded, "of course it should. If the CIA is infiltrating the Medellin Cartel, what are they doing in Panama?"

"Maybe," geography wasn't my long suit "they land in Panama to cross over into Colombia. That's possible, isn't it? They're adjoining countries, right? So why is it such a big deal?"

"Well, well, because...." he sputtered.

237

Sharon Carton

"I mean, don't they have drugs in Panama?"

"Well, yeah, sure," he said, enthusiasm petering out, "there's been a lot of speculation-"

"So there you are," I concluded.

"What, so you don't care, right?" His disgust, or disappointment, was palpable.

"It's not necessarily inconsistent with what Rittenby told me. Besides, what does it matter if the drugs came from Panama instead of Colombia?"

"It's just that," he tried weakly, "there's a completely different political situation in the two countries. I just think it makes a difference whether the CIA is infiltrating a drug cartel in Colombia or conducting a covert operation in Panama, where-"

"What's politics got to do with it?" I was wondering when he had found time to acquire a degree in Poli Sci, too.

"Well, since they've already indicted the key players in the cartel, what's the point of this operation?"

"I told you what Davy said about that. The goal now is to completely destroy the cartel's enterprise from within."

Kevin just shook his head, giving up on me. Defeated, he evidently decided it was easier to drop it than to try to educate the uneducable. Maybe I shouldn't have so carelessly deflated him; he had treated me to a rare display of zeal that I wouldn't ordinarily have wanted to shoot down. Now, however, he hadn't shown me anything like hard proof that Rittenby had lied, and second, I found I didn't really care. Whatever Roger and Velez had been involved in, whatever CIA operation they had been quietly and profitably sabotaging, it didn't change the basic fact: Roger had murdered Ernie, and before the day was over, Roger would pay.

When we pulled into the hotel parking lot, I let

Sometimes You Get Killed

Kevin out.

"Aren't you coming?"

"No," I said. "But you're going to do two things. First, pack all our stuff and tell the desk to prepare our bill."

"Do you have any money to pay it?"

"Don't worry about that. Just do it. And second, and this is important, you're going to call the Center. I want you to tell Roger, that's Dr. Samuels, to meet me, um, at the warehouse in one hour. The warehouse, in one hour. Got that?"

He nodded. "How come?"

"Tell him I've figured out who Velez was working for."

"You have?"

"Just tell him, all right?"

"But is it true?"

I hesitated. "Yeah, for what it's worth, it's true."

"Aren't you going to the police, then?" Oddly, Kevin didn't ask me to share the info with him.

"Eventually," I said. "Just do what I told you. Tell me what you're going to say."

He repeated his instructions. "Why the warehouse, of all places?"

Because it's isolated, I thought, and it'll be a while before anyone finds Roger's body. And because I want to see what's in those packing crates before I get the hell out of this state. "It's as good a place as any," was all I said, and drove away.

The nurse had given me her friend Mary's address, and told me all she knew was that Mary worked nights at this new place. I hoped I would get to her house before she left for work. Mary's friend expressed some skepticism that Mary would speak with me, but I had no such doubts. All I needed was her confirmation of Roger's actions; then I would kill him with a clear conscience. Somehow. Big

Sharon Carton

talk from a man with his ribs taped in place.

Guns are easy to get in South Florida, but even if you don't need to be sane you do need to be solvent. I didn't have any money. I had a checkbook, and an overextended Amex card, but did I want the gun purchase traceable to me? If I took my time and thought about it, I could probably arrange it so that I wouldn't be caught. I couldn't stop long enough to think. I'd kill him and then figure something out. Besides, there was always the chance that the CIA wouldn't want me caught.

I would've felt better walking into a confrontation with Roger at the warehouse if I was armed, but that made me uneasy. Maybe Annie was right. I'd reached a point where I no longer felt safe without a gun. When had that happened? I'd had a gun several years ago, sold it when I was broke, and then went years without one. Then, a year ago, when Ernie had been shot, I bought the Colt. I had gone around for the intervening years, the happy little moron, armed only with aging reflexes and lethal sarcasm.

I told myself now I wasn't smart enough to get by on brains, and that was even scarier, if it meant that guns belonged to the intellectually impaired. A social conscience was nice, but I'd never been a fanatic. I didn't like getting beaten up; all right, my gun hadn't prevented it, but that was just because I hadn't been ready. Uh huh. Maybe I should take Jonah's self-defense class, like Kevin. Yeah, but he was more than ten years my junior. I wanted my gun.

Not that I'd need it for interviewing some nurse. Afterwards, I told myself, I'll stop in Davie and buy a gun.

It didn't work out that way.

I'm not sure exactly when it occurred to me. Waiting in my car, across the street from Nurse Mary's house, where the car her friend had described still sat, I somehow came to understand why I hadn't gone and knocked on her front door, why I was waiting for her to go to work, why I was sitting so still that my muscles were starting to

240

Sometimes You Get Killed

cramp. Frozen in place, I was afraid to move, afraid to think, afraid to doubt. Of course, I kept saying to myself, of course; it was an idea literally breathtaking in its beauty. If I moved, if I doubted, its beauty would fade, its tenuous reality would shatter. Of course, I kept repeating mechanically, of course.

Nurse Mary didn't live far from her new place of employment. After only about fifteen minutes, she pulled into the driveway of a modest, two-story brick house on a quiet suburban street, deep in the heart of Fort Lauderdale. I parked my car across the street, several houses away, and watched her adjust her make-up in the rear-view mirror. Surprising touch for a woman under duress. Then she got out of her car and walked up the path to the front door, straightening the skirt of her uniform as she approached the door.

I quietly got out of my car and crossed the street, staying on the sidewalk a few yards from the house. She gained entry by simply twisting the doorknob and pushing open the obviously unlocked door. The only evidence of a security system was her surreptitious glance upward to a point above and to the left of the doorway before entering. A surveillance camera and an unlocked door? Before she closed the door behind her, I heard a full-bodied laugh; someone was waiting inside, and she knew him or her.

I walked past the house until I could see its backyard. There was another door, and no guards were visible there, either. I figured there was another camera there, too, and an unlocked door. Come into my parlor, said the spider.... Who knew I was going there? Or was the trap meant for someone else?

Looking up, I saw six second-floor windows, some of which were ajar. There were two huge, ancient trees in the yard, and one had grown close enough to the back of the house that it made climbing in through a window a real possibility. My ribs ached, especially since I was breathing so hard, my heart pounding as if I'd been running. Some of it was fear, the tension of a break-in, but mostly it was the

Sharon Carton

excitement of an idea. An idea so enticing that it made a thirty-something man with cracked ribs and polluted lungs climb a tree.

I pushed the window open wider and climbed into the room. A familiar figure, his back toward me, was pulling a tee shirt over his head.

"Yo. Darwin," I said coolly.

He turned abruptly, then that old lop-sided grin lit up his pale face. "Hey, Jack, how ya doin'?"

"Fine, fine. And you? I notice that you're relatively alive."

The grin widened. "See, it's your keen powers of observation that distinguish you in your field of employ."

I didn't know whether to hug him or strangle him. "I trust this isn't a recent thing."

"What's that?" He plopped down on the bed, his face blanching with pain from the sudden impact.

"Your being alive," I replied evenly. "I mean, you've been alive for some time now, right? It's not like you've just recently been brought back from the dead?"

"Huh?"

"Well, I can't be sure. Your face is green, and with that cute little scar on your neck, you're almost an exact double of this guy on the late show who-"

"Whoa, wait a minute. Are you pissed or something? You seem kinda upset. Aren't you glad to see me?"

"Mild understatement, Darwin. The point is, I'm slightly surprised, since a coupla weeks ago I was the keynote speaker at your funeral."

He had been leaning back against the headboard of the bed, but at this he slowly, gingerly eased himself upright.

"That's right, Ernie, and I was amazingly articulate, if I do say so myself. All right, slightly hung over at the time, having gotten shit-faced with Jeff and Jonah the night before, but I've always done well under adverse conditions.

242

Sometimes You Get Killed

Do you have any special attachment to this room?"

"What? Uh, no, but what-"

"Then tie your sneakers. We're getting out of here."

Gratifyingly obedient, he bent over, but I saw him wince with the effort. As I tied his sneakers for him, I quickly gave him a condensed recitation of what had been going on.

He kept trying to interrupt me, but I wouldn't let him speak until I finished.

"What's your hurry?" he protested as I propelled him roughly toward the window.

"Call it a hunch, but I don't think it's gonna be as easy to get out as it was to get in."

"You might be surprised," came a woman's voice from behind me.

I whirled around to face Louise Fischman.

"Hey!" exclaimed a delighted Ernie.

I was less pleased. "Oh, Jesus, not you, don't tell me it was you all along."

Leaving the doorway, she crossed the room to sit on the bed. She didn't appear to be carrying a weapon. "No, Jack," she said, as Ernie left my side and sat down next to the social worker spy. "It wasn't me all along, and it's not me now, at least not the way you're thinking."

"What's he thinking?" asked an unconcerned Ernie.

"He," I answered, "is thinking that our nurturing shrink here has been in cahoots with Roger, keeping you prisoner."

She smiled. "Wrong on all counts, Jack."

I tried to answer, but Ernie stopped me.

"Jack," he said plaintively, "nobody's been keeping me prisoner. I only woke up the day before yesterday. Roger's been hiding me here, for my own protection, until I came out of the coma."

"Your own protection?" I said, dubious.

"Uh huh," Ernie nodded with conviction. "He's

Sharon Carton

convinced Eddie Velez wasn't working alone, and he wanted me safely hidden away from any of his associates."

"Well," Louise amended, putting a hand on Ernie's hand, resting on the bed, "that's only partly true. Keeping you here was to hide you from whoever was working with Velez, but apparently Roger was also motivated by the belief that you were attacked because you knew who was working with Velez, and that when, and if, you came out of the coma you could identify them."

I listened to this with eyes narrowed and mouth gaping. "And you guys all knew about this, but let me go on thinking Ernie was dead?"

"Oh, no," Louise protested, "this was Roger's little secret, until this morning, when he announced to all our personnel at the Center that Ernie was alive, regaining consciousness, and expected to name Eddie's confederates imminently."

"So he's setting Ernie up as a target?" I asked, indignant.

She nodded, grimacing. "That's a fair assessment," she said, "and that's why I'm here."

"Walking into Roger's trap?" I accused, not missing Ernie's crestfallen reaction.

"Of course not," Louise said. "I'm here to get the cheese out of the trap before the mouse shows up. Roger has a way of losing sight of the trivial fact that he's playing with people's lives. I was so relieved to have gotten a second chance with our friend here that I decided I was not going to let him be at risk just to suit Roger's little scheme. We can catch an attempted murderer just as well as a successful one."

"So," I said slowly, "you're telling me we can go?"

"No," she smiled again, with more determination this time, "I'm telling you you *have* to go."

"Lady, you don't have to say that twice. We're gone. we're outa here. I-95, here we come. But," I stopped, "what about the guards downstairs?"

Sometimes You Get Killed

"They won't stop you."

"What, you have a gun or something?"

She shook her head no. "Just take my word for it. I can be very persuasive."

I looked at her.

"Get your mind out of the gutter, Jack," she chided. "The men downstairs are foot soldiers. I outrank them. But I suggest you leave before Roger — who outranks me — shows up, or the would-be killer makes his appearance."

"Come on, Darwin," I said, grabbing his arm and pulling him toward the door.

He was frowning. "What if I want to see who's after me?"

I dropped his arm and stared at him. "You must be fucking joking. I'll pay for the toll call from New York. Let's just get the hell out of here. I've had my fill of South Florida."

"I have your word on that, Jack?" Louise said. "It's my condition for giving you safe passage out of here."

"Darlin'," I drawled, "it's been real. Darwin, you're out that door or I'll save everybody a lot of trouble and kill you myself."

Mercurial as ever, Ernie shrugged, which prompted a wince and a sharp intake of air, then smiled and leaned over to plant a light kiss on Louise's cheek. She placed a hand gently on his cheek, and taking that as goodbye, I pushed him through the door.

The guards downstairs nodded wordlessly as we walked past them. They offered absolutely no resistance. I made sure no one was skulking around outside, then trotted Ernie to the car and shoved him in it.

It wasn't until we'd driven about a mile that I noticed my hands were shaking.

"You okay?" Ernie asked.

I looked over at him, lying back with his eyes closed. "Uh huh," I decided. "You?"

Sharon Carton

He nodded, a pleased smile lighting his face. "Can we spend tomorrow on the beach?" he asked inanely.

"Jones Beach, or Robert Moses, sure," I agreed. "Or we can stop at Atlantic City, if you'd prefer."

"No, I mean-"

"I know what you mean, asshole," I interrupted affably. "We are getting in my car and hitting the interstate, and we're not stopping until we get to New Jersey, at the very least."

"Yeah, at the very least," he smirked.

After a few minutes of comfortable silence, I broke in, "Did it occur to you I might be interested in hearing from you?"

He opened one eye. "I was in a coma, you know."

"Yesterday?"

"Yeah, but Roger told me you knew all along."

"That you were alive?"

"Yeah, and that you were driving down from New York, that you'd started out as soon as he called you to tell you I'd regained consciousness."

"And Roger told you were free to leave?"

"That's what he said, but I don't know, in light of what Louise told us. I can't believe, after protecting me all this time, he was willing to use me to trap a killer."

"Well," I said generously, "he probably did care about keeping you in one piece. I mean, he could've left you in the hospital, but instead he kept you here, and since he didn't even know whom at the Center he could trust, he kept you a secret."

"Yeah," Ernie said, disappointed, "until he got impatient and painted a bull's-eye on me."

"Why do you think he changed tactics?"

"I guess because, when I woke up, he discovered I had nothing worth protecting."

"You mean the names of Velez' associates."

He nodded.

"So what was your big item of information that

Sometimes You Get Killed

you wanted to tell me? You know, the night I came to the Center to meet with Rios."

"Oh, that. Jesus, Mig, I don't remember, that was another lifetime."

"In a manner of speaking."

"Anyway, it must've been about the journal."

"What journal?"

"The one Velez was keeping."

"You found Velez's diary? Did you read it? What did it say? Was there a confession to-"

"No, no," Ernie stopped me, "I just found out that it existed, not what it said. And it wasn't a book. I'm pretty sure he said it was tape-recordings."

"That's it?"

"As far as I can remember, yeah. Of course, I didn't know how important it could've been, because back then I didn't know he was Berto's killer. I didn't find that out until I woke up two days ago. I just thought the tapes might have some information about the people at the Center, including Berto." He opened his eyes and looked at me. "Does that mean you never knew about this journal?"

I shook my head.

"Funny. See, in a conversation with Velez, I happened to mention my writing, and he told me he'd been keeping a journal since coming to the Center. I wondered if he'd recorded anything about the murder."

"And I wonder why no one ever mentioned it to me. Presumably they found the tapes after his death, so-"

"Maybe we can ask Louise."

"We're not asking anybody anything, unless it's in a long distance phone call from New York," I said firmly. "I meant what I said back there, Darwin. We're getting the hell outa here. I've had it up to here with the fucking CIA."

"Yeah, how do you like that," he grinned, "us and the fucking CIA."

"Oh, yeah, I meant to ask you...."

"Yeah?"

Sharon Carton

"That meeting you set up with me and Paul Rios."

"Dr. God. Yeah. What about it?"

"What did you tell him, about me, about us?"

"Oh. Well, I asked him about the night Berto died, and he admitted he was on the control booth that night. So I told the truth about you being an investigator working for Berto's uncle-"

"Which we now know he already knew," I pointed out.

"Yeah," Ernie nodded.

"Did he say he had something to tell me?"

"Not in so many words. He just agreed to keep our secret and meet you the next night."

"Mm."

"I mean, now it sounds pretty tame, but at the time it seemed like the first break in our case."

"I guess."

"Got a cigarette?"

I pointed to the glove compartment, and noticed I was still trembling. I took a long, critical look at Ernie as he concentrated on lighting a cigarette. There was a drawn, weary look on his face, with dark circles ringing his eyes. He'd lost weight he couldn't afford to lose. It made him look younger, somehow, more vulnerable.

It suddenly struck me, the sheer enormity of it: Relief flooded through me, washing away the misery and tension that had gripped me ever since that bloody night at the Center. I felt a broad smile crease my face; the shaking finally abated. Things were all right, in a way they hadn't been all this time, in a way I had thought they never would be again.

Chapter Twenty-Four

"I don't fucking believe it."

"Who's Kevin?" was Ernie's mild reaction. Then, "does this mean we're not leaving yet? Can I go to the beach tomorrow?"

We were back at the hotel, where I had found packed suitcases but no Kevin. He had left a note.

> "Jack -
>
> I called Dr. Samuels, but he had just left the Center. So I left a message with Debbie. Also, in case you come back here before going to the warehouse, you should know I've set a little trap of my own. If I'm right, you and Roger aren't going to be alone at the warehouse. If I'm wrong, I'll be back here in a few hours and we can leave if you want -
>
> Kevin"

"I just don't believe it," I repeated. "Of all the juvenile, asshole pranks-"

"So who is he?"

I took my eyes off the note. "He's a kid whose old man has been footing the bill for this whole shindig." Briefly I explained.

Ernie gave a sniff of disapproval. "My replacement." Nodding at the bandages on my wrists, he said, "Here I thought you had opened your veins out of grief, and all the time you hadn't even noticed I was gone. I'm

Sharon Carton

not even cold in my grave-"

"You were burned, not buried, shithead."

"-before you go out and hire some Ivy-Leaguer to take my place. I'm wounded, Mig, I'm hurt, I'm offended, I'm-"

"Could you also manage quiet? I've got a little crisis on my hands."

Shifting gears easily, Ernie asked, "Why does he think you're at this warehouse with Roger?"

"I thought Roger killed you. I told Kevin to have Roger meet me there -" I looked at my watch "-about ten minutes ago."

"To accuse him?"

"No, to kill him."

Ernie smiled, mollified. "Oh. Thanks, Jack."

"'Thanks'? Isn't the capital punishment on the bleeding-heart-liberal list of fascist no-no's?"

"It's state-sponsored murder I'm against," he said reasonably, "not personally-motivated revenge. One has nothing to do with the other."

"Uh huh."

"So why aren't we at the warehouse?"

"Because, in case it's eluded you, it has been proved to my relative certainty that you're not dead, which means Roger didn't kill you."

"But Roger doesn't know about this change of plans?"

"Yeah, yeah."

"And so we're going to the Center anyway, to find this kid, Kevin, or to the warehouse to-"

"*No. I'm* going; you're staying here. Under no circumstances are you to budge from this room. Do you understand me? Have I been very clear?"

"Uh huh." He didn't mind. "Can you bring back Mickey Dee's if you don't get killed or arrested or anything?"

"I'm touched, Darwin."

Sometimes You Get Killed

"I've said that for years, Mig."

"Call the Center," I said, anticlimactically, as I left, "and stop Roger if he hasn't already gone."

What should have been about a fifteen or twenty minute drive to the warehouse took me more like an hour and a half. Traffic kills. By that time I had convinced myself that, regaining a partner only to lose an apprentice, I would arrive at the warehouse and find Kevin dead, if I found him at all.

The initial delay was caused by what I had thought would be a brief but necessary detour to a gun shop in Davie's redneck country. It was at the third shop that I found a gun, and a price, I felt I could live with.

That's when the trouble started. I gave the guy my Amex card, and he gave me a registration form. Keenly aware of the time, I bucked at the paperwork. The guy turned ugly, not exactly an earth-shattering transformation. I threatened to walk out and cost him the sale. He said if I did that, he'd call the police and say I seemed dangerous and should be picked up.

I filled out the form.

Soon after leaving the shop, I discovered that I couldn't retrace the route to the warehouse. Lost, I drove around west Broward in muddled confusion for close to half an hour. The more confused I got, the faster I drove, which somehow made sense to me at the time. I don't know whether I sped up out of frustration, embarrassment or some misguided notion that the quicker I got all the wrong moves out of the way, the sooner I'd get around to making the right ones.

Maybe because I drive almost everywhere I go, at least outside of Manhattan, I've got a pretty reliable sense of direction. The first and only time I had gone to the warehouse, though, I'd been concentrating on nothing so much as following Rittenby and Oyola without being spotted. I had only found my way out of the maze of

Sharon Carton

deserted roads and winding streets by following their lead.

Finally, I decided to retrace my route of that night by starting from the Center. It worked. I forced my imagination back in time to remember where I'd tailed Rittenby and Oyola to the private airfield, and from there I found my way to the warehouse.

I pulled into the warehouse parking lot just as Roger was stepping out of his car. There were two other cars there, both rentals. Roger waited for me, a dismayed scowl on his normally equable features. As soon as I got out of my car, he walked over to me with long, purposeful strides.

"Didn't Ernie call you?" I said, keeping my voice down.

"*I* called *him*," Roger answered in an exaggerated whisper. "He told me-"

There were two gunshots. Roger and I looked at the warehouse, then at each other, and then, with guns drawn, we ran into the warehouse.

Kevin was standing over Coleman's body. I could see two huge bloodstains blossoming on Coleman's blue shirt. Coleman's eyes were open and staring vacantly, and a thin stream of blood trickled from the left corner of his mouth. A revolver lay on the floor beside him.

Kevin's two arms were extended stiffly forward, his hands wrapped around a semi-automatic pistol I had never seen before. His face rigid with concentration, he was pointing at the dead body. As Roger and I crashed through the door, Kevin swung his body in our direction, arms still extended, hands still tightly gripping the pistol. He swung the gun back and forth between me and Roger, his eyes wild and terrified. His face showed no sign of recognition.

"Drop the gun!" Roger shouted to Kevin.

I stepped away from Roger and trained my gun on him. "Just lower your gun, Dr. Samuels," I instructed quietly.

Sometimes You Get Killed

Roger turned to me, now aiming his gun at me. "You, too! Drop it!"

Kevin, who hadn't yet understood who I was, kept swinging his pistol from me to Roger and back again. Struggling to keep my voice controlled, I said, "Let's just take this slow and easy. I don't know about you two, but it occurs to me that all three of us are on the same side. So, on the count of three, why don't we all just lower our guns. Okay?"

There was no sign of assent from either one, but I went ahead and counted. At "three," Roger very tentatively began to relax his gun arm, not really committing himself until I started to do the same. Kevin, his eyes still scared but now showing the beginning of confused awareness, slowly followed suit. It was only when his arms were lowered all the way to his sides that I saw the tension drain from his face and some color begin to return to it. A flicker of comprehension mixed with recognition. "Jack?"

I nodded, and reached over to remove the pistol from his now limp hands. "It's all right, kid. It's all over."

Kevin glanced in a general downward direction, not really focusing on Coleman. "Do you think he's dead?"

Roger walked between us and crouched beside the corpse, picking up the revolver on the floor. Roger lightly passed his fingers over Coleman's face, and when he was through Coleman's eyes were closed.

Roger then stood up, brushing imaginary flecks of dust from his pants' knees. "Well, young man," he said to Kevin, his characteristic aplomb and officiousness back in place, "perhaps you can tell us what happened."

Kevin eyed me nervously, then looked back at Dr. Samuels. "I want to see a lawyer."

An inadvertent smile curled my lips. "You tell 'im, kid."

Roger's lips tightened. "Under the circumstances, I don't think we're looking at any prosecution."

I shot a startled look at Roger. "Do you know

Sharon Carton

something I don't?"

Roger sighed. "Let me make a call from my car. I'll be right back."

When he was gone, I sat down on one of the crates. Kevin gave a half-laugh, then did the same.

"You believe this?" he said, shaking his head in wonder.

"Coleman was the one you set a trap for?"

He nodded. "That night you got beat up? There was something...the way Coleman...." He stopped, then tried again. "The more I thought about it, the more convinced I became that he only came to finish you off, not to get you help. If the cops hadn't shown up..." his voice trailed off.

"So you figured he must've been working with Samuels and Velez?"

"I kept thinking about how he managed to find you, as if he'd been told where to look."

"By whom? The guys who'd beaten me?" I wasn't convinced. "If he was the one who had it done, why didn't they just kill me in the first place?"

Kevin shrugged. "I don't know, but I decided to set him up. When I called the Center as you directed, Roger wasn't there. I left a message for him, and then had Debbie put Coleman on the phone. I told him I needed to leave a message for Dr. Samuels and didn't know who else to trust. So I said to tell Samuels to meet you at a place called the warehouse, that Samuels would know what that was.

"Then," Kevin continued, "just to cover myself, I got Debbie back on the line and told her to tell Davy Rittenby to go to the warehouse. I mean, he seemed to be the most trustworthy of the ones you'd told me about, since he was the one who'd saved you from Oyola at the warehouse that night."

"So where is Rittenby?" I wondered aloud.

Another shrug.

"So you rented a car and waited for Coleman to leave the Center, then followed him here to see if he knew

Sometimes You Get Killed

the way."

"Yeah."

"Where'd you get the gun?"

"From a guy I used to shoot with down here."

"A guy you used to shoot *what* with?"

"Targets mostly," he said off-handedly. "We'd spent a season pigeon-shooting in competition in Spain a coupla years ago."

"You're pretty well-rounded for a grad student, kid."

He was pleased.

"How'd you get the drop on him?" I asked.

"Oh, that. That was easier than I thought. He'd been wondering why I'd never said anything about that night. I guess he knew how transparent his intentions had been.

"So I said I was working for you, but I had no real allegiance to you. I said that I had pretty much guessed what he was up to in Cuba, and that I wanted in. I think what lent it particular credibility, and desirability, was when I told him that if he'd let me join up, I could offer the financial backing of my father. Then, when he'd relaxed and we were just chatting in a casual way, I was able to draw my-"

"What do you mean?" I interrupted belatedly. "What was he up to in Cuba? Drug-dealing?"

"No," came Roger's voice from the doorway. "Coleman had solicited several of our agents for his own political purposes. I don't know how he found out about our operation, but I guess he had political affiliations."

"Let me guess," I said dryly. "This operation had nothing to do with the drug cartel in Colombia."

"Only indirectly," Roger admitted. "I know what Davy Rittenby told you, but it wasn't precisely the truth."

"Surprise, surprise."

He chose all right with Oyola and Velez, but they couldn't carry the refugee community. That's where Rios came in. And don't underestimate the memory of the Bay of Pigs; Velez might reasonably have expected the Miami

255

Sharon Carton

Cubans to embrace any effort to undermine or even embarrass the CIA."

"By supporting the splinter group."

"That's it."

"But Rios turned him down."

"Not exactly. Paul kept stalling, until Velez had to admit to Coleman what he'd done. Coleman instructed Velez to eliminate Rios before Rios reported him to me."

"But how could Coleman be sure that hadn't already happened?"

Samuels shrugged. "A reasonable assumption, since there'd been no noticeable repercussions. Coleman decided not to push his luck, owing in large part," Samuels went on, narrowing his eyes, "to a telephone call Davy Rittenby heard your friend Mr. Darwin place to you one night."

"What? Rittenby listened in on that conversation? And told Walt Coleman?"

"No, he told Jaime Oyola. Idle conversation. Davy was amused, mostly."

"'Amused'? That one of your agents planned a rendezvous with a private investigator?"

"I'm afraid he didn't take it very seriously. A miscalculation. He *was* monitoring the control booth-"

"It was bugged?"

"Electronic listening device, except that there was nothing to listen to. Just an innocuous conversation with Eddie Velez-"

"Who had just stopped by to drug Rios' coffee-"

"-and wait for Paul to pass out, so he could silently slit his throat," Roger finished.

"Rittenby was listening the entire time," I mused, shaking my head. "Why did Ken Khoragian show up at the control booth?"

"Oh, that. Pure coincidence."

"Wait, don't tell me. He found out about his wife's little fling."

Sometimes You Get Killed

"That's about it."

"All right, I think I've got this straight, all except Ernie. Why did Velez go after him? Was that coincidence too?"

"No, I'm afraid not. When Davy told Oyola-"

"-who told Coleman, who told Velez-"

"-about Darwin's phone call, Coleman suspected Paul had already confessed to Darwin. He ordered Velez to terminate Paul *and* Darwin."

I shook my head again, trying to clear it. "So Davy set off this whole chain reaction."

"In a sense. In all likelihood, only the timing would have been different if Davy hadn't spoken to Jaime. Rios had already been targeted."

"But not Ernie," I pointed out.

"He has only his own ill-advised phone call to thank for that," Samuels retorted.

"'Ill-advised'? He was just about to break open the splinter group. If your agent had either kept his mouth shut, or conducted a more effective surveillance of the control booth-"

"Well, let's not quibble."

I tried to digest all this new information. "You said you called Ernie?" I asked Roger.

"When I got to the safe house, Louise Fischman told me what had happened. It was not long after that that we caught Oyola, at which point I phoned your hotel to tell you two that Ernie would be safe now. Of course, I was under the impression that apprehending Coleman was merely a matter of returning to the Center. Ernie told me about the note from this young man," he said, nodding at Kevin, "and that you'd gone to the warehouse. I called the Center and found out Coleman had taken off. So I came to, well, to...."

"To rescue us?" I smiled broadly at that. "Go on, you can say it."

"Well, to deal with Coleman, more accurately."

Sharon Carton

"And little did you know Kevin had already 'dealt' with him for you."

Kevin spoke up. "You did say something about no charges being pressed?"

Roger looked away.

"Charges?" I said with mock innocence. "Coleman died of a drug overdose. Oh, wait, he was alcohol, wasn't he? Okay, he died of acute alcohol intoxication."

Kevin looked from me to Roger, then back to me. "So we can go?"

Roger smiled. "I think that's-"

"Wait a minute," I interrupted. "Where's Rittenby in all this? Kevin sent him an S.O.S."

Roger's smile didn't waver. "Davy Rittenby requested an immediate flight out to Panama this morning. He couldn't have gotten the...S.O.S."

I was pissed. "You mean you told him Ernie was alive to name names and he flees the country? And you didn't find that suspicious?"

"Oh, no, this preceded my little announcement."

This pissed me off even more. "You mean he takes off in the middle of all this shit? He just leaves us all behind to shoot it out for ourselves? Great, really great." Well, he did warn me. You gotta appreciate a guy who knows his own character. Or lack thereof.

"It was his job, after all," Roger said. "He left something for you, by the way. It's in my car."

The three of us walked out to the parking lot, Kevin and I glancing backward at the dead man.

From his car's front seat, Roger pulled a small, rectangular box, and handed it to me.

I took it, and shook Roger's proffered hand. "If I never see you again," I said warmly, "it'll be too soon."

Roger smiled with polite disdain. "I couldn't have said it better myself."

Kevin reached over, extending a hand to Roger. "Yeah, drop dead from me, too."

Sometimes You Get Killed

Roger shook the hand, then turned and got into his car. As Roger sat in the parked car, picking up his telephone and apparently placing a call, Kevin and I looked at each other, smiled, and gave the spook a digital salute.

"It's been real," Kevin muttered.

"Unfortunately."

"What's in the box?"

I opened it. "My gun." There was a brief note, too. "By way of apology," I quoted.

" 'Apology'? For what? For his role in almost getting Ernie killed?"

"Maybe, or for getting two guys to beat the shit out of me," I reasoned. "I think he had done it as a friendly gesture."

"Huh?"

"Or punctuation," I continued, "for his advice that I leave town."

"That was a friendly gesture?"

"He probably saw it as good advice that I hadn't yet decided to take." I shrugged. "Don't ask me to make sense of the guy. I just figure he had gotten involved to the point of taking steps, pretty unpleasant steps, to get me out of a dangerous entanglement. Beyond that, whether I learned from it or not, what he wanted most of all was to be removed from the problem."

"What's gonna happen to Oyola?" Kevin asked, then saw my expression. "Never mind, I forgot. He took a drug overdose."

"A lot of that going around."

Chapter Twenty-Five

We didn't get back to the hotel for another hour. Before any of us, including Roger, could make it out of the warehouse parking lot, Sergeant DeBiasio showed up. He was alone, and had apparently come to make some kind of arrangement with Roger, who had called him on the car phone.

It turned out that Rittenby had been feeding selective data to the cops through DeBiasio ever since Berto's death. With a few exceptions — like the knowledge of Ernie's whereabouts — Rittenby had been Roger's fair-haired boy, above suspicion, liaison to the local law. The more I thought about it, the more it seemed in character, with Roger for valuing a team player, with Davy for impressing the powers that be.

Ernie viewed Rittenby's defection with less equanimity. "I can't believe he just cut out. Especially since, from what Roger told you, Davy wasn't without blame for what happened to me and Paul Rios."

"Well," I offered, "I think he felt guilty. It would go a long way toward explaining why he was so dead set on getting me out of town. For someone who's so obviously uncomfortable getting close to people, he went out of his way to buck his rabbi Roger and sic two thugs on me, just in order to warn me off. I can understand that if he felt his indiscretion had caused what he thought were two deaths. Three, if you count Velez. Otherwise, it makes no real sense. He wasn't vicious, he wasn't ordered to have me roughed up, so why else?"

"So you don't think it had anything to do with his being half-Cuban?"

Sharon Carton

"Huh?"

"I mean, what you told me about Walt Coleman always trying to turn the Cubans. You don't suppose he had tried to recruit Davy, do you?"

My God. "Coleman's dead. Velez is dead. Rittenby's fled the country. Who-"

"But," Kevin chimed in, "Oyola's not. If Rittenby were involved, Oyola would've named him. No, interesting theory, but improbable. My guess is that Rittenby's only problem is that he was just unequipped emotionally to deal with all that responsibility."

I stared at him, amused. "Such insight?"

"I'm old beyond my years," he said, offended.

At that, Ernie grinned. "And you thought *I* was pretentious?"

"You are," I said. "And before I forget," I turned to Kevin, "you've known for the last two days that Coleman had tried to kill me and you didn't think it significant enough to tell me?"

Kevin looked embarrassed, but Ernie grinned at him. "He hates that," he told the kid. "To him, keeping secrets is like lying, and nothing pisses him off more."

"You should know, Darwin. Like it never occurred to you to tell me you were getting it on with Louise Fischman?"

Now it was Ernie's turn to look embarrassed. "How'd you know that?" he blurted out.

"Are you kidding?" I said. "The only way to miss something that obvious is if you were legally blind."

"Or legally trained," Kevin rejoined.

"Anyway," Ernie grumbled, "if I told you, you would only have assumed she'd killed Berto."

Kevin looked puzzled at this.

"Inside joke," I explained.

"And besides," Ernie went on quickly, "it's him you're mad at, not me."

"I'm waiting for an explanation," I said.

Sometimes You Get Killed

"Well," Kevin replied with affected diffidence, "it's not like I had any proof."

"Bullshit. You figured you'd fucked up by calling him that night, and you wanted to keep it quiet until you could turn it to your advantage."

"Well-"

"Look, kid, I don't mind your showing some initiative, but don't forget whose side you're on. This isn't some game where whoever dies with the most information wins. In this game, whoever doesn't have enough info, dies. Try and-"

"That's catchy, Jack," Ernie commented.

"-remember that," I finished, glaring at Ernie for interrupting me. His grin, if anything, widened, and I couldn't help smiling back. "Oh, fuck it, what do you say? New York?"

"New York," the two answered in comic unison.

Ernie and I dropped Kevin at the Fort Lauderdale airport, where he would catch a flight home. Ernie opted to drive north with me.

On the road, I started wondering about my new apprentice, about when it would finally hit him that he had killed a man. He had seemed pretty collected, but I hadn't forgotten the wild terror in his eyes after the shooting. I thought that, when Ernie and I made a pit stop, I would place a call to Kevin's father.

All in all, the kid had done all right. I could certainly use the regular income this apprenticeship would provide. It meant that, just as I had the last few weeks, I could indulge in pursuing the kind of lost cause cases Ernie usually saddled me with. Picking and choosing my jobs was a luxury I could enjoy, and I had a feeling I might actually be able to work with the kid.

I looked over at Ernie, half-asleep on the seat beside me. It occurred to me that this new arrangement might not sit too well with him. Ernie dealt with change about as well as Davy Rittenby dealt with responsibility.

263

Sharon Carton

Well, I sighed contentedly, if I had a problem on my hands, it was a problem I would be happy to live with.

"What're you grinning at, Mig?" Ernie said sleepily.

"Just imagining Annie's reaction when we get home."

"Oh, I already called her."

"Excuse me?"

"From the hotel."

"Who else did you call?"

"Whom. Nobody else, why?"

"You made one phone call," I said, my voice climbing an octave, "and you chose my girlfriend?"

"She's my friend too, you know. I'm allowed. Besides, I wanted to ask her...stuff."

"Stuff? Articulate as ever, Darwin. Can you be more specific?"

"Oh, you know. Like how the Mets are doing."

"Uh huh." I paused. Of course. He would have asked her about the trial of his ex-lover, Alice. Annie was probably the only one tactful enough to give him the hard facts gently, and not ride him about it. "So what did she say?"

"Stuff."

"You know," I said, deadpan, "she was never really all that upset about you being dead. In fact, she said something about it being kind of a relief, you know, all for the best...."

"Yeah," Ernie said, twisting in his seat to look at me, "as opposed to you, right? You must've been really grief-stricken, Jack. I die, and you get a tan and a replacement."

"Hey, I was in deep mourning, " I said unemotionally.

"Whadja do, hold my wake on the beach?"

"All right, so I got over it. It's not my fault I'm resilient."

Sometimes You Get Killed

"Uh huh," he said, affecting a wounded tone. "You realize my emotional well-being is essential to my recuperation. I could be traumatized by all this. You might want to keep that in mind."

"And I thought Roger had lied when he said you were brain dead."

"So," he said brightly, "how *are* the Mets doing?"

I snorted. "Let's just say you had a better summer than they did."

It felt good. I felt good. It even lasted a while. I don't know whether it was the time he spent at the Center, or the time he spent in a coma, but Ernie was apparently off the drugs. I wasn't counting on its being permanent; for as long as it lasted, it was one good thing that had come from this debacle. It didn't necessarily mean I had used him well, but I was willing to live with the way things had turned out.

Ernie's friend Cathy, whom we informed of Ernie's resurrection in a long-distance phone call when we were safely home, seemed to have a somewhat mixed reaction to the news: equal parts surprise, pleasure and disappointment. I could understand the source of the first part, but I wasn't clear on which of the other two emotions was generated by the change in Ernie's health and which by our dropping the lawsuit.

As for other developments on the legal front, we had been home a month when Ernie got a letter from the New York State Bar's Character and Fitness Committee. It seemed they had gotten a glowing report from the Director of a certain drug and alcohol rehabilitation facility in Davie, Florida, praising Ernie's sterling recovery from his substance abuse problem. With it were included several letters of testimonial from government officials affiliated with this rehab program. The Committee informed Ernie that, in recognition of this development, the disciplinary proceedings against him were dropped. It was a nice touch.

About the Author

*Sharon Carton is a law professor in South Florida, on sabbatical in the Pacific Northwest. She has produced a number of published scholarly articles, including most recently one on a Canadian serial killer and one on the law of Star Trek. More ambitiously, she is writing a book for a seminar she teaches on the link between bias crimes and domestic terrorism. Last year she was appointed Covenor of a UN workgroup on Intellectual Property for its Millennial Assembly. Other than teaching, she has worked in a South London bakery, clerked for a Manhattan Criminal court, interned with a British barrister, and put in two years with the United States Department of Defense. She has six tattoos, which is six more than any other member of the law faculty. She knows all the lyrics to the theme song from **Pinky and the Brain**, which isn't saying much, but she's also proud to say she knows almost all the words to the **Animaniacs** and to **South Park**, too. Her main claim to fame, however, is that she once served as a dead body for her friend's class in scientific evidence.*